Jay Quinn

Metes and Bounds

Pre-publication
REVIEWS,
COMMENTARIES,
EVALUATIONS . . .

"The greatest comfort of surfing comes in the sureness of instinct,' says Matt, the narrator and protagonist of Jay Quinn's fine first novel *Metes and Bounds*. The same could just as easily be said about storytelling, a talent Quinn displays beautifully here. Set on the storm-tossed coast of North Carolina amid the world of rednecks and surfers, *Metes and Bounds* transcends the boundaries of the typical coming-of-age/coming-out novel with a sureness of hand and a quiet wisdom. Songs of innocence, interwoven with songs of experience, create not dissonance, but harmony—culminating in the all-male family that Quinn creates for Matt. It is, in the end, a vision that is both moving and memorable."

Robin Lippincott
Author of *Our Arcadia*
and *Mr. Dalloway*

"It's often said that love makes a family, but when you take Tiger the beautiful surfer and Mark the butch former Air Force pilot, add Mark's son Shane, a young stray named Billy, and top it all off with Matt, the wistful narrator of *Metes and Bounds*, you've got a loving family the likes of which you won't soon forget. Jay Quinn's richly layered debut novel traces, in a lovely North Carolina vernacular, one teenage boy's journey of self-discovery. His longings are electric, his disappointments evocative, his sexual encounters both stinging and stirring in their awkward ardor. I can't remember the last time I enjoyed a coming-of-age story so much."

Paul Russell
Author of *The Coming Storm*
and *Boys of Life*

More pre-publication
REVIEWS, COMMENTARIES, EVALUATIONS . . .

"This finely drawn novel brings back the North Carolina beaches and coastal country of my childhood, both in the gentle rhythms of its prose and the subtle textures of the voices within it. Jay Quinn has written a treasure: a novel with a whole landscape behind it."

Jim Grimsley
Author of *Dream Boy*
and *Comfort and Joy*

"Every coming out is the same: a girl or a boy, a woman or a man, realizes a truth and shares it. And every coming out is unique: that's why *Metes and Bounds* is a welcome addition to the genre. In Jay Quinn's elegant, honest story, the boy is Matt, son of protective, uncertain but loving Southern parents who entrust his teenhood to surfer and surveyor Tiger, a young uncle who left the family circle for the same reason Matt must—to be himself.

There's an earnest love of family permeating Quinn's work. Tiger is in a loving relationship with military man Mark, whose son Shane from an earlier marriage becomes part of the household, as does even a snot-nosed youngster from down the street. Matt's estrangement from his parents is real, but not tortured; he misses deeply a younger brother who died, and he appreciates his older brother. Best of all, the family spats and tears, laughter and love, both Matt's blood family and his adopted gay family, come across as refreshingly real.

So do Matt's fumbles with sex and passion. His first boyfriend, a fellow high schooler, is sweet and callow in the way boys on the cusp of maturity can be. His entanglement with blue-collared Tillett, muscled and menacing with a meanness borne of his own sexual confusion, teaches him the difference between love and sex. And his eventual pairing up with star football jock, Jeep, despite its flirtation with cliche, is rendered by Quinn with a delicacy that draws simultaneous laughter and, if not tears, then at least profound appreciation.

The title? Metes and bounds are land-surveying terms, usually describing boundaries—an appropriate choice for a sweet book about a young gay man just coming to understand his own needs and define his own limits."

Richard Labonte
Book critic,
PlanetOut.com

Southern Tier Editions
Harrington Park Press®
An Imprint of The Haworth Press, Inc.
New York • London • Oxford

Metes and Bounds

HARRINGTON PARK PRESS
Southern Tier Editions
Gay Men's Fiction
Jay Quinn, Executive Editor

Love, the Magician by Brian Bouldrey

Distortion by Stephen Beachy

The City Kid by Paul Reidinger

Rebel Yell: Stories by Contemporary Southern Gay Authors edited by Jay Quinn

Metes and Bounds by Jay Quinn

Metes and Bounds

Jay Quinn

Southern Tier Editions
Harrington Park Press®
An Imprint of The Haworth Press, Inc.
New York • London • Oxford

Published by

Southern Tier Editions, Harrington Park Press®, an imprint of the Haworth Press, Inc., 10 Alice Street, Binghamton, NY 13904-1580.

PUBLISHER'S NOTE
This is a work of fiction. Names, characters, places, and incidents either are the products of the author's imagination or are used fictitiously, and any resemblance to actual persons, living or dead, business establishments, events, or locales is entirely coincidental.

Cover design by Jennifer M. Gaska.

Library of Congress Cataloging-in-Publication Data

Quinn, Jay.
    Metes and bounds / Jay Quinn.
      p. cm.
    ISBN 1-56023-184-X (hard)—ISBN 1-56023-185-8 (soft)
    I. Title.

    PS3567.U3445 M48 2001
    813'.6—dc21
                                                                    00-047214

Acknowledgments

I would like to thank Nicholas Weinstock for his constant support and encouragement for this novel and this author.

Also, Susan Highsmith for sharing the past and her computer. Joe Riddick for everything he is: mentor, daddy, and friend. Mark Berry, Master Land Surveyor, for listening all those long, hot days to a rod dog who wanted to be a writer. Jill McCorkle for inspiration and encouragement.

At The Haworth Press: Bill Cohen, Bill Palmer, Melissa Devendorf, and Rebecca Browne.

And more than anyone, thanks to Jeff Auchter, my heart and my home.

Me

and Tiger had a difference of opinion. I thought it would be worth it to go out surfing. Tiger just looked off and shook his head. A late season hurricane was passing offshore about one hundred and fifty miles east of Cape Lookout. The whole day had been squally while we worked trying to finish staking out a new subdivision. We weren't able to get much done. It seemed like every time we got the transit set up and got going good, we'd get bitch-slapped by feeder bands of rain. With the winds gusting up stronger and stronger, I couldn't keep the prism pole still enough for him to get accurate shots. Finally, Tiger called it quits.

"Man, I can't control the weather," he said as he packed up the transit for the third time that day. The sudden shower had stopped, but the air was dense with the low pressure. I pulled my sodden T-shirt over my head and threw it in with the equipment in the back of the Bronco.

"Let's check out the waves, Tiger," I said as he locked down the lid of the transit case.

Tiger looked over to the dune line, up the street. We both could hear the waves over the wind. They had to be huge. Tiger looked at me and grinned. "Boy, they aren't going to be anything but slop. The wind's going to have to shift and clean them up some before they're going to be worth a damn." I shrugged and looked toward the beach.

We got pelted by a short burst of fat raindrops that stung my face and chest. "Shit," Tiger said and pulled off his T-shirt as well. The wind was warm on bare skin, but surprisingly chilling against the damp cotton. "C'mon then," Tiger said as he tossed his T-shirt in the back with mine and then twisted the key to make the rear window go up. "I'd hate to cheat you out of your first hurricane." He started off toward the beach.

"Don't you want to bring the boards?" I called after him. We kept our boards strapped to racks on top of the Bronco. All summer, if it started going off at a break near where we were working, we'd quit work for an hour or so to catch a few sets. That was one great thing about surveying, especially if your boss was a surfer.

"Hell no, Matt," Tiger yelled back. His voice carried in the wind. "C'mon. You'll see why."

I looked up at the boards strapped to the racks on the roof of the Bronco and reluctantly took off after Tiger. Since I came to live and work with him in the spring, surfing and surveying had become all I wanted to do. Well, surfing probably more than surveying. Tiger said I'd go out and sit on my board if the ocean was dead flat. He was right. Even if I had just started surfing, I didn't intend to stay a kook forever.

I caught up with Tiger on the crest of the dune. The wind's heavy, wet hand was trying as hard as it could to push me back. Stretching out in front of us, the ocean seemed to be fighting with itself. The waves reared up and dumped out sideways on each other. Ugly gray-ish brown foam rolled up the sand from the shore break and then took off in the wind. Tiger looked at me and raised one eyebrow, figuring he didn't have to say anything else.

I squinted my eyes to search out over the water for a break we had surfed not two weeks before. No doubt, this storm was scouring the bottom, reconfiguring the sandbars and changing every break I'd learned over the summer. The ocean could be a stingy bitch with her favors and fickle as hell, but at least she was always there. She didn't just pick up and take off, leaving you scratching your head and won-dering why.

I thought about Chris, my first boyfriend and lover. It was over and I knew it. We lied when he left after his last visit down. I didn't share any pretty college campus up North. No crunching leaves and keg parties here. That was his. Mine was this raw stretch of sand, wind that forced the breath back down into your lungs and an ocean full of waves wrestling with each other. Hell, it was the perfect place for me. I was right at home. I guess when Chris added up everything, I was as contradictory as his wind to my sea.

I found the break.

A couple of hundred yards up the beach, the waves were breaking cleaner and more consistently. They were thick, but had a nice-ish shape every couple of sets or so. I put my hand on Tiger's shoulder and pointed down the beach.

His eyes followed. After years in the sun, they were beginning to radiate a shallow fan of creases out from their corners. The wind pulled back his bleached hair, and his fine gold brows knitted over the bony ridge of his nose. Only twenty-six years old, Tiger already looked as elemental as any part of the scene around us.

I watched him studying the waves where the old break was wearing down, transforming. His topaz-colored eyes were flecked with green and gray. They seemed to cut like a lighthouse beam through the salt spray and spitting rain.

His eyes used to scare me when I was little. I'd seen eyes like that in a cat, but they were weird in a human being. Even knowing him for years, they still made me flinch every now and again. Tiger's eyes held a history of storms. One long look from him and it seemed like he knew your own dark weather as good as his own.

Fair and blond as he was, it was funny that I'd think of storms when I thought of Tiger; he looked more like a sunny beach boy, his bright head flashing in the summer sun. But behind those bright and beaming eyes, inside that tanned gold skin, I knew there were secrets and mysteries that came and went like tropical depressions.

Tiger blew into my life like a building squall at the end of the summer before my senior year. School had started, but it was still too hot for the sport coat and dress slacks I had to wear for Grandmama's funeral. We were all sitting around in the air-conditioned viewing room at Hampton Funeral Home. Aunt Heloise was crying, but most everybody else was standing around talking.

I was real sad about Grandmama and everything, but I was bored as hell. There's nothing worse than being cooped up with a bunch of aunts and cousins that haven't had anything interesting to say for as long as you can remember. But every once in a while they can still shock you. I was only about three feet away from Aunt Ethel and Aunt Dordeen when they started talking to my oldest cousin Rachel about Tiger.

"It just ain't right, Tiger not being here," Aunt Ethel said. "He always was so close with Mama."

"Why, he hain't bothered to drag down from the beach is beyond me," Rachel said.

"You'd think he'd have some respect for her, considering she put a roof over his head and raised him," Aunt Dordeen said smugly. "But then again, there ain't no telling what he thinks or does, slung up way off yonder."

"Why in the world that young'un felt like he had to move off so far away is beyond me," Aunt Ethel said.

"It weren't far enough, if you ask me," my mama said as she passed by on her way back from the ladies room to the sofa where my daddy was sitting. Rachel snickered and Aunt Ethel shook her head.

"Ethel, you know durn well why," Aunt Dordeen said, managing to sound annoyed and know-it-all at the same time.

"Well, Mama, I got my suspicions, but I don't know exactly why myself," Rachel said, sounding just as smug as her mama. "Considering nobody would have nothing to do with him after he run off with that—"

"Rachel, hush." Aunt Ethel interrupted while looking around to see who might be listening. I acted like I was looking for somebody and stepped away only to double around as quick as I could to hear more of what they were saying about Tiger.

I was younger than Tiger by eight years, and he'd been gone since I was ten years old. First he went off to college, then he moved to Nags Head. I didn't ever see him enough to know him very well, but the way I remembered him was nice. But Tiger always had something strange about him.

He always was as different from the rest of us as night and day. The rest of our people are fairly dark. Daddy told me Grandmama's great-grandmama was Tuscarora Indian. Of course, nobody wanted to talk about it much since Indians were considered to be only one step above black people, but it was so far back it didn't seem to matter now.

Tiger was fair complectioned and had blond hair and odd yellow-colored eyes. Daddy said that's why Grandmama named him what she did. Tiger was his real name, not a nickname. Daddy had a story how Grandmama said she had named her other children names as common as dirt and there wasn't much special about them. She made Tiger different from the start. Besides that, nobody would say how Tiger came to be Grandmama's last young'un. Granddaddy had been dead for years when he was born. If you asked, they'd tell you Grandmama was just a pure saint and change the subject.

I had maneuvered back near Aunt Dordeen and them, when a hush went over the viewing room. I looked around and saw Tiger in the doorway. His hair was down to his shoulders in back, with bangs cut short in front. It was sun-streaked, almost white, and he was tanned and looked more like my age than twenty-five in his clean white button-down shirt, faded jeans and high-top Nikes. He lingered at the door a minute, glancing around the room until he saw the coffin.

My older brother, Tommy, and Daddy got up to greet him, but he acted like he didn't even see them. Tiger just walked as if in a trance toward the open coffin, like not a one of us was even in the room. He stood by the coffin and looked down at Grandmama. He smiled slightly and seemed to speak to her but no noise came out. He just stood there looking down at her for the longest time, moving his mouth just a little, like he was sharing a secret with her.

Daddy started to walk over to him. Tommy started toward him too, but Daddy waved him off as he went to Tiger. He came up beside him and put his arm over his shoulder. Tiger looked at him and smiled the saddest smile in the world, like a dog would look at someone who might kick him.

"Why didn't anybody call me, Henry? I would have come," he asked my dad. For a minute Daddy looked confused as he patted Tiger on the shoulder.

"Dordeen said she'd called you herself, but it don't matter, son. The last few weeks Mama didn't know she was in the world," Daddy said.

Tiger shook his head. "Dordeen's full of shit. Missus Gurley, Granny's neighbor, called me this morning and chewed me out for being so sorry. I ain't heard one word from Dordeen."

His voice echoed sharply over the few sniffles in the stiff, suddenly silent room. I looked over and could see Aunt Dordeen's face freeze and then tighten in anger as she rose to defend herself. She walked briskly up to the coffin to confront Tiger.

"I did *so* try to call you! It's not my fault you won't home," she hissed.

Tiger looked at her. "I have an answering machine. Are you too stupid to leave a message?" he asked calmly, but there was no mistaking his rage.

Aunt Dordeen quivered with righteous indignation in her too-small organza dress. "I didn't want the news of Mama's death to reach you over a machine. I thought you were human enough to want to hear it from family. Well, I guess I was wrong. People like you don't even want to act like they got family."

Tiger looked her slowly up and down and narrowed his yellow eyes. "Get out of my face, you lazy, ignorant cow."

A collective gasp went up over the whole room. I looked over at my cousin Wayne. His mouth was wide open, too shocked to even smirk. He and I both remembered that Grandmama always said that Dordeen was a lazy heifer, and we still could laugh till our ribs hurt talking about it.

Reverend Winslow made his way cautiously to the little triangle by Grandmama's coffin. Daddy gripped Tiger by the shoulder, while Tiger and Aunt Dordeen glared at each other. Reverend Winslow stood by Aunt Dordeen's side and said sternly, "Son, remember where you are. This is no time for all this carrying on. Have some respect for your grandmother laying there."

Tiger turned his glare from Aunt Dordeen to the preacher, who flinched a bit when Tiger's eyes hit him. "Who the hell are you?" Tiger said, as he shook off Daddy's arm and took a step closer to the blown-up Reverend Winslow.

The preacher was a biggish man, an ex-football player, and pulpit pounder. "I am Reverend Winslow, your grandmother's pastor, " he said, making himself up to be large and intimidating.

Tiger snorted, "Where the hell did they drag you up from? Mama hadn't been in a church in twenty years."

I looked over at Wayne, who couldn't hold it back anymore; he started to snicker and so did I. I heard Daddy say to Tiger, "Come on outside now; it's okay."

Daddy put his arm back over Tiger's shoulder and half pulled, half walked him out the door. When they had made it into the hallway the room sounded a little like a teakettle with so many people letting out their breath all at once. Then it hissed like a bunch of snakes with all the whispering going on. Aunt Dordeen broke it up by letting out a wail and sinking to her knees by the edge of the coffin. Reverend Winslow bent down to comfort her, saying, "An ungrateful child stingeth like a viper."

Aunt Dordeen sobbed, "He ain't mine; he ain't nobody's but the devil's."

Somewhere, I thought I heard a somebody say "Amen." I barely had a moment to think about what Aunt Dordeen had said to Tiger . . . something like "You people act like you don't have family." I felt a trickle of sweat collect between my shoulder blades and run down to the hollow at the bottom of my back. Even in the air-conditioning, hearing all that, and just what it might mean, made me feel kind of hot and sick and excited, all at the same time.

Before I could sort it out, Wayne punched me on the arm and motioned for me to follow him outside. I concentrated hard following him out the door so I wouldn't forget, so I could think about it all later.

My brother Tommy was standing on the porch looking out to where Daddy and Tiger were leaning on our car, talking in the parking lot. "Damn, Tiger's a pisser, ain't he?" Wayne said.

Tommy looked at him and laughed. "Did you see Aunt Dordeen's face when he called her a cow?"

Wayne shook his head. "Tiger ain't nothing but trouble; never has been."

Tommy looked back out over the parking lot at Tiger and Daddy laughing. He said, "Daddy never thought so."

Something in Tommy's voice caused another bell to go off in my head, but Tommy never missed an opportunity to make me look stupid so I didn't say anything.

"I got some killer sinse bud, but I need to go down to the 7-Eleven to get some rolling papers," Wayne said. Y'all want ride around and catch a buzz?"

"I got my pipe with me," Tommy said. "I don't reckon nobody'll miss us if we ride around some, but you got to drive."

"Cool," Wayne said. They started walking off. Tommy looked back and said, "C'mon. Mama and Daddy ain't gonna want to stay that much longer."

I looked over to where Daddy and Tiger were talking. "Nah, y'all go on. I'm going to stick around."

"Figures," Tommy said.

Wayne snickered as he began tossing his keys in the air. "See you, wuss."

"Yeah. Fuck you." I said.

"You wish, faggot," Wayne laughed, not even looking back. Tommy snatched his keys in mid-toss and took off running down the rows of parked cars with Wayne chasing after him.

I felt kind of shy about barging in on Daddy and Tiger's conversation, but I didn't want to go back inside either. Hampton Funeral Home was the same one my baby brother Henry Junior was buried out of a few years back. Even the new plush wine-colored carpet and velvet cushions hadn't changed the fact the place was hateful, scary, and sad.

Grandmama, laid out for the viewing, looked like she was made of wax. The relatives and folks inside were weird to begin with, and worse right now, walking around with Jesus and death and heaven all stuck out of their mouths. I walked over to where Daddy and Tiger were talking instead of just leaving them to visit and going back inside.

They stopped talking when I walked up. Tiger looked me up and down slowly and said, "You near 'bout a weed, ain't you, hoss?" I was embarrassed. I had grown to over six feet tall in what seemed about a week and I felt like I would never get used to my own body.

Daddy said, "We tried to cut down on his feed, but he takes after his mama's side."

Tiger looked at me and said, "Have you ever seen any paintings by an artist named Mantegna?" I shook my head no, amazed that he would ever think that I had. "You look just like a figure at the foot of the cross in one of his crucifixions."

"I don't know whether that's good or bad," I said.

Tiger nodded, "It's a compliment," then he asked Daddy, "How's the building moratorium affecting your sales?" Daddy started in on a lengthy complaint on the economy and the government, leaving me with my hands in my pockets, staring up at the old pin oak limbs, trying to figure out how to spell Mantegna.

After a while Daddy offered that Tiger stay over with us. Tiger smiled and said no thanks politely. I offered him my room even, suddenly wanting him to stay just so I could listen to him talk.

He shook his head and told Daddy, "You know Sharon Ann likes me 'bout as much as Dordeen does."

Daddy nodded to him and said to me, "Son, go find your mama and tell her to come on; I'm ready to go."

I started to leave but Tiger told me to hold it a minute. He looked back at Daddy and asked, "Henry, can I use your key to get in over at Mama's? I want to take Matt and go get some things that mean a lot to me."

Daddy looked puzzled. "Can't that wait till after the funeral?"

"No," Tiger said sharply. He looked off a minute down George Street and then looked Daddy in the eye. "I'm not staying for the funeral. I'm driving back to the beach tonight."

I was surprised when Daddy just nodded and reached in his pocket for his keys. He found the one he was looking for and began working it off the ring. "Why come you need Matt to go with you?" he asked as he handed the key to Tiger.

Tiger laughed. "You know why. When my so-called sisters find out I was in that house, they'll say I stole. Matt here is going to be able to tell them all I took is Mama's old blue tea pitcher and the pictures of me when I was little," Tiger explained. He looked down at his feet and nudged a small rock gently, then kicked it spinning into the street. He looked up at Daddy and said calmly, "If I ask Dordeen for them I'll never get them, period. They all act like it was never my home, even though I lived there for eighteen years."

Daddy nodded, and then did an odd thing, considering he wasn't a real huggy-type guy. He turned to Tiger and put his arms around him, hugged hard and told him to take care of himself, then letting Tiger loose, he turned abruptly to go. He didn't even say good-bye. Tiger fingered the key and watched him walk between the cars and onto the front steps of the funeral home.

After a moment, Tiger turned and started walking into the parking lot. Confused, I hesitated for awhile before following him to his car. When I caught up, he threw me his keys.

"You look like you're man enough to drive this thing," he said. He had a brand-new, white-on-blue, full-sized Ford Bronco. I unlocked the door and climbed in. He got in on the passenger side and rolled down the window.

Tiger lit a cigarette, and smoked quietly watching George Street turn into the bypass as we headed out to Grandmama's place. I just drove. Tiger rode looking out the window like a lost little boy. We turned off 117 onto 70 and he just stared at the small houses and the churches that had grown schools.

Finally I said, "How do you spell Mantegna?"

Tiger looked at me quizzically with his cat eyes and then laughed. "M-A-N-T-E-G-N-A. *Man tain ya.* You should find the painting I was talking about in an art history book."

We rode in silence the rest of the way to Grandmama's house. I pulled up to the back door and sat with the engine running. I didn't know if Tiger just wanted to run in or what. When I glanced over at him, he was just sort of staring at the back porch.

Tiger got a set look on his face. Finally he told me to shut off the truck and come in with him. Inside, he motioned me to follow him. We walked through the tiny house, room by room. He seemed to hesitate in each one. I knew he had grown up here, but I had no earthly idea how long it had been since he'd visited.

We crossed the tiny hall into Grandmama's bedroom. He opened a drawer in her dresser which looked like it must have been her underwear drawer. Gently, he looked underneath all the panties, slips, and bras for something. He smiled finally and pulled out a worn red alligator pocketbook. He snapped it open, looked inside, and sighed with relief. He handed me the pocketbook, closed the drawer, and stood for a while just looking down at the things on top of the dresser.

Tiger sniffed the air, turning his head slightly, catching some scent of the living presence of Grandmama in the close, still air of the bedroom. I was surprised and a little bit embarrassed when I realized he was crying without making a sound. Watching his every move, more out of curiosity than just nosiness, it felt wrong to be catching him crying.

Tiger wiped off the tears with the back of his hand as he walked past me. Without a word more, Tiger went down the hall to the kitchen. I followed behind him still carrying the red alligator purse, wondering why in the hell he wanted it.

In the kitchen, Tiger looked back to where I was standing and asked gruffly, "You want some coffee, or something else to drink?"

"I guess I'll have some coffee, if you're gonna make some," I said.

"Well, you might as well sit down then, Matt," Tiger said. "It's only instant, but you'll get mighty tired standing there waiting on the water to boil."

I didn't say anything back. I just pulled out a chair, its legs scrapping dully on the linoleum, and sat down. I put the pocketbook down across from me, glad not to hold it anymore, but still curious about what it was all about. Tiger got busy making the coffee, perfectly at home. I watched him fill the teakettle with water and turn on the flame under it. Then he reached into the cabinet and took out the instant coffee and spooned out some into two clean cups. Out of nowhere he started laughing.

"Mama let me drink coffee, even when I was a little boy. Dordeen still lived at home back then and she would fuss at Mama for letting me have it. Mama told her she was too old to tell me no, besides, coffee killed worms in hogs and it would keep me from getting wormy. I was a skinny little thing, and she lived in constant fear that I had worms." Tiger got a big grocery bag from the stack under the sink. He opened the refrigerator and took out an old tea pitcher. He took it to the sink, emptied it, then rinsed it out before stuffing it in the paper bag.

Out of all the stuff in the house he could have taken, I wondered why he wanted that old thing. Grandmama had had it as long as I could remember. Other than the fact that it always was sitting in the refrigerator, magically full of tea sweet enough to give you insulin shock, there wasn't anything special about it. I was sort of in awe of Tiger, but not enough to keep from just blurting out, "Why come you want that old tea pitcher?"

Tiger just stood at the sink for a minute, staring out the window at the backyard. I was starting to get embarrassed for asking, when he answered. "When I was six years old, your daddy took me to the county fair for the first time. Henry was twenty-three and courting your mama."

Tiger turned away from the window and spoke directly to me now. "I won this pitcher at a coin-toss booth, because of your daddy. Mama popped me every time she saw me trying to write with my left hand. Your daddy told her and told her I was left-handed, but she thought she could break me."

Tiger searched my face to see if I was getting what he was trying to tell me. It must have been a strong memory. He looked a little bit like a frustrated and defiant kid just telling it. "Your daddy told me it was okay to use my left hand to pitch with."

Right then the teakettle started to whistle. "I bet Grandmama was tickled when you gave her the pitcher," I said.

Tiger laughed as he turned off the stove and poured the boiling water over the instant coffee. "She wasn't nearly as tickled when your daddy told her I got it left-handed and made her promise to leave me alone."

"Did she?" I asked, as Tiger brought the two cups of coffee to the table and sat down.

"Well, she still grumbled about it, but she stopped popping me when she caught me." Tiger gave me a sly grin. "That was just the beginning of her getting used to stuff about me she wasn't going to change."

I wondered what he meant by that. I thought I knew, but I didn't really feel right asking. Not only was it personal, but asking might end up telling him more about me than I'd learn about him. I'd let enough questions just jump out my mouth for the time being. That's what you learn from having an older brother; if you ask personal things right out, older people will try to mess you up. Dealing with Tommy taught me time and again that if I just listened long enough, I'd find out everything I wanted to know.

Tiger reached for the alligator handbag. He opened it and dumped the contents on the table. There was no money in it, just all kinds of junk. I watched as Tiger sorted out four baby teeth, a Red Cross Beginner Swimmer Badge, some homemade greeting cards, a baby's first haircut certificate complete with a still-platinum curl taped to it, some old newspaper clippings, snapshots, and a birth certificate. When he got to the birth certificate, he opened it, snorted, and set it aside.

"What is all this stuff?" I asked.

Picking up and peering at the photos one by one he said, "My childhood."

Finally, he gathered up everything and stuffed it all back into the alligator purse. Then he lit a cigarette and sipped his coffee, not making the first comment about the alligator purse or all the old saved-up souvenirs inside.

After the story of the tea pitcher, I'd hoped Tiger was in a mood to talk. Hearing all about him when he was little, and seeing all the ordinary stuff come out of the alligator pocketbook made me feel easier about asking questions, but he was stingy with his conversation. I watched him staring out the window at the other end of the kitchen table and decided to break my own rule. I didn't have any idea how much longer he'd sit there before it would be time to go. "Tiger, why does everybody hate you so bad?" I asked.

Tiger looked at me and asked, "How old are you now?"

"Seventeen," I said.

Tiger took a long hit off his cigarette. "How many people in our family have blond hair?" he asked.

I thought a minute. "Just you, and some of Renee's kids."

"Renee's kids don't count though, do they?" he replied. I said I supposed not since Renee was Dordeen's adopted daughter.

Tiger nodded and said, "Your daddy was your age when I was born—he's the closest thing to a daddy I ever had. Some of these secrets are way older than me. You ask your daddy. Ask him to tell you about Nathan Willis. If he thinks you should know, he'll tell you."

I sipped my coffee, which had finally gotten cool enough to drink. Tiger stubbed out his cigarette and lit another one. I thought about what Aunt Dordeen, Rachel, and Aunt Ethel were talking about in the funeral home, just when it got good. I decided to try a different tack. "Tiger, you remember the last year you lived with Grandmama, I came for a weekend?"

Tiger smiled and nodded. "Yeah, I thought you were a pretty cool little kid."

I felt myself warm up, and I hoped I wasn't blushing or something stupid like that. It made me feel good to know Tiger even thought about me when I was a kid, even more, he thought I was cool. When I felt like I could talk without squeaking, I asked, "Do you remember taking me to the movies?"

"Yeah, I do," he said and gave me a puzzled smile.

Tiger didn't have any way to know what all that meant to me. In a lot of ways, it was when I started figuring out what was what. I was only ten years old, but I kept stumbling on pieces of things that I'd pick up and put together to make myself out of.

It was back in 1976 and *Rocky* was playing. I had always wanted to see it. Tommy had seen it five times, but I never seemed to get to go. Mama and Daddy were out of town, and I was staying with Grandmama and Tiger for the weekend. Grandmama didn't want to let us go out that Saturday night. I remember Tiger asking her what kind of trouble she thought he could get us into. Finally, Grandmama relented and we took off. Tiger drove us to McDonald's and we ate in the truck listening to an eight-track tape of Bad Company. Tommy was staying with a friend of his and I remember how cool I felt riding in Tiger's truck with "Shooting Star" blaring out of the speakers when we passed them on their bikes on our way to the movies.

Tiger knew the black girl working the box office at the old Jewel Box Theater. She let us in for free. Tiger bought me buttered popcorn and a cherry Coke and told me to enjoy the show. He'd seen it and he was going to hang out in the lobby with his friends.

I got bored late into the movie, so I wandered out in the lobby to find Tiger. Tiger was nowhere to be seen. The lobby was deserted, except for the usher kid behind the counter. He had fallen asleep.

The Jewel Box Theater was ancient. It had originally been a vaudeville theater about a hundred years before. It had a grand balcony, which was seldom opened up. The only time I had ever been up there was when Mama and Aunt Dordeen took me to see *Gone With the Wind* when I was six years old. Now, with Tiger nowhere in sight, the usher asleep, and no one to tell me no, I decided to sneak upstairs and look around. I snuck under the red velvet rope and started up the narrow stairs.

There were no lights on in the stairwell. I climbed for what seemed to be an eternity, almost getting lost on the landing in the dark. Finally I stood at the back of the balcony looking out over the steep rows of seats to the huge screen. For a moment I felt dizzy, like I was going to fall or something. It was such a strange perspective to see the screen from that height and looking down all those steps.

I had an urgent desire to follow them down to the edge and look down at the audience below. It was hot up there and I crept down the steps to the edge and leaned over. I had a secret thrill looking down at the audience knowing that they couldn't see me spying on them. I thought about spitting down on someone. I decided not to spit, though, not wanting to give myself away. I just looked at the people. It was like being upside down.

Finally, I grew tired of staring down at the audience and made my way across the edge of the balcony and back up the steps on the opposite side. My intention was to go back to the lobby by the opposite staircase. When I got to the edge of the stairs, there was a yellowish glow coming up from the landing. A single dim bulb was burning in a chipped gold plaster sconce like the unlit ones leading up to the staircase. Underneath the light I saw Tiger. He wasn't alone.

On the dim landing, Tiger was leaning with his back against the wall. A tall, dark-haired guy was standing across from Tiger with one arm on either side of him, blocking him from turning either way. The guy had on a fatigue flight suit and I could see the military badges with flaming swords and wings on his upper sleeves.

I froze. Scared, my heart was thumping away so hard I thought I could see it pushing against my sweaty T-shirt. I didn't know whether to call out or sneak back the other way. The man in the flight suit looked like he wasn't going to let Tiger go anywhere. He was looking down at him with a strange look on his face. Looked to me like Tiger was in trouble.

Tiger reached up and slowly pulled down the zipper on the guy's flight suit, then ran his hand inside an unzipped panel to the guy's shoulder. The man kissed Tiger full on the mouth as Tiger began to pull the top part of the flight suit down off his shoulders. He had large strong forearms covered with dark hair and a heavy gold watch on one thick wrist. It took him a minute to work his arms out of the sleeves and then the flight suit fell down to his hips, hanging below the white line of his jockey shorts. The gold light over them made the sweat on his back gleam. Tiger put his hand at the small of the larger guy's sweaty back and pulled him to him.

They kissed while I stood frozen for what seemed like an hour. I snuck back up to the balcony. The big screen was filled with the sweat-slicked muscles of Sly Stallone. Then, in an edit, his face flooded the screen. Contorted with effort, with struggle, it reminded me of the face of the pilot as he strained with Tiger in the dim place I'd just left.

Gonna fly now, flying high now . . .

The theme from *Rocky* played constantly on the radio for months afterward. Every time I heard it, it taunted me with everything I'd seen in the dirty gold light of the landing of the Jewel Box Theater. It would take me a long time to fit that picture together with everything else I was finding to make myself grown. But I did.

Tiger looked at me and absently flicked his ashes into the ashtray. His eyes seemed to read all the clabbered dreams that moment of spying had claimed for me. The memory of him drinking in the pilot's sweaty kisses seemed to come in a dream in the early mornings when I woke up. I remembered how the muscles in the pilot's back shivered like a horse as he moved in to kiss Tiger on the mouth. In my preconsciousness, I savored the memory, still clear as day, of Tiger in the arms of that pilot.

I looked over at the stove. I wasn't really ready to hear any truths or tell any. "I had a real good time that night," I ended lamely.

Tiger followed my eyes back over his shoulder to the clock on the stove. "I have a long drive back to the beach and I got to get you home," he said. He must have thought I was ready to leave, when all I wanted to do was ask him more about that night . . . or not. I didn't know.

He looked at me strangely for a moment and then said, "You're still a good kid. Thanks for coming here with me. I'm really glad I didn't have to come alone." I nodded and opened my mouth to ask him more, but I stopped short of saying anything.

Tiger stood, picked up the alligator bag filled with all the little bits and pieces that told him who he was or at least, who he used to be. He dropped it into the paper bag with the old tea pitcher. "You know, if you ever want to come visit me at the beach, come find me. It's not that big, and your daddy knows where I am."

"Someday I might just do that," I said. Inside, I already knew that whoever and whatever Tiger was, he had answers to secrets of mine, as much as his own. I just had to bide my time and wait.

Tiger

nodded, looking back from the break. "It's cleaner over there, but it's still too gnarly to be much good."

I looked out again. I saw a suddenly clean swell, break left with a tube I could have gone for. Tiger shivered slightly in the wind. I wasn't even chilly.

"You don't think it's worth it?" I shouted to him over the wind.

Tiger shook his head. "It ain't worth getting killed over."

I wanted to go out. I just didn't want to go out alone. I had a nice healthy respect for the ocean. But I also knew the worst thing you could do was not fight the fear. If you let yourself get afraid, you quit going out even on glassy summer days.

"C'mon, Tiger. You and me. It's not that gnarly," I said as I grabbed the back of his neck and tugged it gently.

Tiger shook off my hand and took a step down the dune. He didn't like the fact that I was a bigger guy, even if he was more experienced and wiser. In the big waves, I had more stroke. My arms and legs were longer.

"Mark could handle it," I said as I took the step down to Tiger's side once again. Mark and I could hang when Tiger got tossed around.

Tiger turned and looked up at me. Levelly, he said, "Too bad Mark ain't here. He's got enough sense not to go out in this slop even if he was here."

Tiger pointed out offshore. There was a deeper streak of gray water racing out through the surf, closing out the remnants of waves and sucking down a few trying to form over its back. "That's just one riptide you can see," Tiger said.

"Yeah, I know," I shouted back to him. Riptides can pull you out faster than you can paddle back in, but I knew enough to paddle across them, rather than fight the current. Tiger pointed out another one, smaller, but running like hell. He looked back to see if I got the point. I shrugged.

Tiger turned and headed back up over the dune. I looked out toward the break again. It was holding up pretty well. I wanted to go out. To me, it looked totally worth it. I turned reluctantly and followed Tiger down the dune and back toward the Bronco.

I caught up with him and asked him when Mark was supposed to get home. Tiger looked at his watch. "A few more hours. But then the tide will be shifting. If anything, it'll just be worse," he said definitively.

I looked at him, then back toward the beach. "What are we going to do now?" I asked. "I mean, it's still early."

Tiger unlocked the door to the Bronco and tossed me the keys to unlock my own door. "I have enough running around to do to keep me busy the rest of the day. I have to stop by the house first and put on some business clothes. You can go with me, or you can stay home and study. Didn't you say you had a test this week?"

I got in the truck reluctantly. I didn't want to study and I didn't want to just run around with Tiger. "You think Mark is getting much done at the airport on a day like this?"

Tiger snorted as he got in and cranked up the engine. "He's busier than shit on days like this. Even if the planes are grounded, he'll be using the time to work on an engine."

That sounded logical for Mark. Still, I decided I'd rather stay at the house, even study, to wait and see if Mark would come home and go out surfing with me. "I think I'll just hang out at the house," I told Tiger.

He swung the Bronco out on the beach road, and fiddled with the radio until he got a weather report. The forecaster pretty much echoed Tiger's predictions as to when the winds would shift and clean up the waves. I closed my eyes and pictured the little break behind us. I still thought I could handle it.

We were back home pretty quick. Where we had been working wasn't even a fifteen-minute drive from the house. Tiger pulled the Bronco between the pilings under the house and left the engine running. I got out and started my routine of replacing the stakes we had used during the day with new ones from a bundle of lathe, and checking all the other supplies. Before he trotted upstairs, Tiger told me to pull out the transit case and bring it upstairs. He wanted me to wipe it down and make sure it was dry after being out in the rain all day.

I pulled it out and set it by the steps, then I unhooked the straps from Tiger's board and mine from the racks on top of the Bronco. I stood mine on its rail in the sand between a piling and the stairs, so the wind couldn't get it. I took Tiger's board and the transit upstairs before heading back down for mine.

I looked at it. It looked like it could fly. It was an orange and white, six-two, Natural Art twin-fin. I was just getting used to the speed and control I got from the extra fin. My other board was upstairs on the porch with every one else's. It wasn't exactly a big gun, just six-ten with a single fin. That was the board I would have needed if I was going to go out today. I wasn't that used to big waves. The bigger board would help, I reminded myself, thinking again of the thick waves pounding the break down the road.

Tiger came back down the stairs with a tube and a handful of folders, dressed for business. "I'm going to run some prints of Bayview Heights and take them to the developer. After that, I'm going over to Beaufort to record that easement we did last week," he said. He looked at me sternly as I picked up my board and ran my hand down the rail to dislodge the sand stuck where I'd put it down. "You ain't crazy enough to think about going out by yourself are you?" Tiger asked me.

In a way, it was a challenge. Tiger was my boss and my landlord, but he acted like my goddamn daddy when he thought he ought to. It kind of pissed me off sometimes. I finished brushing the sand off my board and just looked at him.

"Your daddy would kill me if I let you go out and get drowned. You know that don't you, Matt?"

I shook my head yeah. I knew Tiger was responsible for me in the eyes of my folks. I didn't like to be reminded of that. I was grown as far as I was concerned.

Daddy figured Tiger to be a tough boss, but he also thought he'd be a fair one. He also knew Tiger would keep me out of trouble and he counted on it. Tiger's eyes softened and he grinned at me. "Hold on, water dog. This is going to be the swell of your life once it cleans up some. I promise."

I smiled back at him and didn't say anything.

Tiger got in the Bronco and put his plan tube and papers on the backseat. "I'll probably be back before Mark gets home," he said as he closed the door. "If you get bored, there's some mortgage surveys that need to be drafted."

"No problem," I told him. In a business as small as his, the rain just meant you got a chance to work inside to get caught up. Tiger gave me a grin before he backed the Bronco down the drive and took off. I headed upstairs with my new board, not particularly looking forward to either studying or drafting. Even if I couldn't be out surfing, I wanted to be doing anything other than work. But working and studying was what I really came to Tiger's to do.

Though my grades were good in high school, I missed getting any scholarships. That meant I wasn't able to go to college. I damn sure didn't want to take out any loans. I watched my daddy give up every spare dime he had, trying to get rid of the loan he had to take out when Henry Junior, my little brother, got cancer and died. I didn't want a loan hanging over my head.

I probably would have been able to go to college, even without the scholarships, if it hadn't taken everything extra Daddy made to pay off the bills and keep a roof over our heads. My future wasn't looking too bright. A month before graduation, I sat down with Daddy at the kitchen table and told him my bad news about the scholarships.

Daddy listened, his face growing sadder and sadder. I knew there wasn't anything he could do. He'd been wanting me to go on to college for as long as I could remember. Seeing the defeated look on his face, every sad thing in my life caught up with me. I felt bad about the scholarships, I felt bad about Henry Junior and I felt worse making Daddy look like there wasn't anything he could do. I laid my head down on the table and cried.

Daddy reached across the table and patted the back of my head softly like I was a dog while I told him I was sorry for making him feel so bad when it was really all my fault. I had fucked up, not him. Finally I cried myself out and went over to the sink to wash my face. I didn't say anything about Chris, but I kind of felt bad about him and what he meant to me, too. It seemed right then like I was worthless, just a sorry-ass kid.

Daddy stood up and came over to the sink. He gave me a hug, the first time I could remember him doing that in a long time. His shirt still smelled like his car, cigarettes, and Aqua Velva. That was Daddy's smell and it made me feel better, like it had when I was little, even though now I had to bend down to get my head on his shoulder. I got tickled then and snickered. "When'd you start shrinking?" I asked him.

Daddy laughed as he looked up at me. "Raising you young'uns has wore me down to a nub, I reckon." I gave his shoulders a squeeze.

"Sit down at the table, son. I think I got an idea you might be interested in," Daddy said as he pushed me gently away. He poured us both some Pepsi and sat back down at the table with me. "I been talking to Tiger. He's offered for you to go down to the beach and stay with him this summer. He can put you to work helping him. If you work hard, you ought to be able to save some money. I'll give him money to keep you fed and pay your share of the bills for the summer. Then, if you and him work good together, you can stay on for a year and make up your mind what you want to do about school the next year."

I was dumbfounded; Daddy was serious. I listened to him as he went on. "I don't reckon you want to go to school half as much as you want to get the hell out of the house. I don't blame you; I was the same way when I was your age. You always wanted to live at the beach. Here's your chance. You go live with Tiger and work some. In a year, you don't know what might happen." Daddy sat back with a smile. He and Tiger must have been talking about this for a long time. It sounded too good to be true.

"What about Mama? You know she ain't gonna like this one damn bit." It was all I could think of to say. While on the one hand I didn't give a shit about what Mama wanted, on the other, I didn't want to see her mad and hurt either.

Daddy took a long swallow of Pepsi and lit a cigarette. He studied me for a minute then said, "Son, your mama ain't stupid and neither am I. We know things about you that you don't even think we do." I felt the hair on the back of my neck stand up.

Daddy looked away. "Matt, life ain't easy on nobody. Things don't turn out the way you thought they were going to. Life's full of disappointments—that's just a fact. The thing is, we love you and we want to do what's best for you. Right now, we think you need to go out on your own. If we send you to Tiger's, he'll keep an eye on you. We've done the best we could raising you and we're right proud of how you've turned out. From here on out, the rest is up to you."

Daddy sighed and stood up. "You go on to Tiger's tomorrow. Talk to him over the weekend and let me know what you want to do." Daddy hesitated in the doorway to the den. "My show's about to come on."

From behind him, I heard a commercial for herbicides going on about nematodes. My mind was racing. Daddy turned to go into the den. "Daddy?" He turned to look at me. "I'm sorry," I said.

He gave me a warm smile. "You ain't got nothing to be sorry about, son. Your mama and I love you." I felt as light as an empty paper bag. It was the first time my daddy had admitted he knew I was gay. Things weren't ever going to be the same, but they were going to be okay.

"Daddy . . . thanks," I said quietly.

Daddy smiled at me sadly for a moment. "You ought to give Tiger a call and let him know you're coming in early." I nodded.

"You gonna get your mess ready to go?" he asked.

"Yes, sir," I said.

"Well go on and call Tiger, then come watch my show with me. It's been right good lately." He smiled at me and let me know that for now, this was enough. I was grateful for that.

"I'll be there in just a minute," I said. Daddy nodded and went into the den.

I watched him go back to his chair and sit down heavily. I tried to be sad, but I was too excited about going to Tiger's. I called him from the kitchen, like Daddy told me.

The next day, I drove down to the beach first thing in the morning, ready to go to work. Tiger wanted me at his place at seven-thirty. He wanted me to work a day before I made up my mind.

When I pulled up the drive at Tiger's, he was sharpening a machete under the house. He looked happy to see me. As I got out of Daddy's truck, Tiger said, " I hope you got a good night's sleep, hoss. We got eighteen hundred feet of line to cut today."

"I'm up for it," I said confidently.

Tiger just grinned and jerked his head toward the Bronco. "Saddle up, then," he said and whistled for his dogs. They came bounding down the stairs, all gray muscle and flapping ears, to jump in the Bronco and settle happily on the backseat.

When Tiger and I climbed in after them, he handed me a photocopy of some papers and told me to read them. I began: "Beginning at a big rock in a ditch, said ditch being the westernmost line of the parcel belonging to Eustus Tillett, as described in the Carteret County Deed Book Number thirty-one page two hundred and seventy-seven, proceed North twenty-seven degrees eighteen minutes east, three hundred feet more or less to an iron rod . . . "

It went on like that for two pages, talking about finding stumps, iron rods and fence posts along the way. I finished reading it and handed it back to Tiger. He flung it up on the dash.

"You know what you just read?" he asked.

"Sure. It's a land survey from way back, real old timey," I told him.

Tiger laughed. "That's the problem. Half them permanent reference points probably don't exist anymore. Matt, we are going to be doing this boundary survey almost from scratch. It's out in Back Beaufort and it ain't going to be nothing but marsh and mosquitoes all day. If you make it through today and still want to come back, I'll be happy to put you to work, but if you hate it—"

"No way. I'm looking forward to it," I interrupted him.

He looked over at me skeptically. "Well, if it's not what you expected, don't blame me."

We drove back over the bridge at Atlantic Beach to the mainland. After about twenty minutes, we pulled off the shoulder of the road to park at the site and the work part of the day began. Tiger taught me how to use a plumb-bob and how to hold a rod and use the tape. Mostly, I swung a machete to cut limbs, branches, and reeds out of the sight line.

The sun came up hotter and hotter. I dug around in the soft black dirt looking for iron rod markers. I stripped off my shirt and sweated like a horse. The dogs ran loose, chased rabbits and nosed around in the weeds, even went swimming. As I cut line, I hoped they were scaring off snakes.

When I wasn't hacking branches or trying to hold the rod, I stood around waiting while Tiger made field notes in a little yellow notebook. If the sky hadn't been so blue, and I'd not have had so much time to think my own thoughts; I'd have wanted to trade places with the dogs.

Tiger was patient with me, but I knew he was watching me, too. I figured he was thinking I'd be miserable standing outside all day. He didn't talk much—not much chit-chat anyway. I could tell he was working and with that kind of work you don't fuck around and mess up. Tiger was nothing but business, all day.

About four o'clock, we found ourselves back where we started. Tiger made the last of his notes in the little yellow book and whistled for the dogs. They came running as we loaded the transit and tools into the back of the Bronco. When we got it all loaded up, we headed back to the beach. I sat with my window open and let the wind from the road blow across me. I felt completely happy.

"Well hoss, that's about as bad as it gets this time of year. It's a lot worse in the summer. You still want a job?" Tiger asked me. I guessed he was pleased with the work I did.

"I had a great day," I said honestly. "I'd work for you, if you'll have me."

Tiger nodded. "I wish I had you working right now; it's a good thing it's slow. You still got a month before you get out of school, don't you?"

"Yeah, but I haven't missed many days. If you need me bad, it wouldn't be no big deal for me to miss a few between now and then," I told him.

Tiger said dryly, "I'll keep that in mind."

"Since I ain't going to get to go to college, it don't make much difference noways," I said.

Tiger gave me a sharp look. "That's what you think. Your daddy didn't mention the rest of the deal to you?"

"No, I didn't know there was any more to it. Daddy only told me that I could come work for you over the summer and stay for a year to get my head together and save some money. Then, maybe I could go on to ECU after that."

"Look in the back and screw off the lid of the water cooler. There ought to be a couple of beers in there. Get me one and you one, too," Tiger said.

I climbed between the seats and in between the dogs to get to the back. It was worth it for the promise of a beer. When I got back into my seat, I popped the top and handed Tiger his beer, then did the same for my own, wondering all the while what other surprises Daddy hadn't told me about. Tiger set me straight right quick.

"Well, your daddy left out one thing. If you come live with me and Mark, you got to keep on in school. I want you to enroll at Carteret Community come fall, even if it's for only two classes. I'll work with you on your work schedule."

"Whoa, hold on. I didn't agree to go to school," I said, and then really went off about not wanting to do it. Tiger listened to me trying to argue and didn't say anything. I noticed we missed the turnoff to the bridge back to the beach. We drove right past it heading out Arendall Street. Tiger didn't say anything until he turned into the campus.

"Take a look around, Matt. You ain't got to take but two courses. I don't care if it's art, English, or science or any damn thing you please, as long as it'll transfer credits, but this here is part of the deal. It gets too easy to get out of the habit of studying if you don't keep on."

The campus looked good. It was right on the water. Tiger pulled up and parked in front of a brick building. "The admissions office is in yonder. Run in and get you an application."

I drank the last of my beer and looked at him hard. It was like trying to stare down a cat. I went in and got an application.

A month later, I graduated from high school. The next day, I moved to the beach and my real life began. But before that, Daddy had sent me down to Tiger's before. In his mind, I think he had started planning it all out the October after Grandmama died.

I was hanging out around the house watching *Soul Train* when the phone rang. Daddy yelled from the garage asking me if I was deaf. I heard him grumbling, then he picked up the phone in the kitchen. I was watching Don Cornelius and wishing I was dead. I switched over to *American Bandstand,* but the sight of so many happy, heterosexual teenagers made me want to throw up. I switched back to *Soul Train*. Straight black kids' happiness was a lot easier to take.

Daddy came into the den smiling. "That was Tiger on the phone. Seems he's started his own surveying business down at Atlantic Beach."

I was instantly interested. I hadn't hardly even thought about Tiger since Grandmama's funeral. "Hey, that's great. Atlantic Beach is a lot closer than Nags Head," I said.

Daddy eased into his recliner. "Ain't there a football game on? Duke is supposed to be playing State, I think."

I got down on the floor to twist the knob on the front of our old Sears floor model TV that had a built-in HiFi stereo and speakers to run through the channels for him.

"I'm hoping your mama will get us hooked up to cable for my Christmas," he said.

I wanted cable TV too, for MTV. Mama said besides being a waste of money, MTV was of the devil. I knew daddy didn't give a damn about MTV; he just wanted to be able to change channels from his chair. I pictured him sitting there with one of those remote controls, pushing down the little buttons, over and over, driving Mama crazy. I found the game and stretched out on the floor in front of the screen.

"Son, you got any plans for tonight and tomorrow?" he asked, knowing full well I didn't.

"Naw, nothing special," I said, hoping some conversation about dating wasn't in the works.

"I want you to take the truck down to the beach and give Tiger a hand getting into his new place. You remember how to seat a commode, don't you?" Daddy asked me casually.

"Sure. I mean it's been awhile since you showed me, but I could probably handle it okay." I didn't want to sound too interested, but driving down to the beach on my own was lots better than hanging out at home, even to install a toilet.

"Tiger's bought a house in Salter Path and it needs a new stool. I got him a good price on one. I need to stay around here, but I'd sure appreciate it if you'd go down there and get it in for him."

I was secretly elated, then concerned. "What about Mama?" Since Grandmama's funeral, she didn't have two good words to say about Tiger.

Daddy looked at me sharply. "I can handle your mama. Go get your stuff together. Half the day's gone already. It'll take you at least an hour and a half to get down there." I was already on my feet.

It didn't take me long to throw some stuff in my backpack and get back downstairs. Daddy followed me out to the garage and I helped him lift the new Elgin commode into the back of his pickup. He gave me the directions he'd written out, then hesitated for a moment before handing me the keys.

"Matt, you're getting old enough to know there's a lot of different kinds of people in the world. Tiger's always been kind of different. You're smart . . . " He was fumbling badly with what he had to say and though I was scared of what he might say, I couldn't let him just dangle there.

"Daddy, its okay; I think I know what you're going to say. I can take care of myself."

Daddy looked at me strangely. Then he said, "Tiger's had a tough row to hoe, in more ways than one. Just don't judge him too hard."

"Daddy, I asked Tiger, back when Grandmama died, why come everybody hated him so bad. He told me to ask you about a man named Nathan something."

Daddy gave me a funny look, then said, "What did he say about Nathan Willis? What did he tell you?"

I fingered the truck keys knowing I'd hit a sore spot. "Nothing. He said if you thought I ought to know you'd tell me."

Daddy looked out the garage door into the lemony afternoon sun. "You better get going, boy. You tell Tiger I said that's his story. Far as I'm concerned, it ain't nothing to be ashamed of. Tell him I'll come and see what kinda job you did next time I'm down that ways after Christmas."

I was incredulous. "You see Tiger right regular?"

Daddy nodded. "I been looking after Tiger since I was near 'bout your age. Love him as good as one of my own young'uns. You ask Tiger anything you want. Just remember you got to live with any skeletons he digs up. Now get the hell on away from here. I'm missing my game."

He squeezed my shoulder before I closed the door to the truck. As I pulled down the driveway I saw him going back into the house. For the first time I could remember, he looked old and tired. I felt like I'd said or done something that had stripped all the starch out of his proud bantam walk. I didn't let it spoil the excitement of the unexpected trip to see Tiger, though. I just put the truck in gear and hauled ass.

I knew the back way to the beach by heart. There probably wasn't a kid my age who didn't. Every summer, people from my hometown would beg a week's rental from friends or relatives lucky enough to have a place at the beach. We usually stayed at some friend of Mama and Daddy's. They had a trailer in a mobile home park on the ocean side in Indian Beach. Every night we would drive through the live oaks and cicada songs on Highway 12 from Indian Beach through Salter Path then Pine Knoll Shores to the Circle in Atlantic Beach.

The Circle was a full-time amusement park with bumper cars and night clubs, ice cream places and beer joints. There were dance places that played rock and roll, dance places for country music and beach music too. Through their open doors you could see the couples swaying, doing the shag, or gyrating like something crazy. Mama said it had gotten awful honky-tonk, but for a kid it was a wonderland. Tommy and I would beg to ride the bumper cars while Mama and Daddy would stand off to one side watching us. Mama was tense, you could tell, watching us try to ram the living shit out of each other and everybody else. Still she had enough sense not to cry out and embarrass us.

One time we got out and found Daddy with his arm around Mama's waist whispering in her ear. She giggled like a girl and Daddy gave us money for cotton candy and sent us off running into the neon night. I think I saw him pinch her butt, but she laughed instead of asking him if he'd gone crazy, like she usually did when he'd do it at home.

The beach had that effect on people. Outside of the bright lights of the carnival rides and beer joints were guys without shirts idling on the hoods of cars eyeing girls in gauzy halter tops. The warm salty night breezes carried looks that got tossed back and forth, caught and held. Teenagers wandered around the humid dark streets and sudden shrieks followed by giggles let the sleepy folks in the mobile homes and cottages know that sex was in the air.

Nobody seemed too worried about it, though. People let their hair down. Even hard-core religious people acted like God winked at them and turned a blind eye toward their sins when they went down to the beach. With just about everybody half-naked in muggy nights, a big ol' Carolina moon overhead, saying no was about as far from anybody's mind as January sleet.

The beach was magic, and I was always jealous of Tiger for getting to live there all the time. I didn't know much about Nags Head; it was too far away for us to go to. Tommy's friend Eric used to go all the time. He'd come back telling us about *The Lost Colony* play and the good parts where the Indians came out and killed the colonists and stuff.

When I was little, I asked Daddy if Tiger had anything to do with the Lost Colony but he told me no. Tiger worked for an engineering firm on the beach and explained to me that the Lost Colony was on Roanoke Island, not Nags Head. He told me Tiger actually lived near where the Wright brothers flew the first plane at Kill Devil Hill, in Kitty Hawk.

Thinking about getting to see Tiger, I felt happy for the first time all week. The sun was out and I turned the radio station to WDLX. I'd be able to pick up WQDR for soul music and WSFL for rock and roll by the time I hit Kinston. It seemed good to be out on the road and the strangeness of going to the beach this late in the year was sweet.

I was by myself and I didn't have to juggle anything. I was with me and right then I felt like pretty good company. Going through Kinston, I saw this good-looking guy with his shirt off working on his car in the warm autumn sun. I slowed down and checked him out. He must have had a friend or something with a truck like mine because he looked up and waved.

I thought how it would be if he was queer too. Maybe he was lonesome and was just waiting on somebody like me to love and go around with. Then again, he was probably just some redneck with a girlfriend who beat up queers. I waved back like I knew him. What the hell, I was on the road heading to the beach, sixty-three miles an hour, with the radio on. I didn't feel like worrying about it.

I drove through the warm sunshine flicking back and forth through radio stations with no one to scold me for doing it. Following Daddy's instructions, I cut off miles by going back roads after Kinston. I drove past rundown shacks where colored people lived and big farmhouses set way back from the road. The land was long, low, and flat this close to the ocean, and the sky seemed to go on forever in the early afternoon light.

As I drove, looking for good songs on the radio, I wondered if I'd have the guts to talk to Tiger about the past. Dad had said it was his story to tell, and I was anxious to hear it. More than that, I wanted to tell Tiger that I was queer. The bitch of being queer was I didn't have anybody to ask things.

I thought about ways to just launch right into the whole discussion. I decided maybe I could bring it up by telling Tiger I had seen that pilot guy and him necking that time on the stairs at the Jewel Box Theater. I was determined to get to the bottom of a lot of things on this trip.

Before I knew it, I was sitting at the traffic light at the big bridge that humped itself in the middle over the sound between the mainland and the island. I rolled down the window and took in the salty sweet smell of the water and felt the chilly breeze off the sea. Gulls soared way up high, and reflected back on the gray and green water flowing at low tide around the sandbars and reed beds.

Right then, one of my favorite old songs came on over the radio. It was Junior Walker and the All Stars singing, *"What does it take, to win your love for me . . . Oh, I've tried, I've tried . . . "* It was a great moment. I let it stretch out as I drove the truck through the thick of old live oaks and scrub pine through Emerald Isle, with Junior Walker's sax line wailing.

Tiger's house was on a little street between the highway and the beach road. It was not a new house, but it sat up high on pilings on top of a dune. You could see the ocean peeking between the houses across the street from the drive. I parked the truck next to Tiger's Bronco under the house. Figuring he was home, I got my knapsack and climbed up the stairs to the porch.

From the porch you could see the ocean really good. I opened the screen and knocked on the door, but got no answer. Trying the lock, I twisted the knob and the door came open. I called in, but still got no answer.

Wherever he was, I figured Tiger couldn't have gone far or for very long. He'd left the Bronco downstairs and the door unlocked. I decided to take a seat in a rocker and wait out on the porch. I turned back to the view from the porch, looking out over the island a long way. The house faced south so the sun was still shining on the porch, warm and nice. The robin's egg blue sky held a tint of rose in the west and pale yellow toward the sea.

The porch was crowded with empty cardboard boxes and old wooden rockers. I moved an empty box off of a rocking chair and sat down. On a clothesline stretched between the posts of the porch hung a wetsuit and some towels. Two surfboards were leaning against the wall by the door, and a windsock shaped like a dolphin drifted in the steady breeze.

Neatly placed amid all the other junk were rows of those little teeny trees like Japanese people grew. Some of them looked like they were blowing in the wind, some of them looked like tiny ancient trees from fairy tales. It was like a miniature storybook forest in broad shallow clay pots. It took me awhile to remember that they were called bonsai. I wished I could shrink and lay under them in the sun.

I sat for about ten minutes studying the bonsai and looking out over the other cottage roofs before I saw a guy in a wetsuit carrying a surfboard walking up the street from the beach with two big wet dogs. It was Tiger. I stood up and watched him coming home. He stopped and shook his head sideways and one of the dogs took the break as a time to shake too. I waved for a minute before he looked toward the house and saw me. He waved back as the dogs caught sight of me and began to bark deeply. As I went down the stairs to meet them all, the dogs broke into a trot toward me.

Tiger was walking barefoot and still wet. The dogs nosed me casually, looking back at Tiger to see if I was okay. He smiled, asking me if I'd been there long. I told him no and offered to take the surfboard from him. He gave it to me and shook his head like dogs do, spattering me with water droplets.

"Damn swimmer's ear," he said. "Thanks for coming. Sorry I wasn't around when you got here, but the wind shifted offshore and I decided to go out."

I told him no problem and followed him up the drive to the house as the dogs clambered up the steps to the deck. I showed him the new commode in the back of the truck, and he grinned.

"Henry's the greatest. I bought this place and two hours after I closed, I found out the commode was shot." He told me to leave it in the truck, and went around to the outdoor shower. He rinsed off the board first and then started taking off his wetsuit. Just casual as hell, he stripped down to his Speedo and got in the shower.

I tried not to look at his body, seeing as he was a relative and all, but I couldn't help it. He had a nice body, real lean, with a trace of blond hair across his chest and stomach. Watching Tiger strip and shower really got me going. I felt like I ought to be ashamed. He was a cousin, or an uncle, or something. To tell the truth, I wasn't sure what relation he was. That was weird considering I came from a family that would sit around and talk about who married and had who for back like two hundred years.

Still dripping, Tiger told me to come on and we headed upstairs. As the dogs whined and scratched at the door, he hung up his wetsuit next to the other one. I leaned his board against the wall by the door with the others. He pushed open the door with his foot and the dogs scrambled in. The front of the house was one big living room, dining room, and kitchen. Most of the furniture and stuff was already in place. It looked comfortable already, except for the boxes and boxes of books still stacked by one wall. Tiger had obviously been finishing up a built-in bookcase before I got there. Tools still lay in sawdust on the floor.

The dogs were nosing their water bowls around on the floor making a hell of a clang. "Do you still drink coffee?" Tiger asked. He filled the stainless steel bowls for the dogs, then he reached for the coffee pot.

"Yeah, sure do," I said as I watched the tall dogs noisily lap up the water with their big pink tongues. I had never seen dogs that tall and lean, that odd smoky color and with yellow eyes to boot. They eyed me suspiciously as I moved to the counter that separated the kitchen from the living-dining area. "Cool dogs," I said. "What kind are they?"

"They're weimaraners," Tiger said as he reached in the cabinet for a big tin of ground coffee. "This one's Bob Marley," he said of the one sitting by his side eyeing the carton of milk, "and the friendly one's Jimmy Cliff," he said about the one sniffing my knees. I knelt down slowly and stroked the big dog's head. He responded by licking the side of my face. "They're okay once they get used to you," Tiger said encouragingly.

I looked up at Tiger, noticing his skin was pebbled with chill. He smiled down at me, then told me to make myself at home while he went to change. Feeling awkward, I watched him go down the hall in his Speedo.

Accompanied by the dogs, I walked over to the living room and turned on the radio, Tiger's tight little butt burned into my mind's eye. Jimmy Cliff stayed by my side, but Bob Marley climbed up on the sofa and settled in with a big sigh. Tiger already had the radio on a local station where they played old-timey beach music like the college kids shagged to. Looking over my shoulder, I checked to make sure Tiger was still down the hall. Then I rearranged my aching dick.

I thought I must really be a sick person. Not only was I queer, but here I was, drooling over Tiger, too. Incest, damn. Seeing his long legs go up and meet the curl of his unit in the Speedo made up my mind then and there that I'd do him if he gave me a chance. I decided I'd missed all the chances I was going to.

I imagined him coming back into the room naked and chilly, his dick and nuts sort of drawn up from the cool air in the room. I could see the little goose bumps on his legs as I'd just kneel right down in the sawdust on the floor and pull him by the hips toward my warm mouth . . .

"You know about beach music, don't you?" Tiger said from the kitchen. I almost jumped out of my skin. I turned around to see Tiger standing at the counter taking down coffee mugs from the cabinet. He was dressed in an unzipped hooded sweatshirt and a pair of jeans with the knees out. I felt like I had said every word I was just thinking out loud instead of in my head.

"No, what?" I managed to say, before I turned back to look at the radio, then down to pet Jimmy Cliff to keep from staring at his chest.

"Beach music is really the granddaddy of rock and roll. Back in the fifties and early sixties kids could hear these black groups in dance places on the beach all over North and South Carolina. Beach music really opened up black music to white kids around here," Tiger said as he poured two mugs of coffee, added milk and sugar, and brought them over to the living room. He handed me a cup and then sat down on the sofa by Bob Marley, giving him a pat on the neck. "You like black music?" he asked.

I sat down on the floor by the coffee table. Jimmy Cliff laid down by my side. "Yeah, I listen to WOKN late at night a lot," I said.

Tiger smiled and said, "*Soul Serenade,* 11:05 p.m. sharp, right after *Black National Network News.*"

I grinned. He knew exactly what I was talking about. "You know that sax song they play right at the beginning? I love that song, I've always wondered who did it."

Tiger scratched his side through the gap in his sweatshirt and thought a moment, then he said, "King Curtis."

"You want me to get on getting your commode put in?" I blurted out like a fool. Tiger gave me a puzzled look and said, "I thought you were going to stay over till tomorrow sometime."

"Sure . . . I mean, yeah, I'd planned on it, if it's okay." I answered.

"Well, fuck the commode then, we got all day tomorrow to get that done. Actually, I was thinking about getting you to help me put the books in the bookcase, then I'll be done unpacking." I nodded, then he said, "After we get that done, we'll go out on the beach if you like."

"You wouldn't mind?" I asked. I mean I wanted to and all, but Tiger had just come back from the beach.

Tiger yawned hugely and waved his hand dismissively. "Hell, no. We might as well. No telling when Mark'll get home."

"Who's Mark?" I blurted out.

Tiger looked down at me sharply, then his eyes softened. "Matt, you don't mean to tell me your mama and daddy ain't never said nothing to you about Mark and me?" He stared at me then said to himself, "No, I don't guess they would." He sighed, then said, "Mark and I are together—you know—lovers. Have been since I was in high school."

I looked at him and nodded, just like I didn't feel like I'd been hit upside the head. Mostly, right then, I was real disappointed. In my sex-starved mind, I had already been picturing myself blowing him right here in the living room. I also felt satisfied to find I had managed to put so many pieces together of things dropped here and there by Daddy and Mama, Aunt Dordeen, and Rachel. Finally, I found myself wondering why Daddy had been so eager to send me to see Tiger out of the blue just now.

" . . . so I hope you're not freaked or anything," Tiger said.

"Is Mark in the military? Is he a pilot?"

Tiger looked at me, really puzzled. "Yeah. How do you know that?"

"I saw you, a long time ago, in the theater."

Tiger nodded slowly. "I see. Did you ever say anything about it to your daddy?"

"No," I said. I hesitated a minute, thinking. Then I said boldly, "I'm queer too."

Tiger smiled a smile that seemed to start in the middle of his hard-set mouth and spread outward to the edges, lifting them up until they ended, opening for a deep chuckle. "Well, boy, it looks like we got a lot to talk about then. I'm going to need a cigarette for this." He fished in a pocket of his sweatshirt for a pack of Marlboro Lights. "Want some more coffee?"

I shook my head no.

"Well, then let's start unpacking those boxes and put the books in the bookcase. It's just as easy to talk while you're doing something." Tiger slid onto the floor, scattering sawdust and tools by the stack of boxes and then pushed one across the floor to me. "So, you're gay. You must have figured out a long time ago that I was too," he said as I tore the tape off the top of the box.

"Yeah, I did kinda. I figured out it had to be something like that to make everybody hate you so bad."

Tiger began settling books on the bottom shelf. "Did you ever ask your daddy about Nathan Willis?" he asked out of the blue.

I started stacking books on the opposite end of the bookcase, then said, "Daddy said it was your story to tell and far as he was concerned it wasn't anything to be ashamed of. He did tell me that I had to live with any skeletons you dug up."

Tiger nodded. "Nathan Willis is the beginning of the story. Where do you want me to start?"

I thought a moment before I answered. Tiger had so many loose ends. He had always been like walking in in the middle of a movie to me. I realized I had always looked up to him without really knowing him. The few times I'd ever seen him since he left home, he'd always strode in, wearing surfer-looking clothes and acting cool. In a way, I'd always wanted to be like him, even though I didn't know that much about him.

"I want to hear about you and Mark. That time I saw you in the theater? I got to tell you, man. I never forgot that," I admitted.

Tiger looked at me with a direct grin. "Exactly what did you see?"

I felt my face get hot. I wasn't exactly used to just talking out in the open about stuff like this. I reached for Tiger's pack of cigarettes with a questioning look. He nodded and I pulled one out and lit it to stall having to answer until I felt like I wouldn't sound stupid. I handed Tiger some books from my box and said, "It wasn't really any big deal. You guys were just sort of necking." I flicked ashes that weren't really there from the end of my cigarette. "I was just a kid. At first I thought he was going to hurt you or something."

Tiger chuckled and seemed a little relieved.

"Well hey, the movie was almost over, I probably wouldn't have seen much if I'd hung out longer. How did you guys meet?"

Tiger half sighed, and carefully rearranged some of the titles on the bookshelf. "Your daddy got me a job cleaning pools the summer before my senior year in high school. I used to clean the pool at the apartment complex near the base where Mark and his wife and kids lived."

I was stunned—this was too good. Mark had been married, with kids even. No wonder "The Incident" was such a big deal. "Did everybody find out you were seeing a married guy?" I asked.

Tiger shrugged. "Your grandmama found out first, but she didn't really tell anybody. She wanted me to quit seeing him. She didn't have as much problem with me being queer as with the thought of me breaking up somebody's home."

I found this hard to believe and I told him so. Tiger just smiled and said, "Your grandmama was a lot cooler than you know. She had a pretty straightforward way of looking at things."

I knew that, but I didn't want to get into some big discussion about Grandmama. "But you ended up breaking up their marriage anyways," I said.

Tiger looked around at me sharply, but his eyes softened before he said, "Matt, life isn't that cut and dried; neither are people. Mark and Connie, his wife, had problems before I entered the picture. I never set out to break up Mark's marriage, but, technically, I guess you could say I did."

I looked at Tiger. He seemed hesitant to go on. He stopped putting books on the shelves and reached for his cigarettes. I handed them to him and sat waiting for him to continue. He lit one and moved the ashtray between us on the floor. "Mark and I fell in love. At first, I thought it was just horniness on his part, but it went way deeper than that."

"How?" I prompted. Tiger took a long hit off his cigarette and stared out the window for a minute. I felt like he was trying to translate down to me. It was like my French teacher when she went off on a burst of knowledge that was far ahead of my ability to follow. "Matt, we've been together through some rough stuff. At first, Mark got stationed away from me. Mark and Connie's youngest son accidentally drowned. Mark and Connie got a divorce. Mark was an officer in the Air Force. He had that game to play. The first few years we were together we were literally apart more than together. We toughed it out."

Tiger flicked his cigarette against the side of the ashtray and shrugged. He recited the details like a machine gun burst. It seemed like there were things he didn't want to go into, but I needed to know more. "He must have really loved you to go through all that," I said quietly.

Tiger nodded and said, "I'm very lucky. I knew I loved him. It was worth all the bullshit to find out he loved me that much."

"Is Mark still in the Air Force?"

Tiger shook his head no. "He decided to get out. We both love the beach. When he was stationed up in Tidewater, it was easy. We had our own house, and he stayed in the bachelor officers' quarters when he had to be on base."

Tiger smiled. "It was a pretty good life, but there was always the threat he was going to be transferred. Finally, he said fuck it. He got the chance to buy an interest in the airport over in Jacksonville and we took it."

I nodded, but I wanted to know more about his wife and family. When I asked him about them, Tiger winced.

"Connie found out about us after their son died. She was pissed enough to divorce him, but not pissed enough to drag it into the divorce court. I guess having a queer husband is bad enough, but having a queer, poor husband was more than she could stand. She knew he'd get kicked out of the military if she shot her mouth off." Tiger said bitterly.

"What about his other kid?" I asked carefully. As stingy as Tiger was being with the details, I didn't want to shut off the trickle of information he was letting go.

Tiger turned his attention back to the bookcase. He reached for a handful of books and placed them carefully on a separate shelf from the one he had been working on. "His name is Shane. He's going to be twelve in the spring. He lives with his mother and her second husband."

"Does Mark get to see him often?" I asked.

Tiger paused and then stood up suddenly. He walked to the other side of the room and lifted another box of books. He peered into the carton before placing it on the floor by my side and then sitting once more himself.

I watched him take out a handful of slender volumes. They were children's books. They seemed to be worn and well-loved. The corners of some of them were gnawed and some of the pages stuck up slightly where they had been torn out and replaced. Tiger reached into the carton again without speaking. The books he drew out became increasingly newer and more advanced. The last ones looked brand-new.

When they were finally all in place on their shelf, Tiger said, "Connie has expressed her displeasure with Mark by keeping Shane away from him. Since she's remarried, she's loosening up a little bit." He examined the books on the shelf once more before turning back to me. "Mark hopes that pretty soon, she'll let him come visit." Tiger stood once more and went for another carton.

I looked at the covers of the books he had just placed on the shelf. There were old favorites of mine and many of them were about planes and flying. My forgotten cigarette was burning my fingers. I ground it out hastily in the ashtray. "Tell me more about Mark," I said as Tiger returned and sat on the floor. Tiger remembered his own cigarette. It had burned down in the ashtray. He stubbed it out and lit another, then looked at me and grinned.

"Mark's something else; you'll see for yourself soon enough," Tiger said and returned to his task.

I remembered him only as a tall, muscular figure, sweat gleaming gold on his back from the light in the theater landing. It was hard to reconcile that with someone who bought so many books for a child he never got to see. "C'mon, Tiger, tell me a story," I persisted.

Tiger rolled his eyes and half turned to face me. "Boy, there are a ton more books to get put up. What kind of story do you want to hear?"

I smiled. "I want to hear the one that brought on 'The Incident'—you know."

Tiger looked puzzled. "What incident? What the hell are you talking about?"

I read his questioning look as being genuine. It wasn't like he was pulling some typical grown-up stunt, playing dumb so I'd shut up. "I always figured that there was this big incident that turned the family against you. It must have had something to do with you and Mark. I've been wondering what it was for years."

Tiger laid his head back and laughed. I asked him what was so funny. Tiger shook his head and snickered. "Matt, you have an overactive imagination. There wasn't one big incident; it's just years of bullshit."

"What about the time you ran away?" I asked him. Tiger gave me a long look in reply. Frustrated, I said, "I heard Aunt Dordeen talking to Aunt Heloise one time about you running off with some man. They shooed me away when they figured out I was listening to them." Tiger just shook his head.

"I guess Mama must have told them. Your daddy wouldn't." Tiger sighed and continued, "I tend to forget how tiny their lives must be to be so preoccupied with mine."

I was growing impatient. It was no news to me that Dordeen and Heloise were busybodies. "Well, what the hell happened?"

Tiger grinned. "The spring I was a senior, Mark was in Vietnam. I got out of school one May afternoon to find him sitting on the hood of my truck, still in his flight suit. I sure as hell didn't expect to see him. For all I knew he was overseas. He had hitched a ride in on a KC-135 tanker. He told me I had forty-five minutes to make up my mind if I wanted to stow away in the plane with him on its way back to Travis Air Force Base."

Tiger paused and took a hit off his cigarette. He had a secret kind of grin on his face. "You stowed away? On a military plane?" My voice unexpectedly screeched. I sounded like Mama.

Tiger stretched nonchalantly. "It's easy to stow away on a plane when you happen to be sleeping with the pilot's best friend and the crew doesn't give a shit."

"What was California like?" I asked him. I had this insane idea that Tiger got off the plane and went surfing or something.

"I couldn't tell you. Mark and I spent four days holed up in a motel, fucking and eating take-out Chinese food," Tiger said, laughing.

"What happened when you got back home?" I was fascinated.

"The whole family was up in arms. You'd think I had killed somebody, the way they all carried on about me running off to God knows where or for what reason," Tiger said. You could tell by the way he was smiling that he'd enjoyed every minute of it.

"What did you tell them?" I asked.

"I told them I had gone off to South Carolina to go fishing," Tiger said. "Dordeen wanted Mama to kick me out. Your daddy wanted to beat my ass, and Mama, well she just smiled and let them carry on. Finally, when she'd had enough, she told them she'd been handling wild asses for longer than they were alive and she'd handle me just fine without their help." Tiger grinned, his love for Grandmama showing like it had when I went with him to her house right after she died.

Tiger put out his cigarette and grew suddenly quiet. I watched an old resentment come down over his face. "She had gone snooping in my room. She'd found Mark's letters," Tiger said as he looked up at me.

"What did she say?" I asked.

Tiger shrugged. "She didn't give me too hard a time. She did threaten to rat Mark out to the OSI if I didn't stop seeing him."

"What's the OSI?" I asked.

Tiger shook his head, "Office of Special Investigations. Air Force witch-hunters."

I nodded, understanding suddenly how much Mark had gambled. Knowing Grandmama, the threat was real. "Did you stop seeing him?" I asked.

"Hell, no." Tiger said belligerently. "God, all this talking has got me dry as a bone. You want some more coffee?"

I shook my head no. The sun had shifted on the floor and with it the room had begun to cool down. I was so busy listening that I hadn't even noticed.

Tiger stood and brushed the sawdust from his jeans. "Tell you what, let's get the tools put up and the floor swept, then we'll go on down to the beach," he said. "I can put up the rest of the books later." I wanted him to go on with the story, but my butt was sore from sitting on the floor. I stood and stretched as Tiger walked over to kitchen and pulled a broom and dustpan from the space between the refrigerator and the wall. Coming back into the living room, he held them out to me.

"Knowing your mama, I bet you know how to use one of these," he said with a smile. I took the broom and dustpan from him with a grin in return. Tiger returned to the kitchen and poured the dregs of the pot into his coffee mug.

"Tiger, do you think the family will ever get over it—the gay thing?" I asked and began to swipe at the sawdust on the floor.

Tiger took a sip of his coffee, then said. "You know that the family doesn't approve of me, but that's no great loss. Hell, their disapproval is as steady and consistent as love. It's something I've always been able to count on."

I could feel him watching me, even though my back was to him as I turned to sweep. "Did Grandmama ever get to meet Mark?" I asked.

"Your daddy and her came to visit us after I graduated from ECU and went to work full-time in Kitty Hawk as a surveyor. She never came but that one time, but she always asked about him and she never gave me any more grief about us being together." Tiger came over and picked up the dustpan. He knelt down in front of me to hold it while I filled it with sand and sawdust. "Don't worry about it. Matt. People grow more tolerant as they get older."

Tiger stood up with the dustpan and headed for the kitchen after kicking what was left of the thin line of grit under the sofa. "Daddy ain't never done you like that has he?" I asked. Tiger emptied the dustpan into the trash. He stood for a moment looking at me before walking back to take the broom from my hands.

"Your daddy, well, he's the only daddy I ever had. He's also probably is the closest thing to a real Christian I ever met. Dordeen and all the others walk around acting like they're all saved, sanctified, and filled with the Holy Spirit. What a bunch of shit. They have spit like acid and hearts like teeny little rocks. You want to know how to be a real man, look at your daddy," Tiger said with finality. I really hoped that I'd be half like him and half like Tiger.

From the kitchen, Tiger said, "I'll tell you something, Matt. I made up my mind a long time ago how I was going to live my life and I never gave two cents about what anybody thought. Of course, I've had Mark around to back me up and to throw his leg over me at night—that's made it easy. I still love the big fucker, if he does make me crazy sometimes."

Tiger grinned at me. Right then, he looked like a mischievous kid, sunny and happy, no sign of storms or unanswered secrets that I knew were still there behind his glowing eyes.

The dogs barely moved while I took the transit out of its case and wiped it down with a clean hand towel. I rubbed it down lovingly. Besides costing a ton of money, it was how Tiger and I made our living. Finished, I looked around for something else to do. There were a lot surveys I could have drawn up. There was the studying I needed to do for a test I had later in the week, but I really just wasn't into it. What I wanted to do was go surfing.

I went into the kitchen and called Mark at the airport. One of the guys that worked for him answered and told me he was working on an engine over in the hangar. He told me he'd go get him if I really had to talk to him.

I figured Mark would have grease up to his elbows and wouldn't particularly like his concentration disturbed just to find out all I wanted was to know if he wanted to go surfing. I told the guy it was no big deal and hung up.

The dogs were asleep curled up next to each other on the sofa and didn't even move when the wind threw a hard gust of rain up against the windows, rattling them in their sashes. I took a pack of cigarettes from the carton Tiger kept on top of the refrigerator, poured myself some orange juice, and sat down at my place at the kitchen table. Mark had left some papers and a pen at his place. He had a lot going on just then, at work and at home.

I popped the pack of cigarettes three times on the top of the table before I tore the wrapper carefully off the top and remembered meeting Mark for the first time.

Tiger and I had gone down to the beach to stretch our legs after working on the bookcase. As we came over the crest of the dune between the houses Tiger said, "Mark's home."

Sure enough, there was another car parked in the driveway. It was a sporty little Toyota. Tiger's steps quickened and the dogs started barking at a figure under the house as they ran home. I heard a deep voice welcome them by name and I stepped quicker, not only to keep up with Tiger, but to meet a man who loved him enough to give up a family. I found myself moments later standing under the house with Tiger and the dogs, shyly studying the man himself.

He was shucking oysters and dropping the shells into a bushel basket when we came up. Mark didn't stop, but casually pitched one to each dog as they waited patiently for their treat in turn. Tiger introduced me and Mark smiled, revealing a front tooth broken off at an angle that made him look a little like a fighter. He nodded apologetically for not shaking my hand. His own were covered with thick canvas gloves, slimy from the oysters. He only smiled at me, but the look he gave Tiger, brief as it was, was one of unmasked possessiveness and love.

"Long day, hoss?" Tiger asked. "Did you get the Cessna worked on?"

Mark said, "Yeah, everything's okay. I have to fly out tomorrow to courier some rush deliveries. That son of a bitch in Greensboro is crawling up my ass."

Tiger nodded as he walked over and to stand close by Mark. I got to compare them side by side. Mark was taller and bigger than Tiger. Tiger was a little on the short side and lean and sinewy; Mark must have been six-four and built like a running back. Tiger was fine-featured and almost girlish-looking; Mark had a manly kind of handsomeness. His black hair was cut military short and showed a little bit of gray at the temples. Tiger appeared to be made out of gold, but Mark made me think of iron and steel, from his black eyes right down to the salt-and-pepper stubble of a five o'clock shadow along his neck and jaw. I didn't hardly know which one of them to look at first. But, I had to be honest; Mark was my idea of what a man should look like and what I wanted to look like when I got to be his age.

"I thought we might have oyster stew tonight," Mark said. "Old boy down in Swansboro had these out on Highway 24 as I was coming home. Sound good?" Mark directed the question to me.

"Sure," I said, shyly, then added, "I love oyster stew." We hardly ever had it at home; oysters were so expensive. Besides, I was so hungry I probably could have eaten them shells and all.

Mark finished shucking the oysters and handed the bowl to Tiger. "I'm going to take these up and get started on supper. Matt, why don't you help Mark get rid of these shells," Tiger said.

Mark grinned, looking at me. "Boy, I've got a garbage bag with your name on it."

Tiger looked back over his shoulder and said, "Don't let him boss you too bad," as he headed upstairs with the dogs. Mark chuckled, but it didn't take long for me to tell Mark was used to giving orders and getting things done. I held the bag while he gathered up the shells and dropped them in.

Mark had a presence. He reminded me of an older version of my friend Jeep, who was a big guy like Mark. I always thought Jeep was kind of hot, but he was just a kid compared to Mark. Standing beside him, I watched the muscles work under his shirt as he gathered up the discarded shells. He had a natural sexiness about him that you could smell. I had heard some people put out a sort of chemical scent. Mark smelled like clean sweat, oysters, and jet exhaust.

He didn't have an obvious, stare-you-in-the-eye sort of sexiness. It was just a kind of jockish confidence, like he was easy with his size and felt good about himself. That made you feel good about your own self, and before you knew it, you realized you wanted this guy to like you but also like you enough to fuck your brains out.

After we finished cleaning up the oyster mess, Mark unlocked and opened a door in a walled-off part of the pilings under the house. I followed him into a room that seemed to be part greenhouse and part wonderland. There must have been fifty more little bonsai trees like the ones upstairs on the deck, all of them in various stages of being trained and transformed. "Welcome to my hideout," Mark said.

"You do these?" I asked amazed.

"Sure, why not?" Mark asked as he strode over to a workbench that held several small black plastic pots of juniper. Daddy had planted some like it in a spot in our yard where nothing else would grow. Ours were leggy and ugly.

"Blue rug juniper," Mark announced proudly as he touched the little pots. "I found these today in a garden shop in Jacksonville," he said, just a hint of excitement creeping into his voice. "I can usually get regular junipers, but these are hard to come by. Do you mind if I putter a minute while Tiger gets dinner ready?"

"Not if I can watch," I said. Mark smiled and motioned me over to a stool. I sat down while he took out a clay saucer from a plastic shopping bag and set it on the workbench.

"You ever see anybody start a bonsai before?" he asked. I told him no, I didn't think I ever had. "Well, it's not hard. The hard part is the years it takes to see them become what you had in mind at the beginning." Mark picked up one of the plastic pots and knocked it gently against the side of the table to loosen the soil and roots.

After he slid the plant out of its container, he tore away some of the soil and spread it in the clay saucer, then shook off the remaining soil from the roots and looked at them critically. "You have to start by clipping the roots just right." Mark explained. He picked up a pair of pruning shears from the work table and looked at the small plant in his big hands.

I watched him silently as he clipped the roots. This big guy, who flew planes and looked like he could fuck like a stallion, gently trimmed the little plant and twisted wires around its tiny branches. He seemed lost in himself. I kept quiet until he finished.

Mark stepped back from the little tree and admired his handiwork. In the clay saucer, the juniper had become what would look exactly like an old live oak blowing in an ocean wind. Mark packed more soil around the trunk and carefully landscaped the tiny area of ground around it into contours of a miniature hill.

"In about three years, this little fellow will be pretty neat." Mark said.

"It takes that long?" I asked.

Mark smiled at me as he placed strips of moss over the little landscape. "Three years is nothing to a bonsai. If you take care of them, they can live to be a hundred years old."

I was fascinated. I never would have imagined this guy getting into something so weird and beautiful. "What got you into making bonsai?" I asked.

Mark mixed some blue powder into a large pitcher of water and shrugged. "I don't know, Matt. I never really thought about it. I guess I like the discipline and the patience." He moved to the table and fell silent as he watered the new little tree.

"Did you know I have a son?" Mark asked suddenly. I told him

Tiger had said he did. Mark sighed and moved to share the water from the pitcher amongst the other bonsai under the grow lights. "I have a bonsai upstairs that I started when I left his mother. She didn't let me see Shane for a long time." Mark finished watering the plants and put the pitcher away. He walked back to the table and picked up the new one. He examined it briefly and set it down to make a final tiny trim. Satisfied, he placed it with the others.

Mark glanced down at all the pots that held his tiny forest with a gentle smile. He would have really been a hell of a daddy. Big as he was, he seemed lost in his little forest for a moment. Besides the obvious, I began to see why Tiger loved him so much.

Mark looked back at me and grinned. "I guess learning to be patient is the best thing about bonsai, really. Tiger can use up a lot of my patience really quick sometimes."

I laughed.

"Right now, I'm ready to eat," he said. "How about you?"

"I've been ready," I said as I got up from the stool. Mark opened the door for me. With a last look around, he followed me out the door and locked it behind me. Putting one hard hand on my shoulder, he gently steered me up the stairs.

We spent the rest of the night eating and talking. Tiger and Mark encouraged me to tell them my opinions on stuff. I was amazed they even thought I was smart enough to have ideas, much less agree or disagree with them. It was really great to have a discussion with people who might disagree, but didn't get all pissed off and start yelling like the kids I knew did.

We talked about politics and philosophy and all kinds of stuff until it was time to let the dogs out and go to bed. I was warm and sleepy. When Tiger took out the dogs, Mark showed me my room. He asked me if I needed anything. I told him no as he turned on the thermostat for the baseboard heat for me. It was chilly in the room.

"Thanks for letting me visit," I said as Mark started to leave. He turned around and looked at me. "I had a great night and I appreciate it."

He smiled and said, "We'll put you to work tomorrow; besides, it's nice to have you around. Tiger and I don't usually have a lot of company." With that, he smiled again, turned off the light, and gently closed the door after him.

When I woke up the next morning the early sun was shining. The house was quiet and I figured that Tiger and Mark were still asleep. A morning hard-on throbbed companionably between my legs and I stretched out on my stomach grinding it into the unyielding mattress. I considered beating off, but the need to pee was a lot more pressing. Dreading the cold floor, I got up and crossed the hall to the bathroom.

I took care of my business as quietly as I could, and crossed back to my room to slip on my jeans, socks, and a sweatshirt. I figured I'd go ahead and take care of my plumbing chores before I showered. Quietly, I headed down the hall to the kitchen. As I turned at the bar, I saw Tiger at the cabinet reaching for mugs. Mark, wearing only a pair of boxer shorts, walked up behind him, took him by the hips and, bending his knees a bit, ground his crotch into Tiger's butt. Tiger laid his head back on Mark's shoulder and stifled a laugh. Mark wrapped his arms around Tiger's chest and gave him a fierce hug, lifting him off the floor.

As Mark put him down on the floor, Tiger turned toward him and saw me. He grinned and said good morning. Mark looked back and shrugged before letting Tiger loose.

"You're pretty good at catching us like that," Tiger said.

"Timing; it's all timing," I replied.

Mark leaned against the sink and scratched his broad chest. "What the hell are you two talking about?" he asked.

Tiger explained how I had stumbled on the two of them, years ago, at the Jewel Box Theater. As Tiger reached in the refrigerator for milk, Mark poured us all coffee without asking. Mark said, "Those were the days, huh?"

Tiger sat down at the table with sort of a half smile on his face. Mark placed coffee mugs in front of us before sitting down himself. "Yeah, those were the days," Mark repeated. He looked at Tiger with the same half smile. I guessed they'd been together so long now that they shared each other's expressions. I felt as if I'd walked in on the middle of a long conversation that was going on where I couldn't hear it.

"It must have been hard, you being in the service and all," I said to Mark.

Tiger shifted in his seat and started to speak. Mark warned him off with a look and then spoke to me directly. "Matt, you won't get me to say anything against the military. If you want to play a game, you have to play by the rules, even if you think some of them are bullshit."

I nodded and took a sip of my coffee. When I looked up, he held my eyes with a look of challenge and said, "I love the Air Force. It gave me everything I love about my life from making me a damn good pilot to that little cat-eyed bastard sitting there," Mark gestured abruptly toward Tiger.

I nodded again, like I understood. I didn't mean to say anything bad about the military. I sure didn't mean to piss Mark off. As he drank some of his own coffee, I looked over at Tiger, who glanced back and looked away. His lips were a tight white line holding in his opinions. I should have taken a cue from his silence, but I wanted to make amends if I had offended Mark without meaning to. I said, "It must not have been so strict during the war, though. Tiger told me about you taking him to California."

Mark looked at me first with a little surprise, then at Tiger more sharply. "War is hell, huh, boss?" Tiger said.

Mark relaxed back in his chair and reached for his coffee cup. "Hell, no. War can be a lot of fun," he said with a hint of a horny grin on his face.

I pictured Mark flying over a jungle, dodging flack. It seemed a long way from sneaking around with Tiger. Mark noted the confusion on my face. His own took on a distant and kind of condescending look.

"War is different. War is the game we were trained to play," he said remotely, but still with a smile. "How does scrambled eggs, toast, and bacon sound?"

"It don't matter," I said agreeably. I realized the subject was closed. Most military people I'd ever met clammed right up when you tried to get them to talk about war. They always got this look on their face like you couldn't possibly understand what it was all about. I was hungry and breakfast sounded good to me. There was no point in getting Mark to talk more about it. I was just glad he offered bacon and eggs. I figured if I pissed him off, he might offer to cook maggots and leaves or something from a survival training course. He looked right then like he could, and be proud of it.

"Well, colonel, if you're going to start mess hall ops, I'm going to walk the dogs," Tiger said, with a teasing grin.

Mark nodded curtly and said, "Dismissed." Tiger stood and started toward the door. "No salute?" Mark asked as he passed. The dogs swirled around Tiger's legs by the time he reached the door.

Tiger glanced over his shoulder, grinned as he opened the door and said, "Kiss my ass . . . sir." Mark rolled his eyes at me as Tiger closed the door behind himself.

"Sorry little fuck . . . one of these days I'm going to have to teach him some respect," Mark said with mock seriousness.

I let myself grin at him. "You think you can?"

Mark unfolded from his chair slowly as he tightened himself, shoulders back, chest out, square jaw jutting. He looked down at me with a look that left no room for discussion. "If I had any doubt, what . . . so . . . ever, that boy didn't worship the ground I piss on, I'd kick his skinny little butt to death."

As intimidating as he was trying to be, I could still see a glint of humor in his eyes. It kept him from being an arrogant asshole and made him more handsome and charming than I figured he wanted to be. I pulled a serious look over my face and nodded while I reached for my coffee cup. When I glanced up, Mark was already pulling stuff out of the refrigerator.

"How do you like your bacon, Matt?" he asked. "Limp and raw or dry and crispy?"

"Long as it ain't raw, I'll eat it." I could tell he was a little concerned he'd gone too far trying to show me what was what around the house. His pride made me like him more. It wasn't too hard to figure he had a clear idea of who he was, and he was no big fag. Still, when he looked at Tiger, it was as sure as shit that he loved him to death. As hard as Mark drew his lines, I wondered really if he was happy, being queer and all.

"Mark. Can I ask you a question?" I said finally, after watching him work on breakfast and trying to think of the right way to ask what was on my mind.

"Shoot," Mark said as he turned the bacon in the pan.

"Would you do it all over again, the same way? I mean like, Tiger, and not being able to be around your son, and getting out of the Air Force and all?" Somehow, it was like all the effort I'd put into trying to figure out how to ask just that went out the window and I just blurted it out. Mark didn't say anything and I sensed a coldness, like I'd gone way too far.

"Tiger tells me you're gay," Mark said after awhile, as he took bacon from the frying pan and placed it carefully on a paper towel.

"Yeah, I am . . . though I've heard you have to have sex to prove it," I said.

"Well, don't believe everything you hear," Mark said as he drained the grease from the frying pan into a coffee mug. His smile was tight with concentration too hard for just pouring off grease. He started breaking eggs into the frying pan. "Have you ever flown?" Mark asked out of the blue.

"No, sir, I haven't." I answered quietly.

"Have you ever been to an airport or watched a big jet take off?" he asked as he stood watching the eggs. I told him it was nearly impossible not to where I grew up. Mark nodded. "Well, when you're a pilot, there's a lot to do before you ever take off. You have to do a physical check of the outside of the aircraft. You have to go through a checklist in the cockpit. All in all, you got to do a lot of things before you even get permission to taxi out on the runway."

I took a sip of what was left of my coffee. It was almost gone, but I didn't want to disturb him by getting up to get more. Mark stirred the eggs and continued. "For me, I know I'm a pilot. Hell, I was a pilot before I could fly. All I ever wanted to do was just get up there. But I had to pay my dues, complete all my training before I could make it to the end of that runway, in the nose end of that big bitch with the engines running and go."

Mark fell silent again as he carefully spooned the eggs onto a plate and began to place the bacon beside them. Finally satisfied with the arrangement, he turned to look at me. "You get clearance to take off and you pull back the throttle. There is so much power and thrust behind you, you reach that point where you have to commit. You are going too fast to stop and even if you get this feeling in the pit of your stomach that you don't really belong up there, you have to pull up the nose and go. Everything it took to get you to that point is all just past. You have to commit, Matt, or crash and burn."

We heard the scratch and scramble of the dogs and Tiger's light tread on the steps up to the deck. Mark smiled and brought the plate of bacon and eggs to the table. "Once you commit, son, you don't ever want to come down out of that clear blue sky." Mark looked at me intently, trying to see if I got the point. I remembered his odd little trees. Mark just went after stuff with determination and discipline. He didn't seem used to discussing, or explaining why he did things. He just committed and did it. I found myself wishing I was like that.

Tiger opened the door to follow behind a rush of smoky fur that jelled into dogs noisily clanging their steel feed bowls. Mark picked up the bowls and scooped out some dry food as Tiger sat down at the table. "God, it smells good in here," he said.

Mark gave him a smile and picked up the cup with the bacon grease in it. He started to pour some over the dog's food. "Not too much of that. For God's sake, Mark, I ain't cleaning up dog shit all day because of you spoiling those two," Tiger scolded.

Mark looked at me with a grin. "Did I say clear blue sky?"

I smiled. Ignoring us, Tiger asked if there was any more coffee. Without a word, Mark set the dogs' bowls on the floor and refilled our mugs. We demolished breakfast, then just sat talking and drinking coffee. Their yammering back and forth was full of affection without seeming weird. Plus, besides finding out they were cool, neither one of them was hard on the eyes.

Although I was getting to know them so good it felt kind of disloyal to think about them in a sexual way, I did sneak a few looks in the gap of Mark's boxers when he got up to get more coffee. Tiger caught me one time, but he winked at me and I figured he knew I was going to anyway. I couldn't help it. Mark was fine, besides being as easy to talk to as Tiger.

We must have dragged breakfast out for two hours. Finally, Tiger said we better get busy or there wouldn't be day left to do anything else. Mark had to go out to the airport. He left to dress and Tiger and I plotted out the rest of the day. He wanted to get the commode in right away so we could hang out and relax some before I had to head back. Mark came back dressed and told me if I wanted, to get Tiger to bring me over to the airport on the way home and he'd take me up in a plane. He was amazed that I was seventeen years old and had never flown.

Tiger told him to let me get fucked one good time before he got me killed in a twin-engine Cessna. Mark laughed and explained that Tiger wouldn't hardly get in a plane without a quart of vodka in him.

Tiger told me that he preferred to fly with a pilot who wasn't prone to flashbacks of being in an F-15. Mark promised me he'd spare me any barrel rolls on my first trip. I declined for this time, but told him I'd hold him to his promise on my next visit. He gave me a big hug and told me to make sure there was a next visit. I was welcome anytime. With that, he walked over and popped Tiger lightly on the butt. Tiger gave him a grin and told him he'd see him when he saw him. With a hearty, "Later," Mark was out the door and gone.

I pulled a cigarette out of the pack and lit it. It didn't seem like it had been a year since then. Everything seemed to come together for all of us. Mark's business at the airport had really picked up. He was even able to add two new planes to his fleet and hire other pilots to fly them. Likewise, Tiger had gotten busy enough to hire me and keep me on full-time. Back at home now, Mark and Tiger had this instant family of me, Mark's son Shane, and Shane's shadow, Billy.

Shane moved in about the same time I did. Tiger was closemouthed about the reasons for Mark's ex-wife's change of heart and Mark was too delighted to jinx the new arrangement. I didn't dig for details. It was getting to be too much like an episode of *Donahue* to suit me.

Although Tiger kept me busy, Shane and I got to be buddies. I wondered what he thought about his dad and Tiger being together. Shane was at that age where he was noticing sex stuff. Here he was in a house full of queers. Tiger and Mark didn't carry on in front of him, or me for that matter, but there was no mistaking where they slept or how they felt about each other. I wasn't going out with anybody, but I didn't make any big effort to hide the fact that I was queer myself.

Then, not long after Shane moved in, we acquired Billy. Every morning a little boy appeared and sat at the end of the driveway. He didn't come up to the house; he just sat patiently waiting out by the street. One morning, we were trying to finish eating and leave for work. Tiger looked out the door and said, "Who is that young'un that camps out on the driveway every morning?"

Shane slurped his cereal and answered casually, "That's Billy."

Mark looked up from his paper and asked, "Who's Billy?"

Shane looked a little guilty. "A friend of mine," he said.

"Well, tell us about Billy," Mark said and put down his paper.

Shane told us that Billy was eight years old and lived down the street. His daddy was dead and his family was real poor. Every morning, Shane waited for everybody to leave the house, then he fed Billy breakfast.

Tiger looked at Mark and said, "You know who he's talking about, don't you?" Mark nodded. Even I knew about the lady with all the kids whose husband got killed in a commercial fishing accident.

"Don't be mad, Tiger. I feel sorry for Billy, and I like him," Shane pleaded quietly. Tiger looked at Mark. Mark shrugged and went back to his paper.

"Shane, I don't like you sneaking him food. If you want to feed your friend, you bring him on up here and let him eat with everybody else." Tiger told him he couldn't get mad at him for doing somebody a good turn. "Look what you're teaching that little boy, though. He ain't a stray dog that you're sneaking scraps to. If he's your buddy, you can't act like you're ashamed of him." Shane looked down at the table, not saying anything.

Mark had stopped reading the paper and was watching Tiger closely. Tiger lit a cigarette. "Unless you're ashamed to bring your friends up to the house. Are you ashamed of us, Shane?" Tiger asked gently.

Shane looked up quickly, "No. I mean, no, sir. No way. I swear. I was just scared you'd be mad at me for having somebody over when you weren't home. I wasn't allowed to bring my friends over when I lived with Mom."

Tiger nodded and looked at Mark. Mark sat back in his chair. "It's up to you, Mark," Tiger said.

Mark scratched his chest, then looked at Shane sternly. "You have permission to bring your friends over when we're at work, or anytime we're not home. I will hold you responsible for what goes on. Am I making myself clear?"

Shane said, "Yes, sir."

Mark continued, "You are under orders to limit yourself and your friends to conduct becoming an officer at all times. Understood?"

Shane said, "Yes, sir." He stared at his father with something like awe.

Mark looked down at his paper. "Then go get Billy and report back immediately."

Shane scrambled away from the table and out the door. Tiger and I looked at each other, but didn't say anything. Mark grinned, but didn't look up from his paper.

A few minutes later, Shane came in with Billy, who sat himself at the table and started talking.

"Hey. Can I have some cereal?" Billy asked Tiger.

"What kind would you like? We've got—" Tiger got out before Billy interrupted.

"Y'all got Sugar Smacks and Raisin Bran. Can I have Sugar Smacks first?" Billy asked.

Mark looked at Tiger and tried not to smile. "Sugar Smacks coming up," Tiger said as he put out his cigarette and stood up.

"Why come you're named Tiger?" Billy asked him. Tiger lunged across the table and stopped just short of Billy's face with a low growl. Billy laughed. "You're weird, but I ain't scared," he said and wrapped his arms around Tiger's neck. "I like you."

Mark laughed out loud as Tiger got loose from Billy's grasp. He was a scruffy, skinny little boy with long dark hair and eyes the color of Coca-Cola. He was barefoot and shirtless; his hand-me-down shorts were threadbare. He looked like a stray in every sense of the word.

Later, Mark asked how Shane had met Billy. Shane said he'd followed him home one day. Nobody laughed or disputed the truth of the statement. Tiger said that if he knew that when we fed him, we'd have him for life, he'd have told Shane to run him off with a stick. It was impossible to resist Billy. He just didn't get disregard and acted oblivious to sarcasm or teasing. He worshipped Shane, seemed almost hypnotized by Tiger, and thrived on the attention Mark and I gave him.

When Billy more or less moved in, Tiger went over to his mama's house to talk to her. Tiger was concerned she might have objections to Billy hanging out at our house so much. He came home surprised.

"She just about got down on her hands and knees thanking me," he said and shook his head. "She's got four more just like Billy, all of them with that pink-eyed, white-trashy look. I reckon it's about all she can do to keep a roof over their heads. I imagine she'd give him to us if she could get away with it. I told her we'd look after him, but he had to go home to sleep."

Before long, Billy had insinuated himself so deeply into the fabric of the household, it was impossible to remember a time when he wasn't around. He even acquired a set of chores and got disciplined along with Shane for any infraction of Mark's military-style method of child rearing. It was amazing how the two boys responded by bonding and making us a family.

Things around the house settled into a smooth routine. Shane was a pretty cool little kid. He was the spittin' image of Mark. He went with his dad to the airport on some days. Others, Mark let him stay home alone. Shane and I both had chores around the house and we were expected to do them. Mark was firm. Me and Shane both understood real quick how he expected things to be done. Tiger backed off to let Mark run that end of the family.

Mark and Tiger were the ones who really amazed me, though. Mark absolutely loved being a daddy. Like as not, he was always in a clot of little boys and dogs, rolling around on the floor, running them down to the beach, splashing with them in the water. Mark seemed to become like a kid again himself. He laughed and teased and wrestled and made up contests with Billy and Shane. Although he always barked orders and gruffly supervised all their activities, both Shane and Billy quickly came to adore Mark. Mark in turn, adored them. He swaggered around with a fatherly pride.

Tiger adapted to the responsibility of becoming a parent. For awhile, he seemed overwhelmed by the overnight presence of a seventeen-year-old, twelve-year-old, and eight-year-old in his formerly quiet and orderly house. I saw all of the loyalties in his life change. Instead of just Mark to consider, now there was all of us. Even the dogs seemed to abandon him for the energetic activity surrounding Shane and Billy like an electric field. Now, the dogs only sought him out for food, water, and passing affection.

One Saturday morning in July, Mark left with Shane and Billy to go to the beach. He was teaching Shane to surf and Shane had become a total water dog. He had to be threatened with discipline to come home. From the breakfast table, I saw Tiger stand on the deck watching the excited clump of dogs and boys and man make their way down the street, over the dune and onto the beach. Tiger came in the house and filled a pitcher with water and went back on the deck to water Mark's bonsai.

I watched him for a moment as he carefully shared the water over the neglected little trees. In the weeks since Shane had come to stay, Mark's devotion to his little works of art had waned. Tiger gently traced his fingers across the tiny sculpted limbs, murmuring to each of them comfortingly. He seemed smaller and lost among Mark's forgotten substitute children. Brown and bright-haired, Tiger remained a pretty thing, but he seemed older. I felt sorry for him.

I went out on the deck to be close to him and he looked up from tending the bonsai with a slow certain smile for me.

"Your life's gotten a lot more crowded, hasn't it?" I asked him gently.

Tiger looked off toward the beach then nodded. "Do you ever wish we'd all just go home?" I asked. Tiger shook his head no and his answer surprised me.

"Matt, you never stop growing. Even these goddamn little trees here, they don't. Mark says that these here can live to be a hundred years old if you take care of them." Tiger carefully pinched a browned branch from one of the plants and tossed it into the wind off the side of the deck. "Ain't you noticed how happy he is?"

I nodded; it was totally obvious Mark had a kind of happy completeness that even a near-stranger like me could understand.

Tiger sighed deeply, but smiled. "Mark's starting the process to get custody of Shane away from Connie. For once, I don't think she'll put up much of a fight. There were problems . . . " Tiger's voice trailed off and he glanced at me quickly to see if he'd said too much. Tiger was fierce about a confidence. I nodded and looked away. I'd gathered from Shane that his stepfather had beaten him practically every chance he got.

"I'd give Mark anything that made him happy, Matt. If you really love somebody I guess you have to figure the whole, not just the parts that agree with what you want." Tiger smiled into the wind that threw back his sun-scorched hair and picked out the tiny lines around his eyes.

"I'm just taking care of my big-ass bonsai. I want him around for a hundred years at least." I looked at him with a new kind of respect. He responded by shrugging and saying, "I been a lot of things, including a homewrecker. Now, I guess I get to be a homemaker." His smile grew into a grin and he said, "Paybacks are hell."

I stubbed out my cigarette and finished my juice. The rain was still pounding against the windows. I decided I might as well go back to my room and study for my test. I took Tiger's cigarettes before I headed down the hall. As I passed by Shane's room, I stopped and went in. I knew he had snagged my last issue of *Surfer*.

Although I wasn't trying to be nosy, I did run across an issue of *Hustler* under his bed while I was looking for it. I grinned to myself as I tried to place it exactly where I'd found it. While neither me, nor Tiger, nor Mark acted real queer, there was nothing female or feminine in our house, nothing at all. Women or girls might as well have been like dogs or horses other people kept around. I didn't say anything about it, but it kind of worried me. I had wondered if the kid would turn out to be queer.

A couple of weeks after me and Shane had both moved in, Tiger and I headed home early from work one afternoon. It had started to rain. Tiger had to run to the grocery store, but he dropped me off at the house first. I had a couple of lot surveys to work on that Tiger was teaching me to draft. When I went into my room, I found Shane holding this frame Chris had given me with the pictures of me and him in it. He put the pictures down and said he wasn't snooping, he had come in to borrow a tape. I almost yelled at him, but I remembered my brother Tommy yelling at me for the same thing. I told him it was okay.

Shane seemed relieved. He picked up the pictures again and studied them. "Is this your boyfriend?" I nodded and leaned against the door jamb. "His name's Chris, right?"

I told him "yeah" and tried to answer him when he asked me why we weren't together. He accepted my explanation.

"You must miss him a lot," he said as he put the frame down gently on the nightstand. He looked at me and said, "I like girls."

We started talking then. We wandered into the living room and sat down. While it rained, Shane told me all about himself. He told me what he remembered about his mom and Mark splitting up. He told me about living with his stepfather and how the man mistreated him. While he didn't go off on any tangents, I was able to piece together that he wasn't going back to live with his mom.

I asked him how he felt about his dad living with Tiger. He shrugged. "He's my dad. Anyways, Tiger is way better than my other stepfather or whatever. My mother told me about my dad and Tiger a long time ago. She hates both of them."

Shane stretched out on the floor and used one of the dogs as a pillow. "She wanted me to hate them too, but I don't. They seem to love each other a lot." He stared up at the ceiling fan as it spun.

For a little while, the only sounds in the room were its hum and the rain outside. I thought he had finished, then he spoke. "It's good to have somebody who loves you and doesn't try to eat you alive. I hope one day I have somebody who loves me like that." He looked at me and smiled. "Only I hope it's a girl. With blonde hair and big boobs."

Shane was real level-headed for a twelve-year-old. The more I got to know him, the more I liked him. We did stuff together. We surfed together a lot the first few weeks of the summer, but Shane liked to be around kids more his own age. He had Billy, too. Also, Shane got better at surfing a lot quicker than I did. He'd been a big-time skateboarder when he lived with his mom. Now, living with his dad and Tiger, he was turning out to be a real talent.

I found my copy of *Surfer* under the bed on the side by the wall. I fished it out and made sure, one more time, that Shane's copy of *Hustler* was where I'd found it. Satisfied, I went on into my room.

On the dresser were my notes and book for the test I had coming up. But the copy of *Surfer* was in my hand. I looked outside my window and got a sharp slap of rain across the glass for a view. "Fuck it," I thought. "If I can't go surfing, I might as well read about it." I flopped down on the bed and arranged the pillows behind my head. I reached over to the bedside table to get my ashtray and saw the frame with the pictures of me and Chris.

It was a one of those hinged wooden frames that closed in on itself. In it were three of the pictures Chris and I had taken back in May, the night before he left to go back to Philadelphia to live with his dad. The first one was the one of Chris whispering in my ear, the middle one was of him lying on the bed with his arms behind his head and his bandaged knee sticking up, the last one was of us kissing. They were all perfectly focused, clear, and sharp.

I tried to push the memory of the night we took them out of my mind. I opened the copy of *Surfer* and turned to the letters to the editor. This guy down in Miami wrote in saying how he was a gay surfer and how he wished everybody could just get along and enjoy the waves together. He said he dreamed of that day when there wouldn't be any bullshit about it. The editor just replied, "Good luck."

In a way it made me smile. I knew better. Hell, I lived in a house full of queer surfers, except for Shane. Chris claimed to be a surfer, even though he wasn't very good at it when he came down over Labor Day. There was somebody else, but I didn't like to remember him. It was funny, but it was this magazine that kind of got me and Chris together.

The winter before, when I was still living at home, we had a huge blizzard, then an ice storm on top of that. After being locked up in the house with Mama and Daddy for three days, I decided to walk down to the shopping center near our house to at least get a new tape or something.

All of the stores at the shopping center were closed but the drugstore. Eckerd's never sold any tapes except for shitty ones of old top-forty stuff up by the cash register, old hits rerecorded by off-the-wall people with names like "The Original Artists." I looked through the paperbacks instead, hoping to find a decent book. All they seemed to have was stuff like *Love's Torrid Throbbing Savage Fury*. As over-active as my imagination was, I knew better than to even think about any of those. They'd find me in the spring thaw, masturbated to death.

I picked up a copy of *Surfer* at the magazine rack. That seemed to be more the thing to read. The guys were cute, and it made me feel like a little bit of summer looking and reading about the beaches inside. Tiger had promised to teach me come summer, so I might as well start reading up on it now.

"Do you surf or do you just like the pictures?" someone asked from behind me. I turned around and that was when I met Chris. He had on a navy toboggan cap and a ski parka. His curly hair was escaping from under the woven cap. His cheeks were ruddy and he had a big smile on his face. He looked genuinely happy to see me.

"I'm just a wannabe right now; my uncle's going to teach me next summer," I replied. I wondered what he meant when he asked if I just liked the pictures.

"I could teach you. I learned how at Ocean City. I've been surfing for about six years," he said. "You have to get used to falling down as much as getting up at first."

We stood in the magazine aisle talking about different kinds of boards, twin fins versus tri-fins and stuff. He was standing really close to me and seemed to be talking dead into my eyes the whole time. Unconsciously, I took a step back from him.

"I'm sorry, am I crowding you?" He seemed genuinely sorry, not mocking. "I'm real nearsighted. I lost my glasses and I'm trying to save up for contact lenses. I know it seems weird to have someone right up in your face, but you're kinda blurry if I don't," he explained.

"No, you can stand as close as you want," I said, and he grinned. "I mean, you know . . . I'd hate to be a blur. I'd want to see who I was talking to too."

"There are some people I don't care if I can see or not," he said, taking another step closer to me. "Sometimes being nearsighted is a good thing." I felt myself blush. I didn't know what to say to that.

"What are you doing? Just hanging out?" Chris asked. I told him my folks were driving me nuts. I had hiked out to try to find some new tapes for my Walkman. He told me his mom had gone to a conference in Raleigh and couldn't get back home because of the roads. Bored at home, he had driven out to look around. I told him I couldn't believe he was out driving. He laughed and reminded me he came from a place where people didn't freak out in the snow. "I got a lot of music back home. You want to come over and pick some stuff out? We could make some tapes for you," he offered.

I took him up on his offer. It turned out he was offering a lot more.

I gave up trying not to remember. I dropped the magazine on the floor and turned the pictures of me and Chris where I could see them. I ran my hand down my bare chest, over my right nipple. It was small and hard under the breeze from the ceiling fan over my bed.

I ran my hand under the loose waistband of my baggies and found my dick, already half hard. With my other hand, I unsnapped my pants and roughly opened the velcro fly. The surf trunks were still too confining. Reluctantly letting go of my dick, I pulled them off completely and lay back to look at the pictures one more time.

This was no good. I knew it. Chris and I were done. I couldn't kid myself anymore. He told me he had a girlfriend. He was really straight. My dick thought otherwise. It lengthened and arched over my belly, the head hot on the skin just below my navel. I wrapped my hand around it and began to tug, remembering.

We picked out about ten albums and started making tapes. Chris concentrated totally on the taping process. He twiddled and tweaked the levels for each song, all the time giving me a running commentary on recording engineering. At the same time, I wanted to tear his clothes off and fuck the living daylights out of him on the yellow shag carpet. I nodded a lot and tried to move around as little as possible to keep from putting any pressure on my aching dick.

He "engineered" me four tapes, meticulously filling out the little tag board sleeves with the titles and artist for each song. We had screwdrivers and got kinda buzzed. Finally, Chris asked me if I listened to much jazz. I told him only what I heard on the soul stations late at night. He told me there was something I had to hear. He jumped up unsteadily, ran into the living room, and came back a moment later with an album with a yellow cover. It was *We Want Miles* by Miles Davis. He explained his mom's boyfriend had given it to her so she kept it with her stereo in the living room. He cleaned it carefully with one of those wood and velvet album cleaners, then let the needle down on it slowly and leaned back against the side of the bed.

Chris closed his eyes and spread his legs out in relaxation. I watched him as I sat Indian-fashion across from him. He opened his eyes and looked at me. He took my arm, pulling me over next to him. He told me to lean back and relax. I leaned back and I tried to relax, but despite all the vodka and orange juice, I felt like I was a super sensitive satellite antennae. Everything was registering so clear and sharp, it hurt.

Chris nodded at me encouragingly. "Isn't Miles great? Sometimes I get so knotted up inside and so into my own head, I can't think. I come in here, put on this album and just kinda drift away, you know?"

I swallowed hard and nodded. I was about to go crazy. My heart was pounding and I was so full of conflicting thoughts I didn't know whether to jump up and walk home or blurt out how bad I wanted to touch him.

"Why are you so uptight?" Chris asked.

He looked over at me, seemingly innocent and knowing, all at the same time. For a second, I hated him. I hated him for putting me in such a dilemma. I hated him for being so at ease and in control while he was driving me crazy. I hated him for making me feel like I was taking advantage of the situation or reading more into it than there really was. I felt and heard something inside my head kind of ping, like a wire snapping. I looked him dead in the eye and said, "I really want to kiss you."

I'd said it, out loud. I was floating in the air. The floor felt like it had disappeared from underneath me. My was heart pumping like I was gonna have to throw down and fight, or walk a long way home in the cold. It didn't matter which. I didn't care anymore.

"So why don't you then?" he said, staring back at me.

Feeling so calm and still it hurt between my eyes, I searched his face looking for any hint of teasing or deceit. His eyes looked back at mine steadily, his lips were slightly parted and serene. I didn't find any cruelty anywhere. "You don't care?" I asked him huskily, my voice giving away the last of my secrets.

He shook his head and smiled gently, then he put his arm over my shoulder protectively. "I want you to," he said. His arm was heavy and warm across my shoulders. I caught a scent of sandalwood.

Chris moved his arm and put his hand gently on the back of my neck. I leaned toward him and put my lips against his. They were firm and parted against mine willingly. Some little voice in my head that I didn't recognize warned me to go slow.

I kissed him gently at first and then started exploring the texture of his lips. He responded in kind. If I was insistent, he was insistent. If I roughened the kiss with urgency, he pushed back as hard. I grew adventuresome and began kissing his face. I put my hand on the back of his neck and squeezed as I planted kisses on his ears, eyelashes, and nose. Always, always his mouth looked for mine again after I wandered down to the hollow of his neck, over his Adam's apple, and back up his chin. The taste of him was wonderful. I sucked on his tongue and ran mine over his teeth. I wanted to kiss him forever.

Chris pushed me away gently and stood up. He held up one finger and left the room. I heard him in the bathroom down the hall and became aware of the urgency with which I had to pee. I managed to stand up and follow the sound of the commode's flush to the bathroom. Chris was coming out. He pulled me to him and began kissing me again, then he told me to meet him in his room. He needed to lock the front door.

I went into the bathroom and seemed to pee for an embarrassingly long time. I washed my hands and sucked some toothpaste straight from the tube. I rinsed out my mouth and sniffed under my arms. Everything seemed A-OK. I looked in the mirror for a moment and my eyes stared back at me, bright and eager and still innocent. In the mirror, I looked like I was about twelve years old. I didn't want to be twelve; I wanted to be here and now. I snapped off the light and went back to Chris's room.

Chris had stripped down to his jockey shorts and was lying across the bed with his hands clasped behind his head. Outside, the clouds had come back. The late afternoon light filtered through the clouds and reflected off the icy snow outside, bathing the world and this room in a pearlescent light. Chris's pale skin, stretched over tight muscle and bone seemed to glow with moonlight and silver. He raised himself up on his elbows and reached out a hand toward me.

I suddenly felt really shy as I stripped down to my jockey shorts and lay down next to him on the bed. He pulled me over onto my side and stretched out on his side against me. It felt great. I ran my hand from his armpit to the elastic of his shorts, then hesitating, slipped my hand under the band to rest on the smooth skin of his hip.

His eyes were inches from mine and peered at me intently. "Am I blurry now?" I asked.

Chris chuckled. "No way. You look really good this close," he said, and kissed me.

"Chris, I have to tell you something," I said. His mouth found my shoulder and his tongue explored the grooves where my arm attached itself there. I heard him mumble yeah questioningly.

"I ain't never done this before."

Chris sat up slightly. "Never? Not with a girl? Nobody?"

I looked away, embarrassed.

Chris said, "You could have fooled me the way you kiss." He smiled, like he knew something I didn't, but I didn't feel bad about that. I was kind of glad.

"A virgin, huh?" Chris said softly. "Well, that just means it's up to me to make this real special for you." He slowly ran his hand down my back. My spine vibrated like a tuning fork. I shivered half from the feeling and half from some kind of reluctance, now I was where I wanted to be. I didn't want it to go too fast.

"Are you okay?" Chris asked me.

"I just don't want to do anything that might gross you out or something,"

Chris peered at me thoughtfully. I felt more naked than I really was. Finally he asked, "Do you trust me?" I told him sure, aware that my hand on his hip was getting sweaty. "Then just relax. Whatever I do to you, you can do to me, okay?"

I responded by kissing him, and he parted my lips and snuck his tongue into my mouth. He slipped his hand underneath the elastic of my shorts to gently knead my butt. I responded in kind, exploring the hard ridge of muscle on either side of his spine, then following the little hard lumps of bone to the crack of his ass.

Chris rolled me over onto my back and began kissing my chest. He ran his tongue over it, following the shallow groove to my navel and then back up to my nipples. I couldn't believe anybody would want to touch me like that. I couldn't believe how my body responded to the touch. The tuning fork I felt before was like one voice being slowly joined by others until my body was a whole choir singing. Chris moved over me to squeeze the inside of my thighs and mouth my dick through the flimsy material of my shorts. It felt like my dick would rip through the material at any minute. Roughly, he pulled down my jockey shorts and I raised my hips off the bed to help him. Chris's fingernails and the elastic band sliding away made me feel more naked than I ever had before in my life.

Once my underwear slid off my ankles and over my feet, my dick extended straight up toward my face almost to my navel. Chris took it in his hand and stroked it. "You got a nice dick," he said.

This surprised me. I never really gave much thought to whether it was nice or anything. I had heard guys talking about measuring theirs, but I figured that was kind of stupid. What if your dick turned out to be only three inches? How could it help to know that?

Chris was looking up at me, still gently pulling on my dick. He seemed to hesitate for a moment, looking in my eyes, then, bending down, he put my dick in his mouth. I couldn't believe it. It was like he nursed it gently. The sensation was incredible. It would have been so easy to drift away on the feeling, but I felt like I wasn't doing anything for him. I pulled his head off and he looked at me questioningly. "Did I hurt you?" he asked.

"Nope," I said. "It's your turn."

Chris lay down on his back and I sat astride his waist. The little voice inside my head spoke to me again urgently, telling me that now was the time to do all the things I had ever dreamed of doing. I leaned over and pulled Chris's arms back over his head. Holding them there, I kissed him long and hard, running my hands down his forearms past his elbows, squeezing the flat, extended muscles of his upper arms. I let my tongue find all the places it had ever wanted to go. I stretched out on top of him and worked my way down from his pecs to the taunt swell of his stomach.

There was an almost indefinable line of blond hair running from his navel to the elastic of his shorts. I followed it with my lips, knowing it was time to break the first taboo. Kissing was one thing, necking another, and extended tongue baths quite another. Now it was time for me to become a cocksucker.

All the taunted words spoken in anger ran across my mind as I gripped the sides of his jockey shorts and pulled them down his hips. Peter puffer, dick licker, fuck face, ran through my mind as Chris arched his butt and the shorts came down to reveal his thick penis and loose scrotum, inches from my face.

As Chris hooked his toe in the band of his shorts and pulled them free, I cupped his balls in my hand. Like I was engraving it in my mind, I memorized their weight and freedom in his silky scrotum. I put my tongue at the bottom of his dick and followed it up to the swollen head, recording the resistance of the skin and every vein. I took the head in my mouth, gently running my tongue across it, tasting Chris's slick flavorless pre-cum. I took his dick as deep as I could in my mouth and tried to swallow it before letting it go slowly through my tightened lips.

I did this several times until Chris moaned and tried to thrust it deeper into my mouth. I pulled away and looked up at him. His face was turned to the side, buried in his arm. His eyes were closed and his lips parted. He looked like an angel, strong but defenseless. He opened his eyes and looked down at me expressionlessly, still caught up in the feelings of the moment. I wanted to do more. I wanted to make him look at me like that forever.

Gently, I bit the insides of his thighs and he opened his legs for me, allowing his balls to drop between his legs. They almost touched the mattress. I took them in my mouth and teased the loose flesh with my tongue. I released one testicle, holding one in my mouth, while I rubbed it with my tongue through the thin-skinned sac. Chris moaned. I pulled away and wrapped my hand around his dick, stroking gently, memorizing how it felt in my hand. Still gently tugging, I felt it swell as I took it back in my mouth.

Chris gasped and pushed my head away, pulling me up on him by my armpits. "Not yet; not yet. I don't want to come yet," he said. He held me against his chest for a moment. I placed the flat of my hand on his breast and felt his nipple, hard under the palm of my hand. My ear was against his sternum. His heart beat strong and steady, like thunder. He rubbed my back and then rolled over on top of me. He placed his dick between my thighs and began to hump me slowly as he kissed me on the mouth.

Chris ground his cock in hard between my legs and I crossed my ankles to hold him tighter there. He bucked and twisted his hips, holding my wrists in his hands over my head. It felt great, but it wasn't enough. We kept this up for a while, but it was incomplete somehow. I was wet with sweat. Chris felt as slick as a fish under my hands. "I want to fuck you," he said.

I looked up at him and watched a bead of sweat trickle down the side of his face as he searched my eyes. It slid suddenly down his neck to dissolve into the warm shallow sea that seemed to be moving between us.

"I want you to," I said. I had gone this far. I wanted it all.

Chris got up off me and went over to the dresser. He rummaged around in the top drawer and when he found what he was looking for, came back to bed. He lay down beside me and kissed me on the lips.

"I'm going to try not to hurt you if I can help it," he said. "But it is going to hurt some. Will you trust me?"

I smiled at him and nodded.

He kissed me again hurriedly, then tore open a condom package with his teeth and rolled the rubber down over his dick. I tried not to think about why he was wearing a rubber. I didn't want to know. He reached over me and opened a tube of KY Jelly and squirted some on his hand. He rubbed it over his dick and then got between my legs. He squirted more of the lubricant on my dick, then more into his hand.

I gasped as Chris smeared the cold stuff in the crack of my butt. His other hand began to work it slowly over my dick. I relaxed under the gentle tug and pull of his hand, combined with the novel feeling of his other hand touching a place I had never allowed anybody to touch.

I jerked when Chris's finger went in. He quickly shushed me, telling me to just relax. It took a minute, but the sensations his hands were bringing from my groin were incredible. Too soon, he stopped and put his slick hands at the back of my knees, lifting them back and over his shoulders as he positioned himself in front of me. The position was awkward, it made my neck hurt. I made him stop while I put an extra couple of pillows behind my head. Chris hesitated. He gently tugged at my dick.

He looked at me and I looked back at him. His eyes seemed to be saying we had to be in perfect agreement that we were going to do this thing together. Somehow, I let him know it was okay. He grasped his dick in his hand and guided it to my butt. Slowly he began to push. I tried not to resist, but a slow circle of fire seemed to ring his dick as he pressed it inside of me. He let go of it and seemed to move toward my face, his mouth open to kiss me. With a hard thrust of his hips, I felt his dick being buried into me until I felt his sparse pubic hair.

Chris swallowed my cry of pain with his open mouth pressed into mine. It hurt bad. As bad as I wanted it, I wasn't prepared for how bad it hurt. Everything in me wanted to push him away and make it stop. I took my hands and put them around his throat. With my thumbs in the small hollow at the base of his neck, I squeezed. His throat was hard in my hands. I could feel the blood beating in his neck.

The wave of pain passed as Chris stayed perfectly still above me. As I relaxed, my grip on his neck loosened. He placed his face next to my ear and gently shushed me. Ever so slowly he began to slide his dick out and then back in abruptly. Slow, hard, slow, hard. I began to feel like my hip joints were melting. Letting go of his neck, I reached behind him to hold his butt in my hands. The need was getting bigger than the hurt.

Sucking Chris's dick was philosophical. This had nothing to do with that. This was what it was all about. No matter what, straight, queer, whatever. This feeling was hurting and living and crying out loud because it felt so good.

Chris quickened the pace with his hips. His breathing was coming harder and harder in my ear. I became aware of my own gasps as he thrust himself into me. He straightened up over me, sliding my legs off his shoulders and catching them in the crook of his elbows. My hand found my own dick and I began to beat off as he fucked me.

My own orgasm seemed to begin at the soles of my feet and spread upward. Chris felt me tighten myself around his dick and he pulled out quickly, almost making me pass out from the sensation. He pulled off the condom and began to beat off over me.

"I'm going to come, Matt."

I was distracted from my own pleasure enough to watch. He seemed to stop breathing as his jism shot, once, twice, four times. I came as it landed on me, warm and wet. I couldn't tell whose was whose. It didn't matter.

The fan whirred over me crazily now. The wind sent fresh spatterings of rain against the window by the bed. I felt my scrotum contract in my left hand as the head of my dick swelled in my right. I felt my memories gathering my familiar internal ocean into a swell. The wave rushed forward and I pushed my way up on it, riding it, my hand trailing in the wall. The jism spilled like foam over the tops of my fingers first, then shot up onto my chest.

The ride was over. My cum cooled and my wrist throbbed slightly with a small ache as I coaxed the last bit of cum out, squeezing my cock head. My scrotum relaxed. I wiped my hand on the inside of my thigh. I shivered slightly under the fan's breeze and from the memory of closeness, gone. I felt more lonely than I had in a long time. I closed my eyes and caught the last of the memory as it ran like the cold jism down my side.

Chris stretched out on top of me, both of us slick from sweat and cum. Smiling, his breathing slowing, he looked at me searchingly and I smiled at him. "Was I okay?" I asked.

He shook his head. "That was unbelievable."

I pinched his ass hard. "Does that mean yes?"

He wiped the sweat off his forehead and said, "It means it was so good it was almost scary." He pulled up a blanket from the foot of the bed and spread it over both of us. "Just let me close my eyes a minute and recover," he said. To show me he wasn't mad or anything, he laid his arm over me.

Outside, the twilight was turning the room from pearl to deep gray. Chris's breathing slowed and evened out. I realized he was falling asleep. Suddenly, I felt completely alone and more lonely than I had ever felt in my life. It was as sharp a feeling as the orgasm had been.

I was drowsy too, but I wanted to fight it as long as I could. There was too much to feel. Too much to think about. For the time being, all my questions were answered. There were a thousand others waiting in line. But for the first time in my life, I wasn't in any hurry to answer them. Stiff and a little sore, I turned over on my side to get more comfortable.

Chris whispered, "Don't go anywhere right now," then tucked himself into my back, his arm holding my waist. The feelings of loneliness disappeared.

So many things were churning in my mind while lying there with Chris's arm around me, his breath soft on the back of my head. I was aware of his dick pressed into the crack of my butt and the thin skim of shared sweat, spit, and semen bonding us together. The room was filled with a dull gleaming light, like the inside of a seashell. In the center of it we lay together like one creature, some warm, wet bivalve surrounded by mother of pearl. The noise of the world outside was muffled by snowfall and we were as protected and serene as if we were in the bottom of the sea.

I fell asleep.

Even with the rain from the storm pelting the windows of my room, I didn't sleep more than thirty minutes or so. I woke up cold, sticky, and antsy as hell. I knew I had to do something, even if it was wrong. If I kept on sitting around the house, memories would start to beat me up. I rolled off the bed and headed for the shower.

Chris came and went in my mind all the time. I guess it was because he was the first guy I ever fell in love with. He wasn't the only one I ever slept with, but almost. In the shower, I scrubbed at myself almost as if I could wash away the memory of his touch on me. I rubbed the shampoo into my scalp and watched it run down the groove of my chest until it collected briefly in my groin and fell away.

Leaning my head back, I felt the weight of my hair being pulled down by the water. I imagined Chris's memory falling clear.

Labor Day had been hell. Chris came down to see his mom before school started. He came down to the beach after that. We checked into a motel. I wasn't ready to show Chris and me together to the surgical precision of Tiger's cat-eyed gaze. Things were rocky between us and I didn't want Tiger's or Mark's opinion about my relationship. Besides that, I didn't want to share Chris' attention with anybody else, not what with the little bit of time we had.

We hung out some, went surfing together, but nothing was like it had been. Before he had left to go back up north, we had been like two halves of the same thing. In the time we had been apart over the summer, it had changed completely. The easy closeness was gone. Like a fool looking over and over again for something lost in a familiar place, I was stupid enough to try to look for the Chris I had loved so much in bed. I didn't find him at all.

The sex was still pretty good. But sex is more in your head than in your dick, if you're with somebody you love. While Chris slept happily, I sat awake, chain smoking and watching him sleep. He had been my lover, my brother, my friend. That was gone and it didn't seem to bother him at all. I thought he felt it too. Watching the untroubled peace on his sleeping face, I began to hate him in earnest, and myself, maybe more.

Chris had to leave early in the morning the next day. He was cheerful, but I could tell he was already on the road mentally. I was in two pieces. Part of me wanted him gone so bad I could almost hear the seconds click off until he was finally out of my sight. But still, I wanted to hold onto him. I didn't want him to leave me here and go back to whatever his life was away from me.

On the drive back to Tiger's, we didn't talk much. Somehow, we both had said too much in the past few hours. In too many words and too many touches we had played each other out. I really don't think either one of us wanted to know what was next.

Going back over the bridge to Emerald Isle, Chris took my hand. I didn't really want him touching me, but I let him hold my hand and surprised myself by finding his again when I had to loosen his grip to shift gears.

"Matt," Chris said gently. Glancing over, I saw the concern on his face. I felt it was counterfeit. He was leaving. I was staying. My resentment swelled up my throat and made me croak. "We're getting good at saying goodbye, aren't we?"

Chris let go of my hand and stared out the window. "I thought it was the hellos that counted," he said finally.

I reached up to the sun visor and found my cigarettes. Stalling for time and a little guts, I managed to get one lit. The ocean revealed itself in little glimpses through the dunes. Tiger's wasn't that far away and Chris would be gone. "It's not enough, Chris."

Chris slammed his fist against the dashboard and started to speak, then stopped. I heard him sigh. "It's all there is, Matt."

I looked at him across the car. I loved what I saw, but I was sorry to see what I found. I loved him, but what I was looking for, he didn't have. Chris didn't want to hurt me; in his own way, he really loved me. I knew that. I realized there were just some hoops neither one of us could jump through.

Reaching across my own growing pit of emptiness I found his hand again and squeezed it. "I know, Chris." He looked at me. I knew his every expression. For the first time since he came, we had communicated like we used to.

I was still sentimental enough to watch him leave. I didn't wonder whether it was the last time I would see him. Whatever it was that pulled us to each other didn't have anything to do with love. Not anymore. It was something else now. It didn't feel like either one of us was ready to let it go but both of us knew it wasn't ever going to be the same.

I shut off the hot water and let the cold run over me. It felt good. It also cleared my mind instantly. I shut off the shower completely and just stood there, letting the cold water roll off me. I wanted to do something, to change somehow. Getting out of Mama and Daddy's house and moving to the beach was only part of it. I might have an interesting job, a strange and wonderful new family and all that, but inside, I was still just me.

Looking in the mirror while I toweled off, I saw how much I had changed outwardly. Surfing had made my shoulders fill out. I was still pretty lean for my height, but I was more muscular than I had ever been before. Working outside had left me tanned. I looked in the mirror and was surprised to find this surfer guy looking back at me.

Throwing myself into surfing was part of wanting to be something special on my own. Being queer was not really that big a deal when you got right down to it. I used to think that just being queer made me special somehow.

When I met Chris, that's how I felt. I thought all it took to be whole was to have this really hot and intense lover. I redrew my whole picture of myself as Chris's boyfriend. That turned out to be the same as obsessing about being gay. Losing Chris taught me that you can't go looking for yourself in other people. If nothing else, I had to thank him for that.

After he left, I tried to put Chris out of my mind and put surfing into the empty place he used to stay in. All summer I'd been out there, in all kinds of waves, working on trying to connect with something bigger than myself and more demanding than a lover. I'd long been at the point where I'd go out by myself just to get connected with the good feelings the waves brought me. I'd hurl myself down the face of the biggest wave, or try to shred the shit out of the smallest ones just to push myself to the point where my body and mind were exhausted by the effort. It was great. The ocean might beat the hell out of you sometimes, but it never broke your heart.

Combing my wet head, I realized I needed a haircut. The thought of it made me happy. It was a quick fix if you felt like you had to change something, but it worked. I looked at myself in the mirror, seeing the bowl haircut I'd had for a year; it made me look like a kid. I pulled my hair back off my face and tried to imagine myself with a buzz cut. "What the hell," I decided, "hair grows."

In a few minutes, I threw on some clean baggies and a T-shirt. Outside my window, I could see the rain had slowed down but the wind was still up. Deciding it might be cooling off, I slipped off the T-shirt and reached instead for a flannel shirt from the drawer in my nightstand. The pictures of Chris and me caught my eye.

Finding the flannel shirt I was looking for, I pulled it on and then reached for our pictures. I gently folded the sides of the frame in on each other. I slipped the frame under some other clothes in the drawer and closed it. I could feel my heart thumping away steadily between the unbuttoned panels of my shirt. If I really wanted to change something, a haircut wasn't going to be enough. I closed the drawer and headed out of the house.

From the porch, I could see some lightening of the sky to the west. I heard the ocean over the wind and thought about the little break down the road. I figured it wouldn't hurt to take my bigger board along while I was out riding around. I picked it up and headed down to my truck. Halfway down the stairs I changed my mind. I decided that if I still wanted to check out the break after my haircut, I'd just swing back by the house and pick it up.

There weren't a lot of places to get a haircut on my end of the beach. I really didn't want to drive all the way down to Atlantic Beach, so I settled for the barbershop by the post office in Salter Path.

I could park right out in front of the shop; nobody was waiting. I could see the old guy who ran it sitting reading the paper when I pulled up. Nobody much wanted to get their hair cut at two o'clock on a Thursday afternoon—much less on the edge of a hurricane.

He put his paper down and nodded at me when I came in. "What can I do you for, son?" he said.

I looked at the big illustration of old-style haircuts he had on the wall. All the guys looked like Frankie Avalon or G.I. Joe. I asked him if he could cut my hair so it looked like a crew cut after it had grown for about a week.

The old guy chuckled and stood up. "Sure thing. I been cutting hair to request a long time before you met your mama." He swung the big barber chair around for me and I climbed in.

"How long you want it on top?" he asked me as he shook out the big sheet they wrap around you. I dropped my chin and looked at myself in the mirror.

"Long as you can make it, and still have it stand up," I told him.

He grunted as he swung the sheet around me with a flourish. "How short you want the sides?"

I didn't know what to tell him. "Make it proportional, I guess."

The barber smiled as he snapped the collar of the sheet tight under my Adam's apple. "Don't whitewall you, in other words," he said.

I nodded. "I don't want to look like no jarhead down from Camp Lejeune."

He laughed. "Don't worry, son. A lot of the surfers are coming in to me to get clipped. I know what you want." I heard him turn on the clippers and I closed my eyes. Last year, Mama had given me money to go downtown and get my hair cut by DeeAnn, this girl who used to baby-sit for me when I was little. I had needed a change back then too.

"Matt?" DeeAnn screeched. It made me jump. Seeing her after all that time was almost as shocking as her screeching. I remembered her as being sort of plump, with stringy hair. Right then she stood in front of me, thin as a rail, dressed in a black T-shirt, black jeans stuffed into pointy-toed cowboy boots, and sporting a mass of long gold ringlets of hair down to her waist. "My God! Look at you. I was expecting this little boy to come in, not a hot stud!" she screamed.

I wanted to melt and run in a puddle all over the cool tile floors. All the people in the salon started staring at me. I felt like the biggest idiot in the world. "You look pretty good yourself," I managed.

DeeAnn glided up to me and started pushing my hair around on my head. "Goddamn. What have you been doing to your hair? It looks like it's been cut in a Cuisinart." She screeched like she was caught in a Cuisinart herself.

DeeAnn grabbed me by the arm and pulled me toward Sheri Lansing from my French class. "Sheri, please get him shampooed and ready. I have to comb out Mrs. Johnson and then, honey, it's time for major surgery. Nine-one-one. God, somebody dial nine-one-one."

Sheri smiled at me and motioned for me to follow her to the back. "Hey," she said after I'd sat down in the bend-back chair by a sink.

"Hey," I said. "I didn't know you worked here."

Sheri shrugged and tilted me back. "The tips are good. You do know you're supposed to tip me, don't you?"

I nodded. I didn't, but I knew I had a couple of extra bucks more than Mama had given me. I let Sheri shampoo my hair. It felt really good, but sort of strange. Never in my life had I ever imagined Sheri Lansing rubbing my wet head. I was embarrassed and didn't know what to say. Sheri didn't seem to mind. I just closed my eyes and concentrated on the sound of the suds and water all over my head. Finally, Sheri shut off the water, sat me up, and squeezed my hair with a pink towel.

"When do I tip you?" I asked.

Sheri smiled and motioned for me to follow her up front. "When you pay is okay. Just tell LaShonda how much."

I thanked her as she left me in a seat in front of a huge mirror. Sheri mouthed "Two dollars" and held up two fingers before she walked off. Behind me, people waited and chatted. Besides DeeAnn there were two other people cutting hair. One was a middle-aged woman who looked like a Barbie doll somebody had left out in the rain awhile and the other was a very cute guy.

I caught myself staring at him in the mirror. He was blond and had one of those bowl haircuts that was just becoming popular. His hair swung heavily every time he moved around cutting this other guy's hair. Besides his haircut, the rest of him looked pretty nice. He was about medium height, but he had a nice body. He looked neat as a cat. I was noticing his butt in his jeans when DeeAnn appeared in the mirror as well.

"Well, it looks like we have all kinds of things to catch up on, Matt." She smiled at me and glanced at the cute guy. I felt myself turn red. She leaned over to whisper in my ear. "His name is Timmy. Isn't he the cutest thing?" DeeAnn said, following my eyes.

"I like his haircut," I stammered.

DeeAnn fluffed my hair with her fingers. "Uh huh . . . your hair is so heavy. I think that cut would be amazing on you." She twirled me around in the chair to face Timmy. "Timmy, come here. Matt wants to look at you." I couldn't say anything; I was so embarrassed.

Timmy excused himself from his customer, and walked up to us with a smile. "Well, look away," he said.

I tried to smile and say something, but all I could do was sit there. "Don't you think Matt would look fantastic with a cut like yours?" DeeAnn demanded.

Timmy reached over and ran his fingers through my hair. It sent an electric shock through me. DeeAnn stepped aside as Timmy moved behind my chair. He swiveled me around to face myself in the mirror. I looked like I was scared to death. He gathered my hair and lifted it.

"Do it," he said. "You were born for this." I didn't think it was possible to turn more red and not burst a blood vessel. Timmy and DeeAnn began some sort of discussion about my hair texture. Finally, he leaned down and said softly into my ear, "Be sure and let me see how it turns out before you leave." I found his eyes in the mirror and nodded. He had this uppity little knowing look on his face.

DeeAnn stepped behind me as he walked away. She played with my hair a moment, studying my face in the mirror. "Get up," she said. I was confused. I looked at her in the mirror and she gave me a soft smile. "I need some inspiration to tackle your head. C'mon."

I stood and followed her back beyond the shampoo area to a door on the back wall. She opened it and we went into a large room, bare except for a sofa, coffee table, and boxes of hair supplies. She motioned for me to sit down on the sofa, then rummaged among the boxes until she found a purse. She brought it to the sofa and sat down.

"Honey, are you all right?" she asked.

"I'm fine. Why?" I said.

DeeAnn patted my hand, then pulled a joint from a pack of Benson and Hedges Menthol Light 100s she found in her purse. She lit it and took a deep hit before passing it to me.

I took a toke and then another. The pot tasted like ground-up Christmas trees and was really strong. I handed the joint back to her.

"Well, let's catch up. . . . Do you have a boyfriend?"

I choked. DeeAnn laughed. She patted my back sympathetically while she took a hit.

"Is it that obvious?" I asked. She studied me for a minute before she took another hit. Handing the doobie back to me, she said, "Honey, you're too pretty not to be gay. Now, do you have a boyfriend or not?" I told her I didn't. DeeAnn nodded briskly like she was making a mental note and said, "It's no wonder you don't with that butt-ugly haircut. Are you high?" she asked me.

I felt like I had stumbled into a parallel universe. "Oh yeah," I said.

DeeAnn put her arm around me and squeezed. "Good." She pinched the end of the roach to make sure it was out and put it back into the pack of cigarettes. "C'mon baby. I'm gonna make a whole new you." I followed her back out to the chair in the middle of all those people.

I was so stoned, I just closed my eyes and listened to the music coming out of the speakers. I could hear DeeAnn snipping and twirling around my head. She would push my head this way or that and I just gave in to it.

After the snipping and tugging came the low hum of the clippers. I felt them lift the hair on the back of my head and was amazed at the feeling of air on my neck. It was the first time in years my hair wasn't covering it up. I felt light as a bird. DeeAnn sprayed some sweet-smelling stuff on my hair and then I heard the rushing of a hair blower. Stoned as I was, I imagined myself running down a street in the sunshine, my new haircut blowing in the wind mixed up with falling leaves and pine straw, like somebody in a beer commercial.

"Wake up, handsome. You're done." DeeAnn said. I opened my eyes to the bright shop. "This is gonna be good," I heard somebody say in the background while my eyes adjusted. For a second, I saw this cute guy looking at me, then I realized it was me. DeeAnn had given me a surfer cut like Timmy's. My hair lay straight and even across my eyes and just over my ears. For once, my eyes seemed balanced and my jaw was square as if a good carpenter had laid it out like a foundation for my face. My neck looked strong and muscular. I couldn't believe it. I went to look at DeeAnn and felt the heaviness of my hair in back swing with momentum.

"What do you think, baby?" DeeAnn asked with a sleepy smile.

"Goddamn, DeeAnn," I said, then I started grinning.

"Don't shine them dimples at me, heartbreaker," DeeAnn hollered. She swung my chair around to face everybody in the salon. "Ladies and gentlemen, I'd like to present my latest creation. Get up, Matthew."

I stood up and people applauded. "Girl, you is a magician, not a beautician. That boy come in here looking like a dog," LaShonda yelled from the reception desk.

I caught Timmy looking at me with a kind of hot-eyed look. I was embarrassed, but man, did I feel good.

DeeAnn made a deep curtsey and then pushed me toward the reception desk. "He's mine, people. Timmy, get that look off your face. You're going to have to get in line behind me."

I was surprised when everybody laughed. As good as she cut hair, I wished DeeAnn wasn't so dramatic.

After I paid my bill, remembering to leave Sheri Lansing a two-dollar tip, DeeAnn followed me out the door. Out on the sidewalk, I thanked her for my haircut and the killer buzz. DeeAnn gave me a quick hug. "Listen Matt, what are you doing next Saturday night? I'm having a pre-Halloween party at my place. I want you to come."

I was surprised she asked me. I mean, I never went to any parties and I didn't know why she'd ask a kid like me to her house for one.

"It's not costumes or anything; we're going to do all that in Raleigh on Halloween. But there's going to be some cool friends of mine from Raleigh coming down. Say you'll come. It's going to be wild." DeeAnn said. She seemed so sweet, like she really wanted me to be there.

"Okay. Yeah, sure," I told her.

DeeAnn clapped her hands together like a little girl and twirled right there on the street. From her hip pocket she pulled out an invitation and stuck it in my hands. "Everything's written down. Just show up, okay?"

I nodded and smiled, sticking the invitation in my own back pocket.

"Oh, my God!" DeeAnn screamed. "Mrs. Strickland has had perm solution in her hair for days. Kisses, sweetie! You look fabulous!"

Before I could say anything, DeeAnn twirled around and was back in the shop.

All the way home in the truck I kept looking at myself in the rearview mirror. I hardly recognized myself. "Don't Stop Believing" came on the radio and I rolled down the window and blasted it. Even though I felt kind of burnt from the killer pot I'd smoked with DeeAnn, I felt incredible. I felt so good when I got home, I stripped off my shirt and went outside to make good on my promise to wash and wax Daddy's truck.

The sun felt good on my back. I knew you weren't supposed to wax a vehicle in the sun, but I really didn't care. For the first time I could think of, I felt good and I looked good. I stared at my reflection coming off the truck's new shine. I was lean, but not really skinny, I told myself. My shoulders seemed broader without all the hair I had had on my head. There was a sort of fish bone of dark hair that started under my navel and spread down into my jeans. I was almost getting hard finding the new me in the truck's finish.

I was so busy looking at myself, I jumped when I heard a wolf whistle from the street behind me. For a minute I panicked. I thought somebody was fucking with me. "Matt, is that you?" It was my best girl friend, Cathy, sitting up on her horse. She was riding with Trevor Jensen, who she said she didn't have a crush on, but she did. Hell, I had a crush on him myself. He was pure cowboy come to town, that was for sure.

"Hey, Cathy. Hey, Trevor. What's up?" I said as I wiped my hands on my jeans and walked out to the street. Trevor pushed his John Deere cap back on his head and nodded down at me.

Cathy laughed her tinkly laugh and looked down at me. "What have you done? You look like . . . I don't know . . . you look good."

I patted her horse's nose. "I just got a haircut is all. What are you guys up to?"

Trevor leaned the opposite way on his horse and spat. He was chewing tobacco. "Riding horses, man; what's it look like?" Trevor never was real friendly to me. We had said maybe ten words to each other since eighth grade, but he hadn't ever been an asshole.

"I thought they looked kinda big to be dogs," I said.

Cathy laughed her wind chimes laugh. I felt good. Cathy looked over at Trevor. He was just sitting on his horse looking from her to me. "Haircut give you a smart mouth, faggot," Trevor said.

The sun went behind a cloud. Cathy stopped laughing, but Trevor kept on looking at me and started growing a smile at the ends of his mouth. There was a fleck of tobacco in one corner. I felt cold all of a sudden, and ridiculous standing with my skinny-ass self with no shirt on out in the street. I looked from Trevor to Cathy. She seemed to be waiting for me to say something.

I looked back at Trevor. He was grinning. I stared at him and thought of evil things. Things like pouring gasoline on his face and setting it on fire. Things like cutting the smile off his face real slow with a butcher knife. I found his eyes and concentrated, forcing all that out through my own eyes. I began to smile with the most evil smile I could muster. I tried to push those images up into his eyes and brain as hard as I could. His horse snorted and shook his head. Trevor kept his eyes locked on mine. Finally, he looked away.

"C'mon Cathy," Trevor said and nudged his horse into a walk. Cathy looked at me different than she ever had before. I couldn't tell if it was pity or concern on her face. Trevor's back rolled from his ass in the saddle all the way up to his shoulders. It was like him and the horse were one big, mean triumphant thing. "You coming?" Trevor said back over his shoulder. Cathy looked after him. I could tell she wanted to follow off behind him.

"Take it easy, Cathy," I said and turned to go back in my yard. I didn't look back, but I heard her horse's metal shoes clicking on the asphalt. At first, they were different from the clops Trevor's horse's made, then they synced up and faded off down the road. I tried to forget it and concentrated hard on finishing my chore. I rubbed the last bit of wax off Daddy's truck as the sun came back out. The truck looked really good; I could see myself in the finish. It was just me looking back at me again in the shine coming off the quarter panel by the left front tire.

The barber unsnapped the sheet from around my neck and pushed my head down. I heard him squirt the hot shaving cream into his hand. In just a moment, I felt it smooth over the back of my neck. I tried to peek up and look in the mirror across from me. I had been so busy remembering DeeAnn that I had almost fallen asleep again. All I could see were my own eyebrows.

Finally, the barber finished shaving my neck, and I looked up. I liked what I saw. The bowl cut had made me look like a pretty boy. This was a man's haircut. My eyelashes were still awful thick, which made my eyes look feminine, but this haircut evened it all out. I didn't want to be a pretty boy anymore. I damn sure wasn't Chris's pretty boy, or anybody else's, either.

The barber caught me looking at myself and grinned as he rubbed the last bit of lather off my neck. "Boy, you'll be getting the women wet just minding your own business."

I lowered my eyes and said, "You think so, huh?"

The old man laughed. "Count on it, son. That'll be four-fifty."

I stood up and pulled a ten from the wax pocket on the back of my baggies. It was sticky from where the heat of my butt remelted the residual wax while I was sitting in the vinyl seat of the barber's chair. I handed the bill to the old guy and told him to keep the change. He nodded and stuck the money in his pants pocket.

"You'll need to come back in about three weeks, if you like the way it looks. Short hair don't keep its shape when it's as thick as yours."

The old guy ran his hand over what was left of his own hair. "That ain't my problem no more," he said and cackled.

I gave him a grin and headed out to my truck. I didn't blast the radio, even though Prince singing, "Little Red Corvette," came on. Those days were gone, along with getting stoned. I hadn't smoked since I met Chris.

Damn, Chris again. That Prince song made me think of him. I punched through the stations until I found a weather report. When I pulled the truck out onto the highway, I decided to head down to the pier to see how the waves were breaking there. I did sneak a glance at myself in the rearview mirror. I still liked what I saw, but I knew better than to get carried away.

The pier was almost deserted. The hard-core fishing guys

had abandoned it to the surfers. The hurricane wasn't good for fishing, even if you could stand it in the wind out on the pier. For once, the pier owners didn't mind the surfers. On days like this, they bought enough beer, sodas, and hamburgers while they hung out and watched the waves to cover some of the loss of the fishermen.

The pier near our house had its own peculiar segregation of surfers. It was never more apparent than now, in the late fall after all the tourists had gone. Before I started surfing, one side of the pier looked like the other as far as I was concerned, but since Tiger had taught me to really look at waves, I could see that two different worlds of waves and surfers existed together.

The pier, with its deep-set pilings, is sort of like an open-weave jetty that allows the sand to pass through, but still creates its own unique configuration of sandbars and surf zones on either side of the pier itself. It does the same thing with the surfers who come there to park and watch and bullshit and even surf.

On the left side of the pier, the kids surf. Middle-schoolers and high-schoolers mainly. The waves on that side are not as big, but they are faster and provide more of the adrenaline rush that becomes addictive through skateboarding. The waves on the right side of the pier are thicker and break taller and harder than those on the left. On this side the pier's pilings gouge the bottom most deeply in big storms and during the winter. That's where the big boys surf.

The big boys are hard core. They are the construction crews who came for a summer back in the seventies and never left. They are also the locals who grew up surfing on the left side of the pier and through any number of vicious dogfights in and out of the water, earned the right to move to the other side.

I parked in the middle of the lot. To tell the truth, that was the only real place I belonged. By age, I should have been in the water on the left, balls out to earn my place on the right side of the pier. But I was still a kook, and to tell you the truth, I wasn't all that competitive. I didn't surf the pier much. It was too crowded and too aggressive. I wasn't scared of having to fight or anything, it just seemed like too much bullshit to go through for something I thought was personal. I surfed for me, not for some big macho reputation.

The wind felt weird on my freshly mowed head. I looked over to the right side of the pier and saw Randy Tillett's truck from the roofing company among the others there. He was standing by the bulkhead with some of the guys from his crew. They huddled like a tough dog pack, all tense muscle and ready temper. I knew those guys from some of the subdivisions where Tiger and I staked batter boards or piling placements and did mortgage surveys. I knew Tillet better than the rest, but he probably wouldn't admit it.

Tillett looked over and saw me. I acknowledged him with an abrupt lift of my chin. He did the same and then turned to look back out at the waves. The guys from his crew nodded after their alpha dog had signaled it was okay.

I walked over and stood on the edge of their little group. They didn't accommodate my presence, but they didn't ignore me either. These guys were old-school cool. I had earned my right to the fringes because they knew I worked construction, sort of. As a surfer, I was a nonentity to them. I hadn't been on the scene long enough to even register contempt.

"This ain't shit compared to David," Tillett muttered, referring to the hurricane that had passed offshore a few years back. A few of the others grunted in agreement.

One of them gestured to a four-inch keloidal scar across Tillett's bare collarbone, "Ain't that when you got that?"

Tillet nodded.

One of the younger guys from the crew asked, "What happened?" Tillett looked at the guy who pointed it out and shrugged.

Permission noted, he said, "Tillett and me were doing framing up in Rodanthe that year. We went out right after it cleaned up some, but there was all this shit in the water. Plywood, two-by-fours, Sheetrock even. It was real big, head-high, and still kind of gnarly. Tillet pitched out on this monster. When it came down it pushed all this shit on top of him. He got popped by a piece of one-by-six with a nail in it." The guy chuckled. "He was bleeding like a son of a bitch, and was he pissed he had to get out of the water."

Tillett's lower lip curled down on one side and lifted on the other. It was a menacing look of half disgust and half amusement.

"Why'd you have to get out of the water?" a young guy asked.

Tillett gave him the same look. The guy who told the story spit in disgust, then said, "Goddamn, you're a dumb-ass."

Tillett looked at the boy dismissively and said, "Sharks."

Embarrassed by his admission of ignorance, the boy looked down at his feet.

Tillett half turned and looked at me briefly. I saw a flicker in his eyes and I didn't know whether it foretold meanness or something else. "What's up, rod dog?" he said. I shrugged. Tillett nodded and looked away.

"Ain't that new kid—Shane—ain't he your cousin or brother or something?" one of the guys asked me. I told him yeah, but I didn't go into any details. "Kid's ripping," he said lifting his chin toward the left side of the pier.

That meant he was skipping school, if it was Shane. "No shit?" I responded.

"Man, you ought to check it out. Little fucker might teach you something," he said.

It wasn't exactly a challenge, but I couldn't just walk away from it. Tillett looked at me, suddenly interested. "I ain't got to learn what I taught him," I responded, looking him in the eye. The guy gave me a skeptical look and spat down on the sand. I looked levelly around the group.

Tillett's buddy said, "Why ain't you out then?"

I had to graze Tillett's glance to find my questioner's eyes. "I guess I'm like you. I don't need the practice," I told him.

Tillett laughed, then everybody else did. Tillett asked, "Any of y'all checked out anywhere else?"

The tension was broken. A couple of the guys said they had been down toward Fort Macon and commented on a break there. I didn't mention the little break I'd noticed earlier. I was still thinking about going out by myself and I didn't want any of these guys showing up there. After awhile, the crew began to break up.

I told them I'd see them around and started walking over to the left side of the pier. I could feel somebody watching me as I walked away. I glanced back over my shoulder. Tillett grinned. I changed my mind and walked into the pier house. My knees were shaking and my heart was banging away inside my chest so hard I glanced down involuntarily to see if I could see it beating against my sternum. I felt like I could either throw down and fight or dive off the end of the pier, it didn't matter which.

I bought a large coffee from the lady behind the counter and walked out into the fierce wind beating across the deserted pier. Even with the break, I took a seat on a bench looking out over the left line-up. Feeling in the pocket of my flannel shirt, I found my cigarettes while I looked for Shane. I didn't have to look long. He was ripping the big sloppy waves for all they were worth.

His daddy would beat his ass if he knew he had skipped school to go surfing. Mark was too used to military discipline. I cupped my hand around the lighter like Tiger had taught me and got my cigarette lit against the hard wind. Tiger wouldn't rat Shane out, even if he caught him like I had. This time, I was going to let it slide. I wondered what I was going to do about Tillett.

The wind blew the panels of my shirt apart and I glanced down at my sternum again. I was calming down some. I watched Shane eat it on a wave he knew better than to try for. The boy was an animal; he'd try anything. His head popped up like a seal's and he managed to pull his board back by the leash. In one fluid moment, he was back on it and paddling back out into the lineup.

Overhead, the sun broke out of the clouds. The storm was moving off right on schedule. The beach was flooded with sunlight and it looked like a different place, scrubbed and clean in the late autumn light.

I was in love with the beach. I loved how the sky seemed so enormous over me. I loved how the ocean had a sort of phosphorescence in the dark, and how it was as many colors of blue as there are numbers. I studied it under all kinds of skies and different times of day. I loved how everything seemed to be gold, from the sea oats to the sweat-shiny backs of the guys like Tillett, building cottages. Even my own skin had a dark gilding. The air hypnotized me and made me feel like I was walking to reggae music. The old cottages were magical places where people lived suspended between sand and sky.

I felt like I'd come home, for no other reason than it was a place I chose. Mine. I'd found a place where I could be happy. It didn't matter that most everybody I knew outside my little beach family hated faggots and made comments like this wasn't that kind of beach, like South Miami Beach or something. I didn't mind that at all. I knew I wasn't that kind of faggot. I was prepared to go without sex if I could be here and be happy.

The summer had rolled by, one beautiful day after another. I walked down the beach with only the dogs for company many a night. I knew there was fucking going on all around me, but I was either so tired from working and surfing, or I was so in love with the beach, it didn't seem to matter.

I hated to admit it, but I missed Chris for the sex more than anything. I was surrounded by half-naked guys everywhere I looked. Tiger, Mark, and the boy's near-nudity grew to become as sexless as the two dogs. Outside the house was a different story.

Good-looking guys were everywhere. They walked the beaches. They banged nails on construction sites. They sauntered down the street in front of the house. It drove me crazy, but I didn't really know what to do about it. I had never really been with anybody but Chris, so I didn't know how to seduce. I was still hung up on him so I didn't seduce.

It made me feel weird to go out. I didn't really know who to approach, or what kind of signals to put out, and I sure as hell didn't want to get the shit kicked out of me if I picked the wrong guy. I just sort of stumbled along, walking a line between denial and distraction.

It was easy to be distracted. Sometimes, I'd be out setting stakes for a new house and I'd see some guy working building a house nearby. He'd be tanned and his muscles would move fluidly as he guided a roof rafter into place or bent to toenail a stud on a wall frame. I had to force myself not to stare. Some days one isolated movement of a good-looking guy would echo through my thoughts for hours, eating away at my concentration and making me restless and mean.

This meanness was a weird by-product of getting grown and understanding about how sex changed a person. Before I was ever with Chris, back when I was just a virgin, not having sex didn't make me mean. Sex was always something I could just take care of by myself.

It wasn't until I had actually learned how much different and complete sex was with somebody else that I learned you can't ever go back to just this dumb kid, whacking off alone. Having sex and getting it had become this big deal part of my life. Without Chris, without getting *it* regularly, I was fogging out thinking about sex all the time.

One day, Tiger yelled at me for getting foggy while he was trying to get ties to a foundation. I told him to fuck off, but I started paying better attention. I stayed sullen all day. Going home, I could tell he was watching me. He was almost eerie sometimes how he could figure out what was going on with me. Finally, he looked at me and told me I needed to go out, find somebody, and get laid.

I laughed it off, but he was right. Without making any big deal out of it, I decided it was time. Saturday night came and I played cards with Shane and Billy until about ten o'clock. My resolve had hardened. I took a shower, dressed in a new pair of shorts and T-shirt I'd bought that morning, and slipped out of the house to go down to Atlantic Beach.

There's no gay night life on Bogue Banks. No queer clubs anyway. I knew there was a gay bar over in Jacksonville, but I didn't want to drive way the hell over there. I had gone one time when I first moved to the beach, but it was just a bunch of booger drag queens fighting over one or two pimply Marines. It wasn't my idea of a place to find what I was looking for.

I decided to go to Chevy's, this big rock and roll dance place on the Circle. If nothing else, I might get lucky and pick up some drunk frat boy on vacation. I paid my money to get in, and went to one of the bars and bought a beer.

The place was packed. I took my beer and stood over near the dance floor, looking. It was a zoo. There was the whole damn collection of males Eastern North Carolina had to offer, dancing, drinking beer, having a great time, just partying like hell. There was every type of Carolina girl there too. The problem was, they were all looking at each other. I felt like something out of an Anne Rice novel, but I didn't have the predatory charm of a vampire.

The music was good. The dance floor was so packed, I thought, "Fuck it." I chugged my beer and set the empty on a nearby rail, then made my way out on the floor. I could dance by myself if I wanted to. It felt good. I smiled at the other dancers, male and female, and we all floated in and out of one another's gravitational pull. I saw a lot of drunken happy smiles, but I didn't get any lingering looks.

After about an hour, I was drenched in sweat and needed to piss really bad. I was about to leave the floor when I noticed two guys turn from the girls they were with and begin dancing with each other. The song was one of those macho, chanting, anthemic ones, that some guys took as the theme song of their own frustration and anger.

One of the guys pulled off his shirt and lunged at the other who lunged back. They screamed the lyrics in each other's faces and half danced, half wrestled in a sweaty struggle with each other's aggressiveness. A small circle cleared around their intensity and the crowd cheered them on, screaming the lyrics as they met and nearly fucked on the dance floor. I screamed along with the rest and felt my dick thicken my pants.

Abruptly, the song ended and another one began. The guys broke apart and gave each other one brief glance that signaled to me that they must have once fucked as ferociously as they danced. The shirtless guy stalked off the dance floor and disappeared into the crowd as the other one returned to his girl partner.

I left the dance floor myself. I didn't know if I was being led by the radar in my half-hard dick, or the need to piss, but I had to do something. I shouldered my way through the crowd and found the rest room. All the urinals were occupied. The one toilet had its door closed. I stood waiting.

The door to the toilet came open and the shirtless dancer pushed his way out, almost knocking me out of the way. For a minute, our eyes tangled. Mine must have sent a stronger message than I thought. I saw recognition, panic, and anger pass through his in a strangled moment. "Faggot," he muttered as he pushed past me.

I went into the stall and allowed myself a bitter smile as I pissed a long time into the reeking bowl. It had always been my belief that the first one to call you a faggot is the last one to have had a dick in his mouth. My self-satisfaction dwindled with my stream of urine. Deep and bitter disappointment took its place. I wasn't going to find anybody to fuck at Chevy's. I zipped up and left right away. All the revelry and smoky seductiveness was for the breeders, not for me.

Walking across the parking lot, I heard somebody say, "What's up, rod dog?"

Looking around, I saw Tillett sitting on the hood of his work truck, drinking a beer. I walked over. Tillett and I had never spoken much. When we had, it was mostly just grunts of recognition. As it was, I'd have recognized him anywhere.

It was Tillett who had made me go all spacey when Tiger had yelled at me earlier in the week. I was holding the end of the hundred-foot tape to the corner of a porch when I looked up in time to see Tillett begin climbing an extension ladder, one handed. The other hand steadied four bundles of shingles balanced on his shoulder.

Tillett was about six-two and had the kind of body you earn from working, not working out. From my position at the base of the building below, I watched his hard, flat nipple ride on the tight ridge of his chest, then his stomach ripple under its light blond fur, then his ass and calves bunch as he made his way up the ladder with a self-assurance that went beyond posturing.

All I could think of was getting next to that controlled source of power. I could feel myself orchestrating those muscles under the flat of my hands, urging them . . .

"Goddamn it, Matt. Wake the fuck up." Tiger yelled.

Tillett had glanced down from the ladder and chuckled as he transferred the bundles of shingles to the rim of the roof.

Now, he was sitting with his legs spread wide apart, the heels of his sneakers hooked behind the bumper. The cool wind off the ocean blew back the panels of his unbuttoned shirt. I unconsciously walked toward those open thighs.

"What's up?" he repeated gruffly.

I shrugged and looked off toward a straggling couple making their way toward the entrance of Chevy's. "Just looking for the party."

Tillett nodded and reached into the paper bag beside him on the hood of the truck. He pulled out a can of Budweiser and extended it toward me. I took it from him and popped the top.

"Looking for the party," he repeated and snickered. I took a long hit of beer and looked up at him. He let the hand holding his own beer drop between his legs. I followed it with a glance and watched as he tickled his nuts with the tip of his thumb.

Embarrassed, I looked away.

"You're looking for some dick, ain't you, rod dog?" Tillett said in a low growl.

I looked up sharply into his face. My heart was beating and I had to think to control my breathing. Fight-or-flight instinct sometimes was the same thing as lust. A hard kind of amusement shone from Tillett's eyes. I didn't say anything. Tillett slid gracefully off the hood of his truck and to stand within inches in front of me. I caught his scent. It was clean, but underneath it was a note of arrogance and heat. I was aware of his hard chin, shaved and thrust threateningly just below my eyes.

Tillett moved from in front of me and went to the driver's side of his truck. Opening the door, he looked at me and said, "Get in."

We didn't talk. He peeled out of the parking lot, scattering a group of kids. He drove us down toward Fort Macon without looking at me. My heart slowed as I gave myself up to whatever happened. Tillett could either fuck me or kill me. I had gotten into the truck without a second's hesitation or thought to the worst case scenario. I drained the warm beer from my can and squeezed it in my hand until he turned into a small, dark dock area back away from the road. Tillett parked at the end of the rutted oyster shell drive next to an old shrimp boat.

He shut off the engine and looked at me for the first time. I tried to read what I saw in his eyes, but it was too dark. I just felt a heat coming off him across the bench seat. Abruptly, he opened his door and jerked his chin for me to follow him. I got out of the cab of the pickup and watched him cross the dock to jump onto the deck of the boat.

He looked back toward the truck and motioned for me to come on. I followed him onto the deck of the boat and watched as he unlocked the door to the wheelhouse. He disappeared inside for a moment and came back out with an old quilt.

Without a word, he spread it on the deck. He looked around briefly, seeing nobody and hearing nothing but a quiet slap of water against the hull of the boat, he slipped off his shirt and then unsnapped his baggies. He kicked off his sneakers. The sharp sound of the velcro fly ripping apart split the quiet. I watched as he ran his hands back under the waistband and slid them off. His dick reared and bounced as he stepped out and away from the puddle of clothes.

Finally then, Tillett looked at me. I became aware of the slight grin on his face in the dim light. He pulled downward on his lengthening dick and looked at me haughtily, giving me time to admire his nakedness.

"Is this the kind of party you were looking for?" he said as he stepped up to me.

I looked into his eyes. They were a luminous pale blue, like a Siberian husky's. They seemed to gather up the dim light and concentrate it.

"Now ain't the time for you to get shy on me, boy." Tillett said as he roughly reached down and grasped the neck of my new T-shirt in both hands. He jerked me toward his face. "I can rip these clothes off you to help you make up your mind," he said in a harsh whisper, "and its such a nice new shirt."

I took a step back and grasped my T-shirt by its hem. Tillett let go and chuckled.

I quickly peeled off my shirt and stripped off my shorts. Tillett grabbed me by the scruff of my neck and pulled me back to him. I felt the head of his dick hot on my inner thigh as he pivoted us around. He looked searchingly in my eyes for what seemed like a full minute. I stared back into them challengingly. His lips curled in a cruel grin and he pushed me down hard to my knees.

With his free hand, he bent his clubby dick toward my mouth and shifted his stance to accommodate the slight rocking of the boat. His grip on my neck loosened. With a rough tenderness, he squeezed the back of my neck as he urged my face forward.

I fitted my mouth around his cock head and slid down toward his fist holding the shaft. He let go and cupped the side of my face gently in the palm of his rough hand. The hand on the back of my neck held me still. I looked up to find him watching me, almost tenderly. We stayed motionless, joined like that for some time. "Don't move," he whispered with choked abruptness. I could feel the muscles in his groin contracting, making his dick rub against the roof of my mouth.

Haltingly, I slid my hand up over his thigh and side until it reached the hard shelf of his breast. He took his hand from my cheek and covered my own resting on his chest. Gripping it, he slowly began to fuck my mouth. I let my free hand find the hard curve of his ass. He released my neck and covered that hand with his own as well.

I let his dick play through my lips and looked up at him again. He was looking out over the water. I turned my hands under his and grasped them. He looked down at me and I pulled, urging him downward. He lightly squeezed my hands before letting them go. Uncertainly, he knelt in front of me. Tillett's eyes seemed suddenly sad. I touched the side of his face as he had mine. I traced the line of his jaw before placing my hand at the back of his neck to pull him toward me.

He kissed me then, gently at first and then more insistently as he forced me out on my back. Tillett laid his own long torso against me, pushing his dick into my stomach as he rested on his elbows over me. He kissed me as his fingers found their way into my hair. In response, I shifted my weight slightly and curled one leg over his. I grasped his lats in my hands and squeezed them hard before allowing my fingertips to find their way beneath them to trace the hard grooves of muscle connecting his lats to his ribs.

Tillett left off kissing me and hung his head by my left ear. "It ain't supposed to be like this," he mumbled.

I grasped him by the tense knotted muscles of his upper arms. "How's it supposed to be?" I asked him.

He raised his head and looked down into my eyes. I tried to raise my head to kiss him, but he quickly moved and caught my forehead under his palm and pushed my head back onto the deck.

He searched my face again and then rolled off me. He sat back on his haunches and forced me over efficiently. I struggled to get up, but made it only to my knees before Tillett moved behind me. He caught me by the neck again and forced my face down onto the quilt. I felt the tip of his dick against my ass. He began to push.

"No, no, man, don't . . . " I tried to get out, with my face pressed into the dirty quilt. Tillett shoved himself into me and I cried out. I heard him snicker. He started pushing harder into me until I felt his dick buried in me up to his nuts. He let go of the back of my neck and grabbed me by the shoulders as he began roughly fucking me.

I smelled years of accumulated diesel exhaust, fish guts, and motor oil embedded in the quilt. My eyes stung with tears of pain and humiliation. I heard the shirtless dancer and Trevor call me a faggot. Behind me, Tillett was boring a hole into my self-assurance and new pride.

Having found his stroke, Tillett was easing up on me now. The pressure on my shoulders was gone suddenly as he grasped me by the waist. In a moment of pure clarity, my wounded pride raised itself. I

wasn't just going to lay there and get raped. I reared myself up forcing Tillett to sink back onto his haunches to stay inside of me.

I leaned back until I felt his chest against my back. Tillett released
his grip on my waist and held my belly in one hand and my chest in
the other. Past the pain of his entry, I gave myself up to the pleasure in
his thrusts. I formed my self against him, slowing his insistence and
taking control again of the act. I leaned my head back into his shoulder as he lifted us both up onto our knees and measured his stroke.

I felt the hard reality of his body against my back. Tillett's firm
belly melded to the arch of my lower back, his slightly hairy chest
grinding into my shoulders. Finding his hand on my belly, I forced it
down to my own dick. Surprisingly, Tillett took it away long enough
to spit on his hand and then reached for it again. He stoked me in time
with his thrusts as I struggled back against him, countering and facili-
tating his hard pistoning.

Tillett nuzzled his face against my neck, I reached behind and
grasped at the back of his head. He moaned softly, then rationed his
breaths. Too soon, I felt him push deeper and strain. His hand quickened on my dick. Giving up to his unfamiliar rhythm, I clenched myself against his dick and found my own orgasm as he pulled me harder
into him, his free hand grasping me by the inside of my thigh.

It was as hard as I ever remembered coming. I grabbed Tillett's
hand from my chest and put his fingers in my mouth, sucking hard on
them as if I wanted even more of him in me than I had at that moment.
Shuddering, he pushed deeper inside me and held us motionless,
except for the disturbed rocking of the deck beneath us.

I felt Tillet collapse away behind me. The sensation of his exit
damning me for being so easy to have, occupy, and let go. I stretched
upward from my kneeling position and looked down on him, panting
and spent. I wanted throw myself on him and devour his mouth. I
wanted to suck the air out of his lungs. He looked away from me,
shaking his head.

"You got any cigarettes?" I asked him. He motioned toward a pat-
terned place in the dark that was his shirt.

I picked it up and found the pack in the pocket. I lit one and looked
out over the water, my anger growing with the weak soreness I felt in
every part of my body. The cool air from the water chilled my sweat-

ing back. I felt his hot cum clotting inside of me; It made me feel victorious, yet nauseous.

"Give me one, will ya?" Tillett said thickly from behind me. I turned and tossed him the pack of cigarettes and then the lighter.

I watched him light one and look up at me. He shook his head and let go a chuckle. "What's so funny?" I asked him coldly.

Tillett sank back from his crouch, stretched his legs forward and relaxed back on his elbows. He looked at me again and I was surprised to find admiration on his face. "Boy, I don't know who fucked who." He grinned and then arched his head back to exhale a long stream of smoke.

He looked back at me and said, "What're you doing way over there?" I just stood looking down at him. "C'mere," he said, the sudden gentleness in his voice surprising me. I hesitated and he reached out his hand toward me. I didn't take it, but I did sit down across from him on the quilt.

"Hey, don't be like that." Tillett said. He flicked his cigarette over the side of the boat and reached for my hand. I let him take it. He pulled me gently on top of him. With one hand he firmly cupped the space where my buttocks joined and rubbed my back with the other.

I laid my head uncertainly in the space between his neck and shoulder. My anger was running away as hastily as it had gathered. I loved the way the roughness of his hands held everything inside of me, mending the hole he'd torn in my soul.

Tillett was like a dog suddenly turned vicious. Not knowing if he would turn on me added to the excitement I was starting to feel growing like a bruise under his rough hands. I really didn't trust this sudden intimacy, but I wanted to. I wanted to real bad. I nuzzled into his neck and licked the saltiness I found there.

Tillett's body shivered under me. He sighed and wrapped his arms around me. "It ain't supposed to be like this," he said again softly.

Shane pitched off his board to avoid a collision with

another kid who dropped in on him. Anybody else, and a fight would have started, but Shane was too focused. I saw him pump his fists in the air to congratulate the kid who dropped in on him when he got back in the lineup. The kid had gotten a pretty good wave off him, but Shane wasn't just easygoing, he was too secure in his own world to let the little stuff bother him.

The wind blew the ashes off my cigarette before I had time to thump them. The sun, which had blazed out so fiercely, dimmed under a run of clouds. It was as if the temperature dropped fifteen degrees. Shane did a cut back and then milked the wave by pumping the last little bit of energy out of it with a pistoning of his legs.

I leaned back against the hard bench and closed my eyes. I wished I was Shane's age when I started surfing. It would have been so much easier to begin at twelve instead of eighteen. At eighteen, you had too much other bullshit around to take away your focus.

There was all the social bullshit, that and trying to get laid. I thought about this same time last year, back home. DeeAnn had given me the invitation to her party and I'd decided to go. I wanted to be going with somebody so bad before I met Chris. My focus was all messed up. I guess that's what made me find my way to DeeAnn's party.

DeeAnn lived in an old bungalow house on the way to downtown. I'd passed by it a zillion times without knowing it was hers. That night, though, there was no mistaking it. I drove down her street past houses with yard displays of cornstalks and pumpkins, even sheet ghosts hanging from trees. DeeAnn's house was the most tricked out house for blocks around.

There was a black cauldron spewing smoke. There were parts of old mannequins with red paint on them to look like blood hanging from the trees and scattered all over the lawn. Everything was washed with light from one of those revolving Christmas tree lamps. She had taken the cover off and covered it with tinfoil that had cutouts of cats and jack-o'-lanterns. It turned around and around, strewing cats and jack-o'-lanterns over the trees and the sides of the house. It was unbelievable.

I walked up to the front porch through the sounds of music thumping from the living room. There were people standing on the porch, but I didn't recognize any of them. I just nodded and went inside. DeeAnn was dancing in a real dramatic way with some other people in the middle of the living room floor. Other people were just sitting around talking, ignoring the dancers and the loud music.

When DeeAnn saw me, she rushed over and pulled me onto the dance floor. She didn't say anything, but she looked at me in this real dramatic sexual way, but old timey, like Theda Bara or something. She was dressed in some psycho slut outfit with her breasts practically hanging out. DeeAnn grabbed me by the hips and started shimmying down toward the floor, and she stayed there like she was giving me head or something.

I kind of moved my hips, but you couldn't really call it dancing. DeeAnn shimmied back up to face me, then pushed away and struck this pose like Ginger Rogers. She twirled, holding my hand over her head and then rushed back up to me. "Dip me, darling," she screamed. I tried to dip her, but she kept wiggling. She started fumbling with my pants.

"Will somebody throw some water on that crazy bitch?" I heard some guy shout.

DeeAnn let go of my fly and spun around screaming, "Fuck you, Danny."

"You wish," came the reply.

DeeAnn turned back to me and put her hands behind my neck. She started a slow box step, almost kneeing me in the groin in the process. "I'm glad you came, sugar lump. There's beer in the kitchen and I think there's coke in the bathroom. *If Danny hasn't hoovered it all up!*" she screamed.

I was starting to get a headache. "I think I'm gonna go get a beer," I said.

DeeAnn looked me in the eyes and smiled. "Happy hunting," she said, then pulled my head down to her lips and whispered in my ear, "Just don't leave with anybody until you come ask me about him first. There's bad shit out there you don't know anything about."

She drew back and looked at me sadly. I managed to give her a nod and a smile before I pulled away to get away from her.

The kitchen was at the end of the house down a hall. People were leaning on the walls of the hall waiting to get into the bathroom. As I passed, this guy started to bang on the bathroom door and yell, "Come on, faggot, snort it up. Melissa's about to piss in her pants."

A sharp sissy voice came back through the door: "That's the *only* way you could get her wet, asshole."

All I wanted to do was get the hell out of that hallway. It seemed to go on forever, taller than it was wide and dark. Mean-looking people's faces zoomed in looking at me, then laughing hatefully. It was like something out of *The Twilight Zone*. I saw Timmy in the kitchen and tried not to run toward him. He was the only person I'd seen that I recognized or that seemed halfway sane. He was talking to two guys with their backs to me.

I got a Budweiser from a cooler that looked like it was leaking all over the floor. Everything and everybody in the house seemed like they were melting or oozing, it was that trippy. Timmy looked around and recognized me. By the way he was grinning, I couldn't tell if he was glad I came or if he'd won a bet or something. It didn't look like the grin was for me. He lifted his chin and motioned me over. The two guys he was talking to turned their heads to see who he was looking at. One of them I didn't recognize, but the other one was Brent Cox, a guy I knew from high school.

I was really surprised to see him. Like most people who graduated ahead of me in high school, it was like he dropped off the face of the earth instead of only going off to college. I hadn't seen him for two years. He had a mature look to him now, more like a man and less like a boy. He'd been working out. His chest and arms stretched the T-shirt he had on. Brent looked good.

As good as Brent looked, the guy he was with looked even better. He wasn't cute like Brent, all clean and preppy; he was almost mean looking. While Brent looked like he could go to the country club, this guy looked like he couldn't get past the pool hall. Brent looked buffed; his friend looked like he did real work. I heard the rumors about Brent and this jock thug, George Hornby. This guy had the same kind of look to him. I guessed Brent hadn't changed that much.

"Hey, Timmy. Hey, Brent. Long time no see," I said, and nodded at Brent's friend.

Timmy laughed and said, "Brent, don't tell me you've done this one first. I was thinking I was going to get to pop his hot little cherry."

Brent snorted, "Shut up, Timmy. I didn't fuck every guy in high school, especially this one." Brent glanced at his friend, then sized me up mechanically. He gave me a cold smile. "I was wondering how you were coming along. I thought I'd have run into you long before now."

Brent turned to his friend and reached up to squeeze the back of his neck. "Matt used to follow me around with those puppy-dog eyes. Every time I turned around, there was this cute little sophomore *just hoping* I'd notice him."

The guy looked at me and smiled like I was pitiful.

"You were so adorable, Matt. It just *broke my heart.*" Brent said it sweetly, but his eyes were mean as snakes. "I would have done you back then, but I wanted to wait until you had pubic hair."

Timmy snickered. Brent's friend rolled his head back to dislodge Brent's hand that had left his neck and was tracing the lowest line of his cropped hair. I hated Brent Cox more right then than anybody I'd ever known in my life. As bad as Trevor had made me feel a week before, Brent was trying to make me feel worse in a different way. He was such a fucking jerk.

"You thought I was looking at you because I had a crush on you?" I said easily.

Brent eased into his friend's side slightly and smiled sweetly. "Puppy love, Matt. You were just so innocent."

I was so mad, my knees were shaking. I said, "Really? I just felt sorry for you. I wondered how desperate you had to be to suck off George Hornby in front of the whole football team. I was trying to think how hard it had to be living without no self-respect."

For a moment nobody said anything. I watched Brent's self-satisfied face melt and replace itself with embarrassment, then anger. Timmy murmured "Cold," then started laughing.

Brent's friend tried not to smile as he said, "Looks like your puppy grew some fangs, girlfriend." Brent started to say something, but I headed him off at the pass.

"Nice seeing you, Brent. Timmy. Take it easy, what's your name."

As I moved back into the crowd I heard Brent hiss, "Bitch." It made me smile. I wandered back through the press in the hall. It was so fucking hot in the house all of a sudden. I felt my knees shaking and my heart was pumping like I was about to fight. I decided to go out on the porch and get casual again. I didn't know anybody out there, but they couldn't be any worse than the people I knew inside.

Outside, I was surprised to find I still had my bottle of Bud. It felt nice and cold in my hand. I was alone on the porch except for this one guy I couldn't see too good. I ignored him and took a long hit off my beer as a police car passed slowly by the house. DeeAnn's revolving lamp threw cats across it as it sped up and drove away. DeeAnn's party was really turning out to be for shit. I was ready to go home, but I couldn't. I hadn't been gone long enough.

I was trying to think of a good lie to tell Mama and Daddy when the guy at the end of the porch lit a cigarette. In the glow from his hand cupped around the lighter, I could see him looking at me. He wasn't too bad-looking, but he looked pretty old, like maybe he was twenty-six or twenty-seven. "If you want to bum one, I got plenty," he said.

I walked over to him and he shook the pack at me, making a cigarette pop up. I took it and let him light it for me. "Thanks," I said, exhaling a long stream of smoke. I felt kind of cool, like I knew what was going on.

The guy put his cigarettes and lighter back in the pocket of his jacket, then stuck out his hand. "My name's Nash."

I took his hand and shook it. "Matt," I said, feeling his hand against mine. It was cool and smooth.

"You down here from Raleigh too?" Nash asked. I shook my head and told him I was from here. "Bummer," Nash said.

I couldn't think of anything to say. Closer up, Nash was pretty good-looking. He seemed like a regular guy. He slid over on the porch rail to make room like he wanted me to sit down. He smiled at me. I moved over next to him and leaned against the porch rail.

"So, do you, like, work here?" Nash asked. He put one arm behind me to brace himself and rested his weight on it. I could feel it, strong and hard against my back. It felt good.

"Naw, unh-uh. I go to school." I said. Nash nodded. The revolving light threw a jack o'lantern over his face, lighting it up enough for me to see he was probably as old as I thought. He was still kind of good looking though. "What do you do?" I asked him.

"I work for Channel 5. You ever watch *PM Magazine*? I run one of the cameras," he said proudly. I was impressed. He started going off in this low voice about TV stuff. He was kind of leaning in on me. He must have taken a bath in Polo, but it was nice.

I wondered if maybe he liked me. People who didn't really like you didn't sit so close and touch part of you. When you sat next to somebody who was just regular talking, they moved away quickly when they touched you. Nash wasn't going anywhere.

"Getting kinda chilly out here," Nash said. I didn't want him to move. I wanted him to just stay where he was and let me be close to him. I almost put my arm around his waist to keep him still. Nash looked at me with the nicest look on his face. I got the feeling he was enjoying himself too.

"I got half a gram. You want to find some place we can do a line?" Nash said quietly.

I had never snorted coke before, but it was only because I didn't know where to get it and couldn't afford it. My heart started pounding in anticipation of all the things I'd heard about coke. I was scared my heart would explode or something if I snorted.

"C'mon. I know a room where nobody goes in," Nash whispered urgently.

I looked at him, trying not to think about how good-looking he was getting to be or how good he smelled. He could be crazy for all I knew. He could get all coked up and strangle me or something.

"C'mon, you know you want it," he said and stood up.

Nash looked at me and smiled. He seemed like a nice guy. I stood up and followed him into the house. There were a couple of people passed out on the sofa, but nobody was dancing. I saw two guys making out by the fireplace and that weirded me out, kind of. Nash ducked around a corner I hadn't seen by the fireplace. I tried not to look at the guys making out as I followed him.

Around the corner, I could see Nash making his way up a narrow flight of stairs. I followed him up. Outside a closed door in the tiny hall, he held his finger up to his lips to shush me and opened the door slowly. Inside was a nursery. From the light from a Mickey Mouse lamp, I saw stuffed animals and toys strewn all over a room that contained a single bed and a crib. DeeAnn's little half Puerto Rican baby was sleeping in the crib. Nash gave me a smile and sat down on the single bed.

I looked from Nash to the baby laying there as innocent as could be, despite the house party going on downstairs. Nash patted a place on the bed beside him. I sat down. Nash leaned into me so close his lips moved against my ear. "Cool place for a private party, huh? Just me, you, Raphael, and Mickey Mouse."

I could feel his breath against the side of my face. "Raphael has crashed and Mickey Mouse ain't talking. Looks like its just me and you." Nash whispered.

I turned my head to look at him. My heart was beating so hard, it was like I had already snorted the coke. Nash put one hand on my thigh and the other on the back of my head to push my face toward him. He turned his head slightly and kissed me.

His lips were hard against mine, but they moved softly. His mouth tasted like beer and cigarettes, but it was okay. I felt the scratchiness of his beard against my upper lip and chin. His hand rubbed the back of my neck gently and I started to give into it. It was wonderful. I reached over and ran my hand up his back, underneath his jacket. It was tight as a drum. His mouth moved against mine. I wanted more of it. I pulled him closer with my hand against his hard back.

Then, Nash stuck his tongue in my mouth. It was just there so suddenly and there was so much of it. It was gross; it was too much, too soon. I pulled away.

Nash squeezed the inside of my thigh with one hand, and reached in his jacket pocket with the other. He pulled out a lady's compact and set it on the table after he carefully slid over a stack of Doctor Seuss books. He took his hand off my leg and snapped the compact open quietly. Inside, I could see a razor blade, a cut-down piece of soda straw, and a little teeny piece of baggie in the part where face powder used to be. Nash undid the baggie and spilled out the powder on the mirror part. He picked up the razor and went at the coke with furious little chopping motions.

Raphael stirred in his crib, and then sat up to see what was going on. Nash was so busy chopping the coke, he didn't pay any attention. All I could think of was what might happen if the baby started crying. Raphael looked around for something. I watched him as he picked up his pacifier and stuck it in his little mouth. He watched Nash for a second, then he turned to stare at me.

The little fellow had the biggest, prettiest eyes you ever saw. A perfect light blue that didn't go with his dark skin or kinky hair, calm and steady; those eyes looked too old and wise to be in his little head.

Nash stood up and leaned over the compact. He put the straw up his nose and snorted up one line, then another. The quick, sharp sounds of his snorts were loud in the tiny room. Nash straightened up and pinched his nostrils together, then sniffed in deeply again. He looked over at me and grinned, reaching for my hand. I looked at Raphael; his wise baby eyes stared at me just watching to see what I was going to do.

"I don't want to do it in front of the baby," I whispered.

Nash looked over at Raphael surprised, like he just figured out there was a baby in the room. He looked back at me and whispered fiercely, "Damn, man, with a coke slut like DeeAnn for a mama you think he ain't never seen this shit before?"

I didn't say anything. Nash looked at me with a smile. "C'mon, Matt. I already got it cut up. It'll make it better when we get off." He looked back at the compact on the dresser and then back at me hungrily. "Goddamn, you've got me so hot."

Nash grinned at me and stroked at his hard on through his pants. The proof was there right under his thumb, filling up the palm of his hand. He wanted to fuck, not just get high and neck like some dumb teenager.

It was really happening. Right now. I looked back over at the baby. He was still staring at me, wide-eyed and waiting. What did the name Raphael mean? Wasn't that an archangel or something?

Nash started unbuttoning his pants with one hand and pulling down his zipper with the other. Getting them loose, he sighed and eased his hand down between the white line of his shorts and his belly. The head of his dick popped out, covered with foreskin; I could make out the deep purple of the head swelling out of the tight hood it had over it. I could see the outline of the rest of his dick straining against the white fabric. I looked back at the baby, who was ignoring Nash. He was just watching me, waiting.

I looked at Nash. I had a really great-looking guy touching his dick right in front of me. How often could that happen? Nash smiled and slipped his balls out over top of the elastic of his white jockey shorts. It was all inches from my face. I really wanted to touch his dick, play with it. I had never seen an uncut one hard before. I stated panicking. I wanted to do it with Nash real bad, but it was too weird. I couldn't just do up some coke and start fucking in front of this little kid named after an angel.

I looked over at Raphael. He stood up slowly and held onto the sides of the crib. His plump little lips worked around his pacifier for a moment. It was obscene. His blue eyes kept on staring, steady and deep. I imagined my mouth working around Nash's dick the same way. It was all just so wrong.

"I can't, man. I just can't," I said. "I'm sorry."

I stood up and left the room. I left Nash standing there with his dick in his hand, two lines of coke on the dresser, and Raphael in his crib. On my way downstairs, I heard Nash say "Shit." I felt like running. I left the house without saying anything to anybody.

I got in Daddy's truck and drove all the way to Kinston and back on Highway 70. I was real careful to drive the speed limit. I concentrated on the driving so hard, it was like I was taking a driver's test. My mind was going ninety miles an hour, though. It was all just so damn fucked up.

Almost back into town I couldn't take it anymore. I pulled in behind a dark gas station and beat off thinking about Nash's dick and his loose balls filling up his cupped hand. I saw his face as he offered his dick to me. I concentrated on the way his mouth moved against mine and the feel of his tongue slipping into my mouth. I shot off into a Hardee's napkin and threw it out the window into the empty parking lot. I just sat in the truck staring at it. It laid white and crumpled on the dirty asphalt until the wind blew it away. It looked like one of the images from DeeAnn's sad and stupid revolving lamp, rolling off into the dark.

I wanted to cry. The gay part of me wanted it all so bad. The Sunday school part of me kept telling me that it was all wrong. The regular part of me was trying to say it's all okay. I had spent so much time trying to be some of this or some of that, that all I managed to be was a big nothing. I was just coward and a fool, jerking off by myself in the middle of nowhere.

Sitting out on the pier, I almost made myself laugh remembering all that. I couldn't believe I'd ever been that dumb and inexperienced. I'd come a long way since that with Tillett. Sexually, he was like a drug or something. I couldn't get enough of him.

I'd been sneaking around fucking with Tillett again a few more times before Tiger got wind of what was going on. He told me that Tillett was married and had three little kids. His wife was some kind of Holy Roller fundamentalist. "You're playing with fire, hot shot," Tiger said.

"I reckon you ought to know considering some of the stunts you and Mark had pulled when you were my age."

Tiger's eyes blazed at me. My mouth got ahead of my mind sometimes. Although he didn't have to, Tiger coldly reminded me of the facts. The tolerance he and Mark enjoyed on the island was thin-skinned and provisional. We lived in what was essentially a small town. People didn't have much to do but get in one another's business. Tiger could lose work. Billy's mama could forbid him to come to our house, or accuse one of us of molesting him. Shane could be put through constant hell at school, or anywhere he went. Besides that, Mark's custody of Shane could get blown away by me creating a big scandal.

I apologized to Tiger sincerely. He nodded and looked away. I knew he was right, but I still met Tillett down at the boat a few more times. The sex was consistently as hot as the first time. I wanted to tell myself that it wasn't anybody's business what Tillett and I did. I also knew Tillet had a huge reputation as a bad ass and that would protect me.

The problem was I thought I was starting to feel something for him deeper than horniness. I kind of felt like I understood Tillett. He managed to mix tenderness and a rapist's concentrated anger in a way that made me slither. On the one hand, I had this great feeling of power to be able to match his appetite for me. On the other, it was a sweet kind of revenge to have this breeder stud fuck my brains out. It was like fucking every guy who ever called me a faggot.

I knew what the problems were and what my larger responsibilities were to Tiger and Mark, but that was all only in the back of my mind.

Tillett was a coil of anger and had a strong sense of menace that got him his way. He liked sex with me as much I did with him and he wasn't past pressing the point. He got increasingly insistent on us getting together.

It got harder and harder for me to balance the warped sense of power I got from having Tillett want me with the reality that Tillett was bad news. Even though I downright would almost crawl to get the rough fucks he gave out, I was getting over it. Something inside of me that was newer and harder was rebelling at being Tillett's fuck boy. I was also starting to resent the level of humiliation I was letting myself become accustomed to. I was, anyway, until.Tillett beat me up.

The last time Tillett and I were together was just an accident. Tiger and I were working out on Highway 70, near Newport. Coming home, Tiger had asked me to drop him off at a realtor's office and then sent me to get gas while he was waiting. When I pulled up at the pump, Tillett was filling up his truck.

We nodded at each other, and went on doing what we were doing. Tillett wasn't big on "hey, how the hell are ya's," with anybody. He finished pumping his gas and went inside. In a minute he passed by me and told me quietly to meet him in the john. I watched him pull the truck over to the side of the gas station and let himself in. I finished up and followed him.

When I let myself in the door, he had his dick out already. I was kind of annoyed. I knew Tiger would be waiting for me pretty soon. I told him I didn't have time and started back out the door. Tillett slammed it shut with one hand and pulled me back with the other. He locked the door behind me and backhanded me so hard I stumbled. He took the opportunity to grab me by the neck and pull me up next to his face.

"Don't tell me you don't want my dick, pretty boy." I was used to this prison-porno bullshit, but it was wearing thin.

"Go to hell," I said, shaking him off. When I turned for the door, Tillett caught me and swung me around to meet his fist to my gut. I sank to the floor. Expertly, he was in front of me. He grasped my chin hard in his hand and forced me to look up at him.

I focused all my hurt and bewilderment up through my eyes, searching for some of the stingy tenderness that crept into his after he hurt me like this. I saw him fighting it inwardly. His thumb strayed from the clench of his other fingers to trace the curve of my jaw before he twisted it cruelly and leaned down to growl in my ear.

"You don't get it, do you? This is how it's supposed to be. I got a woman to love. I got you to fuck."

I lowered my eyes and felt his hot pant next to my ear. "You like it like this; you come in here for it."

He said it so gently, only the fierce grip he held on my chin and my aching stomach reminded me that I did want it like this, and he would make me whether I did or not.

He stood up, loosening his grip on my jaw only enough to allow access of his dick. Its thick ramming forced reality into a blind emptiness in my head.

"Oh yeah, suck me," Tillett growled and slowed his battering, to encourage me. "Suck me sweet like a pretty boy," he whispered and let go of my jaw to hold the back of my head.

I reached up and grabbed his ass with both hands. I looked up into his eyes to find him looking at me with tenderness. As swiftly as I caught sight of that, his eyes turned ugly and mean. He dug his fingers into my hair and started humping my face for all he was worth.

I dug my fingernails into his butt cheeks and felt them harden against my alarm. He shot off in my mouth with the force of his fist against the back of my throat. Shuddering, he held my face pinned against his groin until I thought I was going to choke and retch on his softening dick and thick, bitter cum.

He chuckled as he finally let me go and moved away to tuck his dick back into his jeans. I knelt still on the filthy floor and looked up at him as I spit what was left of his load on the floor.

He stood for a moment looking down at me. "Don't look at me like that. If you want romance you come to the wrong place." With that, he strode to the door and listened briefly before opening it and striding out.

I stood up slowly and made my way to the basin. I couldn't spit away the truth. Looking in the mirror, I found the reddened imprints of his fingers blending into the deeper red along my jaw where he'd slapped me. I found the swelling of hurt in my eyes. I replaced it with a harder sense of urgency. I had no time to cry.

Tiger started to bitch at me when he got in the truck, but stopped when he saw my face.

"Tillett," he said. I nodded. Tiger sighed and lit himself a cigarette. "For a beginner, you play some rough games."

There wasn't anything I could say behind that. I just drove.

Tiger looked levelly ahead. "You got two choices, Matt. You quit that psycho or I send you home to your mama and daddy." I nodded. Tiger looked at me and said calmly, "This shit stops now." The lines at the corners of his eyes were clenched. "I admit I was listening to Teddy Pendergrass and waiting on Mark while every other faggot in the world was getting peed on or had a fist up their ass and doing poppers, but I know a thing or two about the road you're on." Tiger drew a deep breath and shook his head. "If getting beat up is what you're into, you need to do it away from me."

We rode the rest of the way home in silence while I thought it all out.

Life got back to normal, but I didn't. I felt like I was just me watching me on television. I went back to work. I walked the dogs on the beach. I played cards with Shane and Billy. I didn't mention what was really bothering me. Mark took me down to the little greenroom with his bonsai, now scraggly and wild-looking from neglect. He pinched, watered and trimmed, trying to give me an opportunity to talk. I didn't. Tiger kept me hustling on the job, but he didn't press me to talk. He only watched and saw.

A whore's a whore, and I felt like one now. I hated what I had let Tillett turn me into. Worse, I hated to take responsibility for turning myself into a masochistic little cunt.

It seemed like forever since I was just a dumb happy kid beating off to space aliens with Calvin Klein underwear physiques. I missed that. I missed Chris and the old days from just last spring. It was all gone so quick and completely that the emptiness rattled around inside of me, hard and real as chains. Tillett fucked my head up bad.

It really came down to the fact that fucking Tillett wasn't making me who I wanted to be. Tillett showed me a dirty part of myself that I had to admit to, but I hated. I really didn't need that in the world I was trying to make for myself on the beach.

I didn't see Tillett again until today out in the parking lot.

"What's up, rod dog?" I heard his voice behind me say.

Involuntarily, I jumped. Tillett laughed as he sat down beside me. I flicked my cigarette away. "What's up?"

Tillett looked around at the deserted pier and leaned back next to me. He spread his legs in relaxation and didn't move when his knee connected with mine.

"You and me ain't partied much lately," he said without looking at me.

The same fight-or-flight instinct arose that I felt back in the parking lot. I wasn't sure how I was going to handle it, but I was sure I wasn't going with him down to the boat. A hot, slithering part of me still wanted to. Goddamn, I wanted to. "Naw, man. We haven't," I said warily.

Tillett allowed himself to look at me for a moment before he turned away saying, "I've missed you."

I nodded and he acknowledged it with a slow sideways glance. "Me too," I admitted before I could catch myself. Tillett steadily watched the lineup in the break below.

"How come we haven't gotten together then?" he asked. In his voice I heard a familiar hurt and a familiar hunger.

I thought about Jeep. "I've been seeing somebody." I answered. It was the truth. Tillett raised his eyebrows and glanced over at me.

"Girl or guy," he asked gently.

I hesitated before I said, "Guess."

Tillett snickered. "You been getting properly pounded, huh?"

Pretending to look at the lineup wasn't getting this where I wanted it to go. I quit pretending and looked directly at Tillett. He returned my gaze and what I saw there made me feel sorry for him. Just like any other bully, his ego was easily threatened. I knew my way around bullies. I was a pretty boy. I looked around at the empty pier, just like Tillett had done before I said huskily, "Not as good as you, Tillett."

Tillett laughed and let his hand drop to his lap. "Probably not as big, neither," he said as he traced the outline of his dick through his shorts with the back of his thumb. "So what are you doing with him?" he asked as he gave me a searching look.

I looked back out over the water. I didn't say what I wanted to, I just said, "He's queer, like me. He ain't married and got kids."

Tillett nodded slowly. "I figured it'd come down to that. Sooner or later, all you pretty boys turn into your mama. You want to fucking get married."

I reached into my pocket for my cigarettes and lit one expertly against the wind. I settled back against the bench again, acting all cool and calm behind that little remark. If I let him make me mad, he'd just encourage me to the point where he got hard, and I got fucked harder. With us, fighting had become foreplay.

There was the fact too that Tillett had landed a fair one. I damn sure didn't want to turn into my mama, but I didn't want to be Tillett's jailhouse bitch either. I wanted to be something else, but what I wanted to be Tillett couldn't handle. I looked over at him. He looked a little hurt. That was a last-ditch ploy on his part. It had always worked before.

"Tillett, I'll make you a promise," I said.

"What's that?" he grunted as he looked around once more.

"When I need a real man, I'll find you," I said earnestly.

Tillett gave me a crooked genuine grin and looked around. "Oh yeah?"

I owed him something for the happy grin, as easy as it was bought. "Count on it," I said and leaned in close enough to him to make him uncomfortable. "You are the hottest fuck I ever had in my life," I said with all honesty. I stood up.

I looked down into Tillett's Siberian husky eyes. The hard glacier cruelty melted a little and he nodded. "See you around, Tillett."

Tillett looked back out over the surfers. "See you around, rod dog."

I walked off, glad I'd made it away without any new contusions and glad I'd escaped being in some queer country and western song.

It was funny. I walked out of the pier house wishing I could tell Jeep. He'd think it was funny too, or he would have a long time ago. Things were different now.

As I was walking to my truck, I felt suddenly lighter and taller. The sun was struggling from behind the clouds again. The waves at the pier were big, but they didn't look like more than I could handle. I decided to run back to the house and get my big board. I still had a little time before the tide shifted.

I jumped in the truck and swung it out onto the beach road. I caught a glimpse of myself in the rearview mirror. Maybe haircuts could change your life. The English Beat came on the radio singing "Save It for Later." I loved that song. I rolled down the window and blasted it.

Back at the house, I parked my truck and left the engine

running while I pounded upstairs to get my board off the porch. It was like I could hear it calling to me, reminding me that we hadn't been out in a long time. I picked it up and a sudden gust of wind swung us around. I began to get really excited. It was me and my board. I was just gladder than shit for that. It would have been hell if I had to drive up and down the beach looking at breaks with Tillett and his crew.

It's a feeling that's hard to explain. I don't know if other people who surf have such a strong affinity with their boards. From hearing them recount surfing stories, it seemed like a lot of them do. I mean, I really never heard anybody giving their board a name or anything. It would be like giving your dick a name; you don't go around telling people. But there was an emotional attachment to every board. It was like a best friend; you can remember every detail of how you met.

Saturday morning of the weekend I came down to see if I'd like living at the beach and working for Tiger, Mark and Tiger had a surprise for me. I heard them go out with the dogs and fell asleep again until I heard them come back. I got up when I smelled coffee. They were sitting at the table in their bathing suits.

Mark got up and offered to get me some coffee. I accepted and sat down at the table, watching him pour it.

"There's a little swell coming up this morning," Mark said as he looked at the big diver's watch on his wrist.

Tiger nodded. "It ought to get even better; the wind's shifting."

Mark looked at me. "You still want to be a surfer?"

"I'd like to give it a shot, for sure," I said.

"Can you swim?" he asked, and took a sip of his coffee.

"I imagine I could keep from drowning," I offered back confidently.

Tiger stood up and said we had better get a move on if we were going to get some breakfast and some errands run. Mark swallowed the rest of his coffee and stood. "We thought we'd take you out for breakfast. We need to run down the beach for some stuff. Is that all right with you?"

I said sure. Tiger drove us all the way into Atlantic Beach. Just past the light, he pulled into the parking lot of a surf shop. The surf shop didn't even look like it was open. Tiger and Mark piled out of the car and I followed along with them. Mark rapped on the door. In a moment, a young guy came to turn the key and let us in. Mark and Tiger shook hands with the good-looking guy and introduced me to him. His name was Eric. It turned out Mark was giving him flying lessons at his place over at the airport in Jacksonville. They talked while Tiger wandered over to the surfboards, stacked in a rack on the back wall. I looked at the swim trunks.

"How tall are you, Matt?" Tiger asked. I pulled a light blue bathing suit by Gotcha off the rack and told him I was six-one or six-two. "C'mere a minute," he said. The damn bathing suit was thirty-two dollars. I didn't have much more than that, but I wanted it. Mark and the Eric guy wandered back toward Tiger, who was pulling out an orange and yellow board from the rack. Bathing suit in hand, I went to see what he was looking at.

"Good board. One of the best used ones I got," Eric said.

"How long is it?" Mark asked.

"Six-ten; that's why I've had it so long. Everybody wants something shorter and faster," Eric said as he took the trunks from my hand. Tiger told me to hold the board up straight in front of me. "It cleaned up real well," Eric said.

Tiger grunted. "I just hate giving Wave Riding Vehicles any of my money."

Mark laughed; Eric looked puzzled. "The guy who used to run WRV in Kitty Hawk pissed him off years ago and he still carries a grudge," Mark explained.

"Well, this is a custom board. You don't find many guns like this anymore, especially a single fin," Eric said.

Tiger told me to hold the nose and he picked up the board from the bottom. He examined the fin box, and ran his hands over the rails before turning it over. "There's some pressure dings on the tail."

Eric nodded. "A board that big is going to skimp some on the glassing to cut down on the weight."

Tiger nodded and eased the tail back down to the floor. "What do you think of it, Matt?" It looked beautiful to me. I wished I could afford it. I nodded and didn't say anything.

"It's a good first board," Mark said.

"My first one wasn't as good as that," Eric said.

"Well, you want it?" Tiger asked me. My mouth must have dropped open.

"Happy graduation," Mark said. I started grinning. I couldn't think of anything to say.

"Eric, you got any Balin leashes?" Tiger asked.

Eric nodded, carrying my trunks to the counter. Tiger took off with him. Mark looked at me, smiling. "You need to pick out a nose guard too." I gripped the surfboard in my hands lightly. It felt good.

By the time me and Tiger left Mark with Eric to settle up, I had the board, a leash, a nose guard, the Gotcha bathing suit, and two bars of Doctor Zogg's Sex Wax. Me and Tiger fitted the board to the rack on top of the Bronco. Tiger explained that they wanted me to have it. If I was going to be living at the beach, and wanted to learn to surf, I might as well start with something nice.

I told him it was an awful lot of money, and that I really appreciated it.

Tiger winked. "It ain't as much money as you might think. Mark's trading half of it for flying lessons. Around here, locals look after each other. If you'd just walked in off the street, you'd have paid through the nose." I couldn't stop grinning. "Welcome to the beach, hoss," Tiger said, grinning back.

After Mark had finished squaring up with Eric in the surf shop, Tiger drove us out of Atlantic Beach and back to Salter Path. The beach was coming back to life. Houses were open and flew jaunty new windsocks shaped like fish and God's eyes swung merrily from live oaks and porch rafters. People crossed the road warily, laden with lounge chairs and beach stuff.

We stopped for breakfast at a small restaurant and got a table up front so we could watch the Bronco and keep an eye on my new board. I was so excited, I hardly tasted my food. Mark and Tiger started telling me surf stories mingled with beginner tips. Finally, breakfast finished, Mark said we'd better get a move on, if we were ever going to do more than talk. Tiger suggested we drive around some and check out a few breaks while our food digested.

We drove around for an hour before heading back to the house. I changed quickly into my new trunks. Mark gave me one of his old wetsuits to wear. It was a little loose in the shoulders, but the water was still too cold to be out long without one. Finally, we started toward the beach. Mark carried out a long board; Tiger didn't carry one at all. I asked him why not, and he looked at me, grinning. "I hope you don't think you're going to take off and shred without no lessons."

My board fit under my arm like some newfound appendage. The waves were small, but were breaking maybe a hundred yards out. Mark left us on the beach and trotted out into the water. Tiger told me to lay my board down as he juggled a new bar of wax. We squatted by the board and he began rubbing the wax across its clean, shiny deck. After a moment, he handed me the wax and began earnestly explaining the fundamentals of surfing.

He sprinkled a little bit of sand on the board and I worked it in with more wax, listening intently to every word he said. Finally, we went into the water. Mark sat on his board beyond the break, looking over his shoulder at the incoming sets. I took a deep breath and strode in behind Tiger.

I fell. I fell a lot. I swallowed seawater. I inhaled seawater. I scraped my face on a shell on the bottom after a particularly clumsy fall.

Waiting between sets, I saw fins break the surface of the water not fifty feet from where I sat on my board. I guess I sort of yelped and pointed. Tiger looked over to where I had gestured and caught me by my ankle as I started to paddle off.

"Hold still, Matt," he said as he pulled me backward effortlessly. "Just be still and watch."

After a moment, first one then another and another porpoise curved out of the water cleanly. "Them's porpoises. You ain't got to worry about sharks as long as you see porpoises. They fight sharks," Tiger said.

He stood in chest-high water by my board, helping keep it steady as I tried to learn to time my kicks to be fast enough to actually catch the wave. I looked back at the porpoises gratefully. "Get ready," Tiger yelled. I started kicking, I felt Tiger give an added push to the board. I drew my feet up under me and began to balance and stand. I fell off the side.

Finally, I managed to stand up. I angled the board left, steering with my left foot and trying to ease up the weight on my right foot behind me. It seemed like I was going in slow motion. I could see behind the wave. I could see it rising from nothing ahead of me and hear it closing out behind me.

It seemed to go on forever, but if I was up ten seconds, it would have been a big deal. Finally, the rising ahead stopped. The wave gave out. I fell sideways behind what was left of the wave and felt the board tug at my ankle as it followed the wash in the opposite direction. I stood and pulled the board back to me. Tiger and Mark were both whooping and hollering. I laid lengthwise on the board and paddled back out. It was about the happiest I'd been in my whole life.

I left the dogs barking their resentment at being left behind and went downstairs to strap my board onto the racks on top of the cab. Now that I had faced up to so much bullshit with Chris and Tillett, I was just happy to be going surfing. I felt ready for this challenge. I pulled out under the threat of rain again, but it didn't dampen my enthusiasm. Right then, I would have felt like going surfing even if it started to snow.

Driving down the beach road, I started thinking. I was doing okay as long as I didn't get all fucked up about being queer. I had started surfing after I'd gotten bored with figuring out that angle. Surfing meant a lot more to me as a person. My victories and missteps were mine. My board didn't turn on me or leave me.

I'd never say it to anybody, but in my mind, surfing was just an extension of being queer. I laughed to myself, imagining the guys at the pier hearing that. In some ways, being a surfer and being gay were a lot alike. You're only queer when you're fucking another guy. The rest of the time, you're just wearing the clothes.

The same thing with surfing. If you had a tan, and walked around going "Dude" all the time, you were just another cartoon, like gay people on television. No, being a surfer meant you got out, faced your own fears and lack of expertise, and did it. It was like being queer. The rush came from getting better at it. Walking away from anything alive, from a Tillett or a chest-crushing wipeout, well, that was a victory. Hell, anything you loved could kill you. It didn't make any sense to just stay on the beach and watch.

I made it to the unpaved road where Tiger and I had been working earlier in the morning. I parked the truck and sat taking off my sneakers, listening to all the tones of the wind and the water. The wind was still up, but it was singing instead of screaming. The water sounded thick still, but the grinding had lessened.

I took my board off the racks and started up the dune. Cresting the top, the beach spread out in front of me in Vistavision. The tide had gone out throughout the day and it was just changing now. Because of the storm, it was still running higher up on the beach than it usually did. The ocean looked gray here and less friendly than it did up by the pier. There was no one out here. It was totally deserted.

I looked over to the break I'd spotted that morning. It was breaking overhead and cleaner than it did at the pier. The sun suddenly came out and the place turned the menace to magic. The rough water blued from gray and the shore break glistened like a load of tossed silver coins.

With the sky opening up over me, the break calling, and my board singing under my arm, I wished Tiger was here. It wasn't that I was scared. I was intimidated a little, but not scared. I just wished I had somebody around to share this perfect moment. Jeep crept into my mind but I pushed him back out. Jeep didn't surf.

I made my way down the dune and knelt in the sand to give my board a once over with some fresh wax. The waves were louder here, and looked bigger. As I strapped my leash around my ankle and looked out, I pushed back the fear. I tried to replace it with a calm, centered sense of confidence. I thought about the bubble in the circle when I held the prism pole for Tiger to get a bearing and distance.

Standing up, I faced the water and took a step forward. I could do this. This is who I was. I wasn't Chris's pretty boy or Tillett's bitch—not here. I started to run toward the water, the shock of it hard and real as I ran into a lull in the shore break and flung myself onto the deck of my board. I began to paddle out furiously, taking advantage of the back tow toward the sandbar.

Ahead of me a thick wave closed out suddenly and I timed it so that I could duck-dive through it. The white water sheeted over me heavily. I kept on paddling. More white water rushed toward me from a larger wave that had closed out just after the first. I took a deep breath and rolled over backward with my board over me. The water lifted the board and me with it. After it passed, I found the bottom and pushed myself back up on the deck.

Frustrated, I began paddling out again, alone and determined. I made it outside at last and sat on my board, watching and timing the sets. Instinct began to take over. Timing every second of the approach of the mountain with my skin and my eyes and ears, I turned my board back toward the shore and began to stroke and kick. I felt the familiar rise of the water under me, higher and faster than ever.

Calmly, I felt the internal signal to get my feet up, then angle the board with my right foot. I still crouched, feeling the board fall away under me as I shifted my weight to accelerate across the face of the wave, moving sideways as it gained its forward momentum. I trailed my fingers gently across the wave's face. It was beautiful and for a short while, it was forever.

The waves had very little pattern to them. Some came in heavy and thick, their lips closing out quickly with all the force of a load of concrete dumping on my head. Then, the trough would be confused before a smaller set came at me, noisy and fierce as a loose pack of bulldogs, more trouble to try to ride than they were worth. All they did was push me out of the zone. I turned my board around and paddled back out.

Ahead of me, the set started to build again. Fast. I managed to hit the first one just as it started to peak. The wave went under me, lifting my weight on the board as effortlessly as if I was nothing. I went down abruptly, the bottom of the board smacking in the back of the wave. The trough was short.

The wave ahead of me was bigger than its brother and threatened to pitch out quick. I kicked harder and gripped the rails of my board, forcing the nose down. Tucking down my head for a duck dive, I let the hard face of the wave pass over me. There was always a serene moment when my forward thrust through the wave was countered by its own thrust toward the shore. Then, it was stillness, encompassed by the wave itself, timeless and womb-like. Immediately, I pushed through, and the wave pushed away. I settled down its back to feel myself pulled forward into the next trough.

I didn't try anything complicated at first. To be honest, I was happy just to be competent in those confused and mean conditions. Even so, my confidence in the bigger waves grew. In the effort and timing of matching myself to each new convergence, I was surfing beyond myself. I synched up with some kind of eternal rhythm. The seawater composition of my blood remembered the language it spoke before there was a me. It wasn't about me. I was just a part of something much larger and more special than my own insignificance.

The waves demanded more of me than ever before. I quit fighting them and tried to just exist with them. They rewarded me with some of the best rides ever, then pounded me for any miscalculation or show of arrogance. When it was good, the exhilaration lifted me farther out of myself than even the best sex I ever had or dreamed of having. I never noticed when it began to get bad. Aching and tiring quickly in the rough water, I demanded more of the ocean.

I got cocky. I fucked up.

The mechanics of a bad wipeout are as varied as any combination of timing, tide, and experience. I didn't pay attention. The tide was coming in and piled the waves up on one another with the help of the wind, which had passed on, but had driven the water ahead of it for days and hundreds of miles. I did something stupid. I made some arrogant misstep and the ocean laughed. I learned what it meant to be insignificant.

All I had time to think was "Oh, shit," before the water came down over my head and my board flew out from under my feet. The power of the breaking wave forced me to the bottom and held me there. I felt my board tugging at the leash attached to my ankle hard enough to drag me around under the water. I tried to fight my way up just in time to feel another wave, piled against the one before, come down on me again before I even reached the surface.

It seemed like I was under water for a full minute. My lungs ached and I pushed at the sand below me, fighting against the weight of the water on my back. After what seemed like forever, the pressure lessened. Forgetting to go up arms first, I shot up, never thinking to check the direction of the leash's pull against my ankle. I surfaced briefly in time to have the next wave slam my board on my head. I felt something sharp glance my right eyebrow as I forced myself deeper under the water again instinctively, to get away from the board.

I felt the drag away from me as my board followed the white water. I managed to stand up. The waves had pushed me into shallower water. I gulped in air and coughed. The force of a new wave breaking behind me drove me to my knees and dragged me along with it as it pushed me toward the shore.

Looking for my board, I struggled up before the rush of water backward could beat me in the head with it again. The place over my right eye started to sting and my head began to throb with a dull insistence I could hear. The water pushed my board toward my left side. I grabbed it and got it under my arm as I staggered through the shore break and up onto the beach.

I made it up onto the dry sand before I stumbled to my knees. I crawled the last small distance to a patch of sea oats at the base of the dune. Sitting down heavily, I looked back out over the water. The sun was low in the sky. A shallow run of clouds threatened to dim it further. I felt something warmer than the saltwater running down the side of my face and clouding my right eye. I touched my eyebrow lightly and drew away my fingers from the sudden piercing sharpness it caused. I looked at my fingers; they were bloody. One of the fins must have sliced me.

All of a sudden, I felt like I was going to pass out. I lay back on the dry sand and looked toward the sun as the clouds ran across its face. The light surrounding it changed to a Technicolor dream of pinks and oranges and golds against the deeper bluish clouds.

The throb in my head worsened, making me nauseous. Letting my head pull me backward, I stretched out on my back in the cool sand. I felt much more comfortable. My aching body made its own claims against my head as I looked at the sky again. It was incredibly beautiful. God himself had thrown the colors against the sky with all the abandon of a happy little kid. Henry Junior used to throw paint around like that. I smiled. Then I passed out.

The morning light was gray, then pink, growing to a hot orange around the few clouds over the ocean, a block away. I was twisted in the sheet on the scratchy sofa in the living room of the trailer. Henry Junior was balled up all sweaty, sleeping next to me.

As usual, Tommy had the tiny bedroom next to Mama and Daddy all to himself. Even on vacation he couldn't quit being the oldest. I needed to pee awful bad, but the bathroom was next to Tommy's room and I sure as shit didn't want to wake Tommy up so he could boss me around. I stood a good chance of waking up Henry Junior and then I'd have to look after him. The morning was all mine as long as no one was up.

I managed to get up without disturbing Henry Junior. I slipped outside and walked under the shed attached to the side of the trailer.

My mama's brother kept his boat under there. Looking out for snakes, I slipped behind the boat and peed on the ground. The boat shed gave me the creeps. There were skins left behind by molting snakes in the rough pine rafters overhead. Rustling like parchment paper, they stirred in the morning breeze. I picked my way carefully back to the front of the trailer.

Henry Junior was waiting for me on the metal top step of the trailer rubbing his eyes. "I got to pee too," he said.

"Shhh, Henry Junior, you gon' wake everybody up," I whispered fiercely.

"Take me," Henry Junior had to do everything I did.

"Go pee in the house," I said.

Henry Junior shook his head no.

I was irritated. Now that Henry Junior was up, I wouldn't have a chance to do anything. "Go on and pee then," I said, gesturing back behind the boat.

Henry Junior looked fearfully down the side of the trailer and back at me. "Snakes," he said "Take me, Matt."

I felt mean. "Don't be no baby; go on and pee."

Henry Junior grabbed at his crotch and his little mouth twisted, "Scared, Matt." He raised his skinny little arms to be lifted. I sighed and picked him off the top step and carried him under the snake skins and past the boat.

I stood him on the ground and took his hand to lead him to the grass. Henry Junior pulled his little underwear down to his knees and arched his back. As he peed, he kept looking quickly left and right, fearful of the cottonmouth moccasins Daddy had convinced us lurked everywhere. Finishing, he pulled his underwear up quick and dashed past me through the boat shed back to the trailer steps. He spotted his treasures he had taken from the beach lying around on the ground where he left them the night before and bent to pick up a dried skate egg casing by the steps.

Trying to get away from the snakes, he had left his little underwear under the curve of his butt. I followed him and pulled up the waistband. "How come you so scared to pee back there? You got to be a big boy."

Henry Junior rubbed the egg casing on his leg and said, "Daddy said snakes could jump right out and bite me on my pecker and if they did they wouldn't let go until it thunders," he said, shivering.

I tried not to laugh. Henry Junior could get on my nerves, but he was right funny sometimes. "Henry Junior, Daddy's full of shit. It's turtles that bite you and don't let go until it thunders."

Henry Junior fingered the egg casing gently and studied me carefully. "Is there turtles behind the boat?"

I shook my head no.

"Where is them turtles?" Henry Junior asked.

I shrugged. "Turtles hate people and is right scared of them. You'd have to pee right on one to make it mad enough to bite you."

Henry Junior nodded like "now I know."

I felt something drag dully against the bottom of my foot. I drew up my legs to get away from it as I looked around for Henry Junior.

`"His back isn't broken," I heard Mark say. I wondered what he was doing at my uncle's trailer.

Somebody started tugging on my eyelids. It made a sharp pain over my right eye. I lifted my arm to push it off.

"Christ, he's bleeding again," I heard Tiger say.

"I have to check his eyes," Mark answered abruptly.

"Matt! Matt, wake up." Tiger commanded.

I gave in to the pull upward on my lids and became aware of a deep, echoing pain in my head. Dim gray light flooding into the blackness made the throbbing worse. I was so cold.

Mark looked down seriously into my eyes. "One of his pupils is slightly larger than the other one. He's probably got a concussion." He looked away and I followed his glance to Tiger, kneeling next to me.

"Tiger, my head hurts bad." My voice sounded all high and whiney, like a little kid.

Tiger looked across to Mark and said, "I know, baby."

I struggled to sit up.

"We got to get him to the hospital," Mark said. Tiger nodded.

"I don't want to go to the hospital; I'm all right," I said, and tried to stand up. "Easy, boy," Mark said as he rose with me.

"I don't want to go home. Don't call Mama." My head was pounding and I didn't feel like I could make it to my feet.

"I'm all right; just let me rest a minute," I told Mark as I started to lie back down.

"Do you think you can carry him?" Tiger asked.

"Hold on, hot shot," Mark said as he slipped an arm around my waist. "I'm going to pick you up."

I felt him fit an arm around the small of my back and another under my knees, then lift me against him like I was nothing. He was so warm. Laying my hurting head against his shoulder. I wanted to go to sleep so bad. I had to find Henry Junior. I was responsible for him. I felt something tug at my ankle and heard the sound of velcro ripping apart. "Where's my board?" I demanded.

"Tiger's got it. Don't worry about it." Mark said as he turned and began to carry me up the beach. Every step he took made my head pound worse.

"Tiger?" I called. I was scared that he was mad at me.

"Right behind you, baby. I'm right behind you."

"Don't be mad at me, okay?" I pleaded.

"I'm not mad at you," Tiger said gently from behind me.

"You won't call Mama and Daddy?" I felt Mark hesitate in our climb up the dune and turn to look backward. "I don't want to go home. Don't make me go home. Please."

Mark stopped. I felt the wind pour over me. We must have been at the top of the dune. The wind had moved offshore. The waves were going to be so good in the morning. I felt Mark's arms tighten around me briefly.

"We're not going to make you go anywhere, Matt," Mark said. I heard Tiger's footsteps scrunch against the sand as he walked past us.

"We're just going to ride over to Morehead City and get you to the hospital," Tiger said from ahead of me now.

Mark began to move us cautiously down the other side of the dune. Though it was getting dark, I could see my truck and the Bronco down the road. "Tiger, promise me you won't send me home," I demanded.

Mark shushed me gently and bent to kiss the top of my head.

Chris and I were in his car. We pulled up in my driveway at dusk the day he left the first time. Mama waved from the kitchen window. "I'll call you in a few days," he said.

I watched Mama move back and forth in the window as she got supper ready. "Don't," I said.

Chris took my hand. "Why not?"

I looked at him. "It's going to be really hard for awhile. It'll just make it worse."

Chris nodded. "When can I call?" His hand was sweating in mine.

"Wait until I get to Tiger's. You still got his number?" Chris told me he had it written in his address book. I took hold of the door handle.

Chris looked toward the kitchen window. "One more kiss . . . for a promise?"

Mama moved out of sight. I kissed him then. He opened his mouth against mine and sucked in my breath before he pulled away. I opened the car door and got out.

"Hey, don't forget this," he said and handed me the wrapped present. "Think about me, okay?" he said.

"Don't worry," I replied. He shifted into reverse and smiled. I patted the car as he pulled away.

I went on in the house. I couldn't watch him drive off. When I walked in Mama slammed down a pot lid. "I cannot believe you, sitting out in the driveway like that," she hissed as she turned to glare at me. "Have you gone crazy? There is no excuse for you just advertising to the whole world your . . . your . . . deviantness."

I stood still while she pulled open the silverware drawer roughly. She snatched out a handful of flatware and slammed it on the counter. "You may think you can go off and act like a girl, but you won't do it in my house. Do you understand me, Matthew?"

I looked at her, feeling like I was a hundred years old.

"You better answer me, boy," she said.

She was fighting mad but I was nowhere near up to giving as good as I got. "I'm sorry, Mama. You don't have to worry about it happening no more."

She glared at me and took a step toward me. "You're durn right I won't. You ain't so grown nothing can be done with you. I'll beat you half to death myself before I let you make a fool out of this family."

She was just getting started. I knew she could go on like this for a long time. "I ain't worked and done right all these years to raise a bunch of perverts who just go around throwing their nastiness up in my face."

She sounded like she was about to cry. I couldn't stand that, not now. "He's gone, Mama. He's gone back to live with his daddy."

Mama's face stayed red, but she didn't say anything. I felt like the floor underneath my feet was cracking. The tears came up in my eyes. I tried not to but I could hear my voice shake. "I'm sorry I upset you. I promise it won't happen ever again."

Mama's face softened and all the meanness seemed to wilt out of her body. She just looked tired.

"I'll go wash up and then I'll set the table for you. Okay, Mama?"

She nodded and turned back to the silverware drawer. "You better hurry. Your daddy'll be home any minute."

The doctor who was sewing up my eyebrow kept asking me all these stupid questions. It was really distracting to try to watch his small neat movements over my eye. The answers were simple but I couldn't seem to communicate in any way that the idiot could understand. It just made my damn head hurt worse.

When he finally finished tugging at my eyebrow, he told me he was going to take some X rays of my head. For just a second, I panicked. What would he be able to see? I had too much hidden in there. After snipping the ends off the stitches, he went away.

It seemed like I had lain on the cold table forever. People in scrubs kept wandering back and forth at the end of the gurney I was lying on, ignoring me. Then, when I wanted to go to sleep, they wouldn't let me. They kept fucking with me. Talking to me, jabbing at me.

A big, fat black lady was lying on a gurney across from mine. She kept on moaning, "Oh, Lord Jesus. Oh, Lord Jesus." Every time I thought she'd shut up, she'd start again with the Lord Jesuses. Then some body would come in and poke at me again. It was starting to really piss me off.

I wished all these people would just go off and let me die. My head hurt. I knew people who died before. It didn't seem so bad.

Jeep's mama died before Thanksgiving. I had never gotten around to going over to see him and I felt bad about it. In the weeks that his mama had been so bad-off sick, he'd been missing Wednesday Family Night our folks dragged us to at the church. I hardly ever saw him around school, and to tell you the truth, I was glad I didn't in a way. We were just Wednesday Family Night friends. Once his mama passed, though, I knew I should say something. Mama had told me Jeep's mother was real bad-off sick. She also told me I ought to go over and see Jeep.

I thought about it. It wouldn't really be such a big deal, me going over to his house, but I couldn't handle it. First off, I didn't know what to say to him. I wondered what on earth I could say to Jeep that wouldn't come out stupid and sanctimonious. I knew what it was like to watch someone you loved die. When Henry Junior was dying, it just got on my nerves for people to try to be all compassionate and shit. I mean, I knew they were sincere, but they couldn't really touch what I was feeling. It was too personal.

I really understood where he was coming from, but underneath that, I was scared of getting too close to Jeep. I didn't want to admit it, but I was scared I'd start caring more about him than I should. In the years I'd been friends with Jeep, I kept him at arm's length. I knew that I was attracted to him, but I almost liked things better the way they were. I fought real hard not to fuck that up by thinking about him in a sexual way.

I felt like a big phony. In a way, I was lying to Jeep, but hey, being gay was one big juggling act anyway. It seemed like God and everybody else thought being gay was wrong. I couldn't help but feel like I was right. But being right just required how right you had to be at the time. I didn't like lying, or feeling guilty all the time. Worse, I hated feeling responsible for having to figure out everybody from God down to Jeep's tolerance for the truth.

At breakfast, the day of Jeep's mama's funeral, Mama said I could sign out of school at lunch to go. Daddy had to be on the road that day and I think she kind of wanted me to go with her. The problem was, I had a big French test that day that I really didn't want to have to make up. I made a deal with her that she would pick me up on the way from the church to the cemetery and I'd go with her to that. After the cemetery we could go by Jeep's house and pay our respects. It would take some timing, but I knew we could pull it off.

I didn't want to go at all. But there was something I knew that Mama would never say. She hated going to the big cemetery outside of town. Henry Junior was buried out there. It had been a long time now since he died, but still it tore Mama up every time she had to go out there and bury somebody else, even just a church acquaintance like Mrs. Loftin. Mama thanked me and gave me a big hug before she reminded me to try and dress a little bit better than usual.

It was an ugly day. The sky was gray and the wind wouldn't give me any peace. I had been hoping that it would clear up by the time Mama had to pick me up in front of the school, but it didn't. I waited out front for her, relieved about my French test, but dreading the rest of the day. I was thinking about how I'd hate to put my mama in the ground on a day like this, when I saw her car turn the corner. I was so relieved, I reached around to hug her when I got in.

Mama seemed to understand. The day had her weirded out too. It was a cloudy day when we buried Henry Junior, but it was spring then and the dogwoods were already blooming. At least we found some peace in that. Today didn't promise spring. It was just depressing with all the trees bare and a cold wind scattering what was left of the leaves in dirty gusts down the streets.

We drove out to the cemetery, not talking much, but glad to be with each other. I loved my mama. She got on my damn nerves most of the time, but I did love her. Sitting there in the car with the heater blowing, I smelled her perfume and sensed her strong love all around me. I felt pretty lucky to have her.

At the cemetery, I took Mama's hand and walked with her up to the tent over the grave. Jeep and his daddy and some folks I didn't recognize were sitting in the mourners' chairs right in front of the coffin. I could just see them from the back. Jeep's broad shoulders seemed like they were going to split the seams of the cheap navy blue jacket he had on. The cold wind picked at his dark hair and ruffled the petals of the flowers and wreaths by his mama's coffin.

It was getting colder. I looked at Mama. Her eyes weren't watching Reverend Winslow; they were scanning the cemetery looking for a place she knew by heart. The wind burned my eyes and made them tear, but Mama's were hard and strong, staring out over the flat bronze markers and artificial flowers in autumn colors. I squeezed her hand and she briefly returned the pressure without looking at me. She was seeing something else.

Reverend Winslow finished droning, and people started moving past the mourners, shaking their hands and whispering to them. I felt like we needed to get in line. I whispered to Mama and tugged at her hand, but she pulled away. Distracted, she said, "You go on up, son; I'll catch up to you in a minute."

I knew where she was going. I didn't want her to go by herself.

"It's okay, son. Go on up there. We'll be going by the house. I'll speak to them there." She didn't even look at me; she just took off.

I got in line and watched her walk across the cemetery by herself. The wind snatched at her coat, but she put her head down and made her way across it, like she was wading in heavy surf. I moved with the line, looking after her until she was out of sight.

I shook Mr. Loftin's hand and he thanked me warmly for coming. I hadn't seen anybody else Jeep's or my age there. None of his buddies were even standing off to one side like they usually did, big and nervous as horses. There was just a bunch of grownups there. I smiled at Mr. Loftin and then moved to stand in front of Jeep. A lady from the church was leaning down over him with one arm across his shoulder. Jeep was staring blindly at his mama's coffin, not crying or anything. He looked like he didn't even know where he was.

I had brought him a joint of some really good sinse Tommy had gotten lately. I was going to give it to him at his house. Now, I wondered if that was the right thing to do. The church lady moved on and I offered him my hand, but Jeep just looked up at me. I put my hand on his shoulder and tried to squeeze it. It was too big, my hand just sort of lay on top of it, pitiful like. I found his eyes. They looked totally empty and kind of surprised, like an animal's when it gets hit by a car.

"Matt, thanks for coming, man," Jeep said finally.

I nodded at him and smiled. "I was thinking about coming over to your house after . . . "

I caught myself and didn't finish. Jeep nodded and looked around. I knew he didn't see anybody else from school. He tried to smile, but got stuck not even half way there before he looked away.

"See ya in awhile, then," I said. Jeep nodded again and looked past me to see who else's pity he had to endure. I tried to squeeze his shoulder again and then moved off. I had to go get Mama. Right then, I felt as if if I didn't find her quick, I might never find her again.

She was over by Henry Junior's grave. Her back was to me, but she had her shoulders held back and she looked strong, even in the hateful cold wind that was tossing plastic petals across the flat faces of the grave markers and making the cypress trees shiver and sigh. I walked up beside her and put my arm around her waist. She moved into me briefly, but then took a couple of steps away. I knew she had to make herself strong and hard right now, or she wouldn't be able to leave here.

I didn't want to leave Henry Junior here myself. I hated the goddamn place. Nearby, there was a big white statue of Jesus holding one lamb around his neck and reaching down to pat another one standing by his knees. Jesus had this look on his face as if he was trying to be all gentle and stuff, but to me, he looked as if he was smirking at some private joke.

"Mama. We got to go, honey," I said softly. Mama didn't answer me, but she stuck back her hand for me to take. Her hand seemed so tiny in its gray leather glove—a little girl's hand. I took it and she squeezed my hand. There was so much strength in it, I was amazed.

Mama turned around to face me in the wind, her eyes dry and steady. "Yeah, we got to go," she said, and gave me a brave smile.

Neither one of us made much effort to talk on the way over to Jeep's house. We just rode past the houses where people hadn't taken down their Halloween stuff and other places that had put out a few Thanksgiving decorations. It wouldn't be long until folks started decorating their yards for Christmas. This was the in-between time that just looked cold and sad. I thought about Christmas coming and tried to cheer up.

When we got to Jeep's, there didn't seem to be too many people around. Mama knew the church folks and she got busy in the kitchen, putting out all the cold fried chicken, tuna noodle and green bean casseroles, and chocolate cakes and banana puddings that the neighbors and friends had brought over.

None of Jeep's friends had even come to the house. It looked like I was the only person under thirty-five there. I found Mr. Loftin talking to some men in the living room and asked him where Jeep was. He pointed down the hall and said, "Thanks for coming." He sounded like a recording, going, "Thanks for coming," over and over. It was real pitiful.

I walked down the hall and looked at all kinds of pictures of Jeep and his mama and daddy from the time he was little. Jeep's mama had started off looking pretty, but the farther I went down the hall, she looked worse and worse. There was one picture that couldn't have been taken very long before she died: Jeep stood between his mama and daddy in his football uniform.

He looked bigger than both of them to begin with, but he looked like a monster in that picture. All of them were trying to smile at the camera, but Jeep just looked determined. His daddy looked like he was trying too hard and his mama looked like a skeleton. Most of her hair was gone from the cancer treatments and her clothes hung on her. It was as if all the life had been sucked out of her by growing the huge boy-man in the football uniform next to her.

I felt as if I'd seen something too personal, like I'd gone snooping in their dresser drawers or something. I turned away from the picture and looked for some clue as to which door was Jeep's. From behind a door to my left, I heard bed-springs creak. I walked over and knocked on it. When nobody answered, I said, "Jeep. It's me, Matt." There was a sort of a choking sound on the other side. I opened the door gently.

Jeep was sitting on the edge of his bed in his jockey shorts and a pair of black dress socks. His dress clothes were scattered all over the floor. He didn't look up when I came in, just sat there with his head hanging down, staring at the floor. I felt embarrassed for him, sitting there in his drawers, so I closed the door behind me. Jeep still didn't say anything to me; he just sat there.

I had never seen him with his clothes off. I knew I shouldn't be looking at him like that, but I couldn't help it. His huge shoulders were squared back as he held onto the edge of the bed with his hands. That made his triceps stick out as if carved out of stone. His chest was broad and he had a sprinkling of dark hair across his square pecs. The rest of him looked to be hairless until his thighs. I glimpsed between his legs.

I felt ashamed looking at him like that. It was worse than looking at the picture outside, but I couldn't resist. I knew I couldn't just keep on standing there checking out his body. He seemed so defenseless; it was all wrong. "Hey, man. Don't you want to slip on some sweatpants or something? It's kind of chilly in here," I said gently.

Jeep looked up at me and I realized he was crying. Tears were slipping down his face and he didn't make an effort to hide them. I felt so sorry for him. I didn't know what else to do, so I went over and sat down beside him on the bed. I didn't want to touch him. I just remembered all the times I'd sat across from him up in the storeroom when we skipped Youth Now at church and how I'd wanted just to lean against him and feel safe. I thought maybe if I sat next to him now, it would sort of be like that, only in reverse.

Jeep looked at me with the most pitiful look in the world as I sat down next to him. I didn't know what else I could do but just be there, close by. He turned to me, put a big arm across my shoulder, and buried his face in my neck. The sobs came out of him against his will, as if he was fighting to hold them in. He was heavy, leaning on me like that. I put my hand on the back of his neck and lay down with him on top of me.

"Go ahead, hoss. Let it out. It's okay," I said as I pulled my legs up on the bed to hold him. He did the same, settling all his weight on me and holding on like I was dry land and he'd been drowning. I held his neck with one hand and stroked his back with the other as he cried and cried. He tried to say stuff, but it mostly sounded like moans, or chunks of things mixed in with the crying. I lay under him and let him talk into my neck. I had heard footsteps in the hall outside come to the door, pause and then walk away, respectful of his loosened grief and my place to catch it as it fell.

I stared at a *National Geographic* poster of the constellations he had stuck up over his bed with thumbtacks and tried not to think about how good his strong back felt as my hand stroked his sobbing into tears and finally into whimpers. From down the hall, I could hear people talking, rattling dishes and silverware, even an occasional bit of laughter. Outside Jeep's room, people's lives were going on without his mama. I hoped he knew everything was going to be all right.

Jeep nuzzled his face into my neck and sighed. I was aware of his big body as it relaxed into mine. Jeep wasn't crying anymore, but he seemed not to want me to leave or to get up off me. I still stroked his back, like he was just a big ol' dog.

He shifted his weight and I was surprised to feel his erection through my jeans. I was more surprised when he kissed my neck, gently, with his lips closed tight. He raised his head and looked at me with a mixture of shame and fear. "It's okay," I whispered. Jeep looked at me searchingly for a moment and then closed his eyes and kissed me.

I was surprised but I wasn't. In a way, it felt perfectly natural kissing Jeep. It was like finding out somebody you had known for a long time was really good at playing the piano or something and you never knew that about them at all. I began kissing him back. I let the hand that had rubbed his back trail down and rest on his ass. It felt full and smooth. I squeezed it and Jeep responded by grinding his hard-on into my leg.

There was a light tapping on the door and a woman's voice said, "Jeep, honey. There's some folks out here who want to say good-bye."

Jeep got up so fast, it was like he dematerialized off me and reformed at the door. I had no idea a guy that big could move so fast. "Okay, Aunt Sheila. I'll be right out," he said.

"Come on then, honey . . . " the voice said and its footsteps turned, hesitated, then went off down the hall. Jeep turned and saw me lying on his bed. He must have felt his erection straining against his jockey shorts, because he sort of moved his hand to cover himself up. He looked like he was caught between hell and a real hot place.

"I'd better be getting dressed," Jeep said gruffly. He tried not to look at me, just turned and opened his closet door. I got up off the bed and straightened my clothes and shook my hair. It felt all mashed up to one side after Jeep had cried on me. I didn't know what to say. I walked over to where Jeep was pulling on a pair of jeans. I tried to touch his shoulder.

"Don't," he said harshly.

I felt as if he'd punched me. I took two steps back and looked at him. Jeep pushed his hard-on into his jeans, zipped them up, and reached for a sweatshirt. I watched him pull it over his head. He stared at me coldly while he pulled his sweatshirt down over his chest.

"Jeep—" I began.

He cut me off saying, "Don't say nothing. Please. Don't."

My own dick was aching as it pushed at my jeans. I shoved my hands down into my pockets to hide it and felt the joint I'd brought him. I pulled it out and tossed it onto the bed. He looked at it, surprised. "For you for later," I said.

Jeep picked up the joint and stared at it like he didn't know what it was. He looked up at me and started to say something but didn't.

"I gotta go," I said. Jeep nodded and looked away like he was real ashamed.

One more time, I got stopped right when the going got good. It was like I was supposed to have a permanent case of blue balls or something. I felt sorry for Jeep, but I couldn't feel sorry for myself. I wanted to laugh. My whole life was just plain ridiculous. I opened the door and went to get Mama, hoping she was ready to go. I sure as hell was. The hell with feeling guilty and all weirded out. I just needed to beat off.

How could I have a hard-on when my head hurt so bad? A light was coming through a door and I didn't know where I was. I looked around and saw Tiger, sitting watching me. "Hey," I said.

"Hey, yourself," Tiger said, and stretched in his chair by the bed.

"I guess I fucked up pretty bad, huh?"

Tiger nodded and rubbed his eyes.

"I'm in the hospital."

Tiger got up and came over by the bed. "How's your head feel?" he asked as he rubbed the short bristly hair back from my forehead. It felt funny somehow.

"Like it's been run over by a Mack truck. Why did they cut off all my hair?"

Tiger chuckled softly and said, "They didn't. You were buzzed when we found you."

This really puzzled me. My eyebrow felt funny. It was a smaller hurt than the inside of my head, more pinched by something than in a vise. I reached up to touch it, but Tiger gently took my hand.

"Am I going to die or anything?" I asked him.

Tiger squeezed my hand and grinned. "No. You have a concussion and a nice cut over your eye. They'll probably let you go in the morning, if you're back to making sense." He looked down at me with some trace of amusement lingering in his eyes.

"Oh, shit. What did I say?" I dreaded knowing, but I figured I might as well find out the worst.

Tiger shook his head and let go of my hand. "Nothing much. A little about Jeep, Henry Junior. Nothing I could get any money for anyway. Go back to sleep, now."

I wanted to. My head hurt so bad. It was good to know I wasn't going to die, but I felt really scared somehow. Tiger stroked my forehead gently.

"Are you going home now?" I asked him. I sounded so little, my voice betraying my fear.

"Nah, I'd better stick around and keep you from hurting the night nurse," Tiger said. "You threatened to cut her when she came in to take your blood pressure."

It hurt me to laugh. Tiger shushed me. I lay there and felt the coolness of his hand on my forehead, familiar and comforting. "You didn't call Mama and Daddy, did you?" I asked him urgently.

Tiger's hand paused on my brow, briefly, then continued. "No. We'll call them when you get to feeling better. Go back to sleep, now."

I gave into the comfort of his cool strong hand stroking my hair. I slept.

Tiger

Tiger left about seven-thirty, when they brought in my breakfast. Satisfied by my appetite, he left to go home and shower, promising me he'd be back later in the morning. The food lady came for my tray and asked me if I wanted the television on. My head still hurt, so I told her no. What I really wanted was to go to the bathroom. She told me to wait until she could get an orderly to help me and she was out the door.

I waited forever and no one came. I thought I would burst. Finally, I thought the hell with it. The bathroom was only five steps away. My head throbbed when I sat up, but it went back to a dull ache after a moment. Swinging my legs off the bed didn't make it any worse, so I ventured to stand. I was swimmy-headed for a second, the room slowly moving off to the left, like clicking a Viewmaster, then it locked itself back to stillness.

I made my way shakily to the bathroom. I didn't trust my aim, so I just sat down on the toilet. It felt so good to sit there; I just rested awhile. When I got up to wash, the mirror gave me a shock. I had to hold onto the edges of the sink to steady myself.

With a rush of recollection, I felt the fin glance my face and the board come down on my head once more. When I shook off the memory, I found my face in the mirror again. My swollen right eyebrow was stitched for an inch up my forehead. The ends of the wiry suture stuck up like stray hairs. My eyes seemed a little out of square, like a cartoon character's do when they get smacked with an anvil.

I had forgotten about the haircut. It made me chuckle. I sure wasn't a pretty boy anymore. I looked like one of the baby Marines who came down to Atlantic Beach from Camp Lejeune to fight on a Saturday night. Only I looked like Sunday morning. I thought about the scar on Tillett's collarbone. Now I had a surfing story all my own. It made me feel deeply satisfied, even proud.

"What the hell are you doing out of bed?" I heard from behind me.

The face of a guy I knew from community college appeared in the mirror. My mind was so crazy, I fully expected to see anybody appear in the room behind me.

"You were supposed to wait until I got here." The guy sounded bossy.

I was about to ask who the fuck he thought he was talking to until I realized he was wearing scrubs. I turned unsteadily and told him, "You ought to be glad I did get up, or you'd be changing a wet bed right now."

He chuckled and came into the bathroom. "You better be glad I didn't have to do that. I'd have to whup your sorry ass."

He slipped his arm around my waist and I gratefully put my arm over his shoulder as he led me back to the bed. My headache was coming back worse.

"I heard you were a bad-ass," he said, turning us back at the bed so I could sit down.

"Who told you that?" I asked him as I lay down.

He lifted my legs for me as he said, "Let's see, the ER doctor. The X-ray tech. Oh, and my girlfriend. You threatened to cut her last night when she came in to check your vitals."

I closed my eyes against his smile and apologized. When I opened them, he was still standing by my bed.

"No problem. Hey, Matt, how many fingers am I holding up?" he asked. I told him three. He nodded. "You'll be all right. You're lucky. Your doctor says you could have drowned if you hadn't made it out of the water."

I thought about Tillett, playing the origin of his scar off like it was no big deal when the kid at the pier asked him about it the day before. I just shrugged, trying my best to mimic Tillett's old tough-guy response.

He laughed. "You surfers are such idiots," he said, not unkindly. "Keep your butt in bed; your doctor's already making rounds. He ought to be in any time now."

"Thanks," I said.

"No problem. You want the television on?" I told him okay, since everybody else seemed to want me to have the damn thing on. I told him to make the sound low. He smiled and switched it on as he left.

I didn't really want to watch it; nothing was on but the morning news. It was distracting, though. If I pushed myself out toward it, the pain in my head lessened to a dull back beat. I watched as the camera pulled back from the lady newscaster to include the sports guy. I could barely hear what they were talking about, but that was okay by me.

Suddenly, Jeep appeared as a sweaty talking head over a pair of padded shoulders. He was playing defense in ECU's coming game against somebody. The camera pulled back to include the sports guy holding up the mike. I couldn't make out what Jeep was saying. Irritatingly, the volume was too low for me to catch his low drawl.

I studied his earnest face and wished he was here in person, instead of just stuffed into the screen over the bed. I missed his solidness. I was so tired of being tough and I hurt. I wanted to just lean against him, like I wanted to lean against him all through high school.

Jeep's mama and daddy started going to our church when I was in tenth grade. When his mama found out she was sick, they came looking for Christ at our church. It didn't take something like that for us to go; Mama and Daddy took church seriously. When somebody came looking for Christ downtown at River Street Baptist, Mama was right there, holding open the door for them.

The first night the Loftins showed up at Wednesday Family Night, Mama dragged them over to sit with us. Jeep Loftin looked like he'd rather be anywhere than there. I sort of knew him from around school, but I didn't *really* know him. He played football and had a reputation as being a big dumb ox. He had a mean look that kept most people out of his way. In the world of high school, Jeep was a Scred jock.

Screds were the opposite of the Proud Crowd, the rich kids who seemed to run everything and do everything. Screds were active dis-joiners. Hell, they were little baby thugs. Jocks could fit in with either the PCs or the Screds because of their athletic abilities and the blind eye teachers turned on their bullshit. I never had any problems with Jocks or Screds because I got high. PCs got high and acted like they didn't. Screds got high and made sure you knew it. Jocks got high, but only with each other. I just got high and didn't make a big deal about it. One thing I had learned early in high school, reefer took you anywhere you wanted to go socially.

Anyway, Mama and Daddy went on and on getting to know the Loftins and me and Jeep pushed our food around on our plates until time to go to Youth Now. On Wednesday nights, high school kids in the church had to go to this group called Youth Now. I hated it. I didn't really want to go to the basement of the Christian Life Activities Center to share my Christian experiences with other teenagers and creepy Youth Now counselors.

Mama embarrassed me by making a big deal out of how I had to take Jeep down there and introduce him around. She acted like we ought to join hands and skip down to the Youth Now meeting or something. Mama seemed to think all kids never really got past kindergarten.

I cut out with Jeep dragging along behind me like I was taking him to an ass-whupping. Outside the fellowship hall, I decided to skip the shit. "Look, man, I got half a joint. You want to cut out and burn it?"

Jeep gave me a sly grin. "Dude," he said. I took it as a yes.

When I started skipping church in eighth grade, I covered the Christian Life Activities Center inch by inch finding places to hide and hang out. My favorite place was an empty storeroom on the fourth floor. It was supposed to be kept locked, but it was up so high and so far out of the way, nobody bothered. It was full of dusty old carpets and office furniture. I spent many a Sunday morning up there, sitting in an old armchair looking down over the town, daydreaming, and by the time I started high school, catching a buzz. I decided to take Jeep up there with me.

Timing was everything if you wanted to skip out. You had to appear to be going downstairs, but really just hang out until you could duck up the stairs past the committee meetings and stuff going on the first three floors. Nobody really checked to see if you went to Youth Now, so I got away with it most times unless some old busybody reminded me I was supposed to be downstairs and watched me until I went down.

Jeep followed me upstairs quietly and we managed to duck an old man hanging out by the stairs on the third floor. We got into the storeroom without a hitch. While Jeep cracked the window, I fired up the doobie. We couldn't risk turning on the light, so we just sat watching the sun go down, getting high.

Reefer makes some people stupid. It makes other people real quiet and others silly. I had a tendency to become a really good listener. Fortunately, reefer made Jeep a good talker. Jeep, normally an introvert, became downright chatty when he got high.

I had no idea he was a thoughtful, smart guy. Once I got him talking on a subject I could listen to him forever. We talked about other stuff that night and about a lot more other stuff on Wednesday nights after that. I enjoyed Jeep. Our paths didn't cross much at school, but when they did, we joked around and said shit like, "I really got a lot of affirmation out of Youth Now."

We hung out every Wednesday night all through high school. Jeep kept getting bigger and bigger. He was six-three and weighed in at two hundred and two pounds according to his stats in the programs given out at football games. I never went to any of them, and in a way, Jeep seemed to respect that. We never talked about football anyway. He didn't have to be a football player around me.

We never talked about sex stuff much either. Jeep dated around, but he didn't keep a steady girlfriend. He said they were too expensive. I wondered sometimes if he might be thinking about some of the things I was thinking about, but I never brought it up. In a way, I didn't want to know. I wanted him to be just sort of cool and out there. If I found out he thought about doing guys too, it would be too weird. When I was around him, I got away from wondering about gay stuff like he got away from football.

There were times, sitting up in the storeroom with Jeep, that I wanted to scoot across the dirty carpets only two feet and just sorta lean against him for awhile. Jeep was so big and solid, he made me feel like I was little sitting next to him. He gave off the steadiness and calmness that reminded me of a big animal or what grown-ups were like when I was small. I dreamed about being able to hide against him, feeling him warm and strong behind me. I knew it was crazy because he was my age, but he seemed strong enough to shelter me somehow.

Of course, I never did it. Not until that time in his room after his mama passed away. He avoided me after that. The night before Thanksgiving, my friend Cathy and I were riding around getting high and having a pretty good time until she pulled into the parking lot of a 7-Eleven and asked me to go get her some cigarettes and a Coke. I went in, got some drinks and bought some cigarettes for myself. I needed some Marlboro Lights. After a night of smoking Cathy's Kools I felt lousy. I paid the lady behind the counter and looked outside.

Jeep and this girl, Gwen, had pulled up in the space next to Cathy's car. I didn't know Jeep was dating Gwen. She was a total slut. The 7-Eleven lady shoved my change at me and I gathered up my stuff. Jeep came through the door and tried to act like he didn't see me. I nodded at him and he ignored me. He walked right past me. I watched him get a six-pack of Bud Light out of the cooler. When he turned around, I saw his face fall when he realized I was still standing there.

I turned and went out the door. It was a bright, clear night, and the stars were like little diamonds. While I got in the car I tried not to think about the poster over Jeep's bed, or kissing him. Cathy started talking. She seemed to take forever to pack her cigarettes, open them up, and light one. I looked over at Jeep's car. Gwen was fiddling with the tape deck.

It surprised me how badly I wanted to stab her. Jeep came out of the 7-Eleven and got in his car without appearing to notice me sitting two feet away. Cathy finally cranked up the car and we pulled off. "Fuck you, Jeep," I thought to myself. "Fuck you."

I didn't run into him again after that until I went to get my wisdom teeth out, right before I met Chris. I looked over into the waiting room and there was Jeep, sitting all by his lonesome. He watched me come in and sit across from him, like a snake had just crawled into the room and might just bite him.

My mouth hurt so bad, I didn't really care what he thought. I nodded at him and then stared at the fish tank Dr. Paulson had installed in one of his waiting room walls. We must have sat like that for five minutes before Jeep finally said, "What's wrong with you?"

"I got to get my wisdom teeth cut out," I mumbled, trying not to move my sore jaw.

Jeep shook his head knowingly. "I got mine out last week. I'm getting my stitches out today."

I grimaced at the word "stitches." Jeep laughed, but it was a nice laugh. "Man, it ain't the stitches; it's when he puts his knee on your chest to get enough leverage to get 'em out. I still have a bruise on my sternum."

I just looked at him in horror. He smiled. Trying not to work my swollen jaw anymore than I had to, I said, "He can dig the motherfuckers out with a butcher knife if it'll make them quit hurting."

Jeep nodded sympathetically, then eyed the glass door of the receptionist's area. He saw me catch him checking it out. It pissed me off. I leaned back in my chair and stared at him before I said, "Don't worry. Nobody can see you talking to me."

Jeep looked at the fish tank and turned red from the neck up. I leaned forward and rested my elbows on my knees and put my aching jaw in my hands. Real low and quiet, I said, "It's you with the problem, man. Not me. I ain't got no problem with nothing."

Jeep glanced back at the frosted glass door as if it was the only thing between us and the listening ears of the whole world. He looked at me pleadingly, but he didn't say anything. I felt sorry for him. I really did. I felt sorry for myself too because I'd lost my friend and I knew it. Well, I didn't feel bad about a little kissing and some grinding, especially under the circumstances. I was big enough not to let it get in my way and I still had some pride.

Jeep hung his head, but he was gripping the arms of his chair hard. I remembered how strong and pitiful he looked sitting on his bed, just like that, the day of his mama's funeral. I sure was glad I didn't feel ashamed of myself for being gay. It was a rotten place to be and he was in it in his own way.

"Jeep. Did you know after my brother died, my daddy stayed drunk for three whole days? I ain't never seen my daddy drunk before or since, but right then, he went a little crazy. People do that when somebody they love dies." Jeep looked up at me slowly. "I ain't never told another soul about Daddy getting drunk like that but you. I ain't never gonna tell nobody else. I'm just telling you because I know you had to have gone a little crazy yourself when your mama passed. It ain't nothing you should feel bad about. Okay?"

My jaw ached something horrible from getting all that out. Touching it just made it worse. I winced and sat back in my seat. Jeep looked at me with relief written all over his face, just as bold as if somebody had taken a florescent magic marker to it. I'd said the right thing. My mouth hurt saying it, but it was okay.

A dark shadow passed over Jeep's face. He said, "Matt, I ain't like that. I'm really not . . . you tricked me."

The glass door slid back and the receptionist told me to come on back. I stood up and told her I was coming, and she shut the door. I looked down at Jeep. He looked like he'd just missed being caught stealing or pissing in the fish tank or something. I was mad as hell, but it was easy to remember feeling so miserable about sex stuff, even stuff that didn't quite happen.

Jeep couldn't even look at me. I spoke to the back of his head. "If that makes you feel better to think that way go ahead. But I know I'm not somebody who would do that to a friend."

He looked at me for just a second and then turned to stare again at the swirling blue and orange and yellow fish. I turned around and took my hurting mouth and went to get my own bruised sternum. I tried not to think about Jeep any more after that. No big deal. No big deal until this summer, anyway.

"Dude," my doctor said cheerily as he rushed into the room and came to a gusty halt at the end of my bed, blocking my view of Jeep on TV. "How many fingers?" he demanded. I told him four. He rubbed his pen along the bottoms of each of my bare feet and didn't smile when I flinched.

"Okay, Matt. How old is Henry Junior?" he asked as he approached the edge of the bed.

"He's eight forever, man. He's dead," I snapped. I wondered what kind of shit I had said while I was so fucked up. The doctor nodded gravely.

"Do you remember what happened to you yesterday afternoon?" he asked. I nodded and he asked me to tell him. I repeated as much as I remembered. He bent over to shine a mag-light in my eyes and stood up back up, seemingly satisfied.

"So, am I going to live?" I asked him.

Turning his interest away from my face he glanced down at me and picked up my wrist. Finally he dropped my wrist and answered. "Yeah, you'll live, if you stop acting like you're going to live forever. That was a crazy stunt you pulled yesterday, surfer boy. A millimeter further or a pound heavier and you never would have made it back up on the beach."

I started to protest, and he silenced me with a glance. He pulled up the chair by the bed and leaned close to me with a seriousness that made me nervous. "There's something else. Your personal life is none of my business, unless it makes you sick. I have to ask you. Have you been having unprotected anal and oral sex?"

I looked at him and swallowed hard. He studied my face and sat back in his chair. He obviously was waiting for an answer.

"What do you mean *unprotected?*" I asked finally.

"You're a bigger idiot than I thought," the doctor sighed.

"How did you—" I began before he cut me off with an upraised hand.

He glanced down into the folder in his lap and searched for something. "Your luck's holding. You're negative for any venereal disease. But there's worse out there. A lot of men who screw around with other men are coming down with a disease called AIDS."

I was so shocked to get hit with that, I couldn't say anything. I had heard something about this disease thing that was killing gay guys, but that was way off in San Francisco and New York, not Nowhere, North Carolina.

"It is a killer and there's no cure," the doctor went on. He reached in the pocket of his white coat and pulled out a stuffed envelope. "Here are some brochures I want you to read. You're also lucky that somebody told the girl in the lab they thought you were cute, or I wouldn't be having this little chat with you for several days. She was so curious or mean-spirited that she rushed your AIDS test results. As it is, you don't have to worry while the results come back."

I took the envelope and held it stupidly. Relief, shame, and a certain kind of nakedness flooded over me, as though the doctor and lab tech had rewound the tape inside my head to find pictures of Tillett fucking me on my knees.

"Son, you better start acting like you got some sense," the doctor said wearily. He looked me in the eye and said, "This is 1983, not 1953. I'm not judging you; I'm just telling you. Death is very, very real. Your hard head saved you this time, but your hard dick might kill you yet."

I broke his gaze and nodded. He stood up briskly then and said, "I don't see any reason why you can't go home. Take it easy for a few days. Don't take anything stronger than Tylenol. If you get spacey, or forgetful, or if your head begins to hurt worse, I want to see you back in here immediately. Understand?"

"Yeah, no problem."

"I want to see you in my office in a week to get your stitches out. Read those brochures and if you have any questions, just let me know."

He was on the way out the door when I asked him, "When can I go surfing?"

He stopped and looked back at me with some admiration mixed with consternation. "Not until your stitches come out. Take the time to think about playing a little more safely," he ordered, and then added, "everywhere."

I watched him leave and then turned back to the television. Jeep was long gone. In his place, the weatherman was talking about the hurricane's progress up the coast. I didn't want to think about what I might have said that prompted the doctor to check me for AIDS, or VD for that matter. I bet the whole hospital knew about my sex life.

I wondered if anybody heard anything that they'd take back to Tillett. That was the real fear. Tillett would kill me for sure and it wouldn't be by fucking me to death either. I groaned around my throbbing head. The phone rang next to my bed. It sounded like a drill going down my ear.

I found it and picked up the receiver quickly before it could ring again. It was Tiger. I told him he could come get me. The doctor said I could go home. I asked him where my bathing suit was. "They cut it off you when we brought you into the emergency room," Tiger said.

My embarrassment throbbed inside my head. "Oh, shit. What else?" I said out loud. Tiger asked me what was going on. "Oh, man. The doctor was in here just now ragging on me about unprotected anal sex and this gay disease," I whispered into the phone. "Tiger, what in the hell did I say last night?"

Tiger didn't say anything. I groaned.

After a moment more of silence Tiger asked gently, "What did he say?"

I told him about the AIDS test and that I was negative and all. "I just can't figure out what made him think to test me in the first place." I imagined myself offering to do somebody in the ER.

"Settle down, Matt." Tiger hesitated, then said, "I had to give him your medical history. It's part of the questions they ask. It's no big deal, hoss."

I didn't say anything.

"Matt, think about it. You were bleeding. Those people had to come in contact with your blood. Until the X rays came back, we didn't know if you might need surgery. I thought they were scared you might have hepatitis or God knows what. Forget about it," Tiger said calmly.

I felt myself begin to relax. My head throbbed slightly less. "So I didn't say anything about Tillett?" I whispered into the phone.

"Oh, so that's what this is all about," Tiger said tersely. Neither one of us spoke. Finally, Tiger continued, "Well, I guess you have a reason to be concerned. Tillett's a psychopath. But I wouldn't waste anymore time worrying about that. You ought to be thanking God he didn't give you anything but a few bruises."

"And Jeep," I added without thinking.

I could hear Tiger sigh. He liked Jeep.

"I'll come on over and bring you some clothes."

"Thanks, Tiger," I said.

"No problem, hot shot. Somebody else wants to talk to you," he said. I heard the dead spot as he handed over the phone.

"Hey, Matt," Shane said. "You got stitches; cool."

"Why aren't you out surfing?" I asked him.

"I'm grounded. Billy ratted me out for skipping."

"I didn't mean it," I heard Billy yell in the background.

"The waves are going off, Matt. Overhead and glassy. Dad says I have to miss the whole swell. Hold on, Dad wants to talk to you," Shane said.

"Matt, the doctor says you can come home?" Mark asked gruffly.

"Hell, yes. As soon as Tiger gets here," I told him.

"You really scared me, son. I want your ass back here as soon as possible," Mark said roughly.

"Yes, sir."

"By the way, you're grounded too," Mark said more gently and then added, "and I really like your haircut. Airman, first class."

I laughed then and told everybody good-bye.

I lay back to wait for Tiger, impatient to get home to my family. I found the white envelope the doctor left me camouflaged in the sheet like some poisonous chameleon. I opened it and read through the brochures telling me about blood and sperms, viruses and condoms.

It made me sick to think about some of the stuff I'd done with Tillett. I figured I didn't need to worry about Chris, but then my mind started thinking about who all he might have been screwing, girls and guys. There was only one person of the three I'd had sex with I could be sure was clean.

My mind wandered off, looking for Jeep. My head hurt a little less when it found him waiting quietly as he always did.

Tiger

let me come back to work because I was bored after only one day spent not going out with him, but he kept an eye on me. When I looked draggy-assed, we'd knock off early. Two days after I got out of the hospital, we quit work about three o'clock. When we got home, Tiger went in to make some phone calls, while I put up the equipment.

Shane came downstairs to help me. He didn't have anything to do after school, since he was grounded. "Man, I'm bored," he said as he handed me the last bundle of stakes to put in the back of the Bronco.

"No homework?" I teased as I locked up the truck.

"Damn, you sound like Dad," he said resentfully.

"Wanna help me take a look at my board?" I offered. "I need to see if I can fix it." My board was in better shape than I was, but it still had a pressure ding along the left rail where it had hit my head. The glassing had cracked and let some water in next to the blank.

"Sure," Shane said gratefully. He had to be lonesome as well as bored. Billy had a cold and was sick at home.

"C'mon, then," I told him. "If we can't go out, we might as well see if we can't get my board fixed up."

We stomped up the steps to the deck and Shane took my board from its place by the living room window while I moved some bonsai so he could set it on the railing.

"Do you think it matters if there's still water in it?" Shane asked as I pushed my thumb on the glassing, making the thin layer of water more obvious.

"There ain't that much to worry about."

"I bet you could suck it out," Shane said, and grinned. I moved to pop him one, but he skipped backward, laughing.

I ran the palm of my hand over the crack on the rail. The edges were still together and almost smooth under my hand. I heard the screen door slam behind me.

"The important thing is to mend it so it doesn't get any worse," Tiger said.

"I bet we could patch it ourselves," Shane said confidently.

"Well, hell, yeah," I said looking at Tiger. "If we had a patch kit."

"Tiger, can't we leave and go down to the surf shop to get a ding repair kit?" Shane pleaded. Tiger looked from Shane back to me and then back to Shane again.

"I saw your homework. Go on, but you better be home before Mark or the grounding will turn into total lock down." He looked back at me. "Understood?"

I promised we'd go straight there and come straight back. Shane and I ran downstairs and jumped in my truck to head down to Atlantic Beach. Shane fiddled with the radio, and looked out toward the beach, yearningly. Coming up on the pier, I asked him, "You suppose going straight to the surf shop means that driving through the pier parking lot is okay since it's on a straight line with the road?" He grinned in reply. When he did that, he looked just like Mark.

We turned in at the pier and parked over on the left side. There was no one out on either side of the pier; even the parking lot was deserted. The waves had gone flat after the storm passed, leaving the ocean as calm as a lake.

"I can't believe Dad made me miss the swell," Shane said. He looked stranded and restless.

"Hey, me too." I offered. "But I guess it was us that fucked up, right?"

"I guess."

I backed the truck up from the bulkhead and went back out on the beach road. Shane finally settled on a station and sat back. Winter was coming and winter was a dangerous time on the beach for kids Shane's age. It was too easy to get high, goof off, and fuck up. I wondered what he was going to do to keep busy, besides school.

"Matt, does your head still hurt?"

"Nah, it's no big deal anymore."

Shane nodded. He drummed on the dashboard with his fingers and shifted restlessly in his seat. "Matt, can I ask you something?"

"Shoot," I told him.

"It's personal," he warned.

I winced. I didn't know what would pop into his twelve-year-old head next. "Okay, but I ain't got to answer if I don't want to," I said.

Shane looked across at me and asked, "Why didn't you want Tiger to call your folks and let them know you got hurt?"

I wasn't expecting this. I was anticipating more of a question about fucking or something. I didn't really know how to answer him.

My life back home had started to seem like some long bad time I'd gotten through. It didn't have anything specifically to do with Mama and Daddy though. Thinking about it, remembering it, it seemed like a cold and too-tight place compared to the beach. Back home, everything was right up on me. There were no open spaces to breathe.

In a way, I did sort of miss my folks, but Mama and Daddy came down to the beach together to visit a few times. Daddy had popped in by himself when he was near the beach, but he only stayed long enough to have a quick drink or bite to eat.

Mama seemed tense on her first visit, but left satisfied and calmed by the actual normalness of the household. Mark seemed to mesmerize her, but he had that effect on a lot of people. He really turned on the charm for her, though. Mama found him hard to resist; she preened a little in his presence. She treated Tiger politely but you could tell there was some kind of real gap that kept her from genuinely liking him. It was just strange the way she acted around him, like I was his fault or something.

Despite all that, it seemed to me like Mama was starting to relax some. I think she halfway wanted to come down to the beach and find me all miserable, but when she saw how happy I was, she began to cool out some. We began to ease into a respectful truce, she and I.

Mama was most taken with Shane and Billy. They, in turn, were taken with her. I watched them as they deferred to her and seemingly became gentle and tame in her presence. It made me wonder. It made me understand a little better how straight people worked. It also made me understand her much better. I never had any awe of her and I think, as I grew older, she sensed her powerlessness to manipulate me as she did Daddy or Tommy.

Still, I remembered how she had acted when my brother Tommy left home. For a solid week, she and Tommy argued and fussed back and forth. It might as well have been one person arguing with himself. When it came to Tommy, Mama might as well have pinched a piece of herself off and made him; they were that much alike.

Me and Daddy just stayed out of it as much as we could, considering most of the fighting was at the supper table. No sooner than Daddy could say "Amen" and Tommy reached for a bowl, Mama would go off about living in sin, or how she raised us, or some such shit. It'd end up with Tommy banging out the back door, Mama announcing her nerves were shot and going to lie down, leaving Daddy and I to deal with the leftover emotions and dishes.

By the fifth night of helping Daddy wash up, I asked him why he didn't make them quit fussing. Daddy just grunted and said the weirdest thing. He scrubbed at some burnt-on rice and told me, "Son, it took Tommy near 'bout two days to get away from his Mama just trying to come into the world. After twenty years, you reckon she's just gonna let him waltz out the back door?"

I was tempted to ask him how long it took me to get born, but I figured I didn't really want to know.

After she blew up so bad the night Chris left, Mama didn't say anything else. I didn't give her a chance. I stayed out of her way as much as possible. I was obedient and polite no matter what she asked me to do. She watched me, though. She watched me like a hawk. I was so miserable about Chris leaving, I had just about quit eating. After the second week, she waited until I asked to be excused from the supper table and said, "Henry, you got to say something to him. He's just starving himself to death."

Daddy put down his knife and fork. I didn't get up; I just looked at him. He didn't want to say anything to me; I could see that on his face. Mama sat watching us both.

"Son, you got to eat," Daddy said. He looked at me and then at Mama. I wished she'd just not have said anything and let him finish his meal in peace.

"I'm sorry, Daddy. I ain't trying to worry y'all or nothing." Daddy looked embarrassed and Mama sighed. "May I please be excused?" I said.

Mama threw her napkin down and snatched my plate. "Go on up-stairs then. You make me sick with all this carrying on."

She stood up and carried my plate to the sink, rinsed it off, and stuck it in the dishwasher. "How are you ever going to be any kind of man . . . carrying on like a teenage girl that's had her heart broke? You need to wake up and smell the coffee, Matthew. Unless you change, your whole life is going to be just like this, time and time again." She sat back down at the table.

Graduation was then just two weeks away. The day after that, I was going to get the hell out of there and go to the beach. If I could put up with all the nothingness I was feeling without Chris, I could put up with Mama for two more weeks. I didn't want to fight with her. God knows, she knew how to hurt me real bad and I had all the hurting I could stand right then.

"Is this what you want out of life? 'Cause let me tell you one thing, just such as this is all you're going to get. The Bible says if you sow the wind, you'll reap the whirlwind."

I looked at Daddy pleadingly. "Daddy, can I please be excused?"

Mama snorted. "Go ahead, ask your daddy to let you off the hook. He'd rather let you run off and live with a bunch of queers than straighten your ass out."

Daddy turned red in the face. "That is enough. I'm sick and tired of both of you. Matt, go on and leave the table. Your mama and I are go-ing to have a talk about who's the head of this house." He glared at Mama. She stood up and went back to the sink. He looked at me. "Didn't you hear me, son?"

I stood up and slid my chair under the table like I'd been taught. "Y'all don't fight over this. It ain't worth it. I know you ain't happy about me, but its just the way it is. I'm gonna be all right. Let's just don't fight no more. I'm gonna be gone soon and everything's gonna be fine. I promise."

Mama wouldn't turn around and look at me. Daddy sighed. "Go on upstairs, Matt. I want to talk to your mama." I hesitated, looking from Daddy's face to Mama's back. "Go on," he said irritably. "If you ain't learned to mind me, you will."

I left the kitchen and went upstairs. It was just something else to be miserable about.

The morning I left to move to the beach for good, Mama got up early to see me off. She offered to make me some breakfast, but I wasn't really hungry that early. I told her I'd just stop at Hardee's for a biscuit or something on the way. I could tell she wanted to talk. She watched me across the table as we drank coffee before I left. I was scared of what she might say. She wasn't like Daddy; she wouldn't let me off so easy. Given the chance, she'd want to have a big discussion about the queer stuff and I just wasn't up to it.

"Matt, honey, your daddy told me you and him had a chance to talk last night," she said finally.

"Yes, ma'am, we did." She didn't say anything else; she just reached across the table for my hand. I took hers in mine and looked at her. In the hard light under the table lamp I could see her struggling. She looked like she might cry, but was determined not to.

"I'm gonna be all right, Mama," I said.

She squeezed my hand. "I know, son. I gave it to the Lord. You just remember how you were raised and you'll come back someday."

"I ain't going to the moon, Mama; I'm just going down to the beach."

Mama shook her head. "That ain't what I'm talking about and you know it, Matt. I know you ain't that way, like Tiger and them. That foolishness don't come from my side of the family."

She sighed and let go of my hand. I held my breath while she stood and went to the refrigerator. I really didn't want to get into a long conversation about "that foolishness" as she called it. It made me feel disloyal to Tiger, and to myself. I was about into "that foolishness" as deep as I could get.

"Your daddy'll be up soon. He'll eat a good breakfast this morning." She took out eggs and bacon and laid them on the counter while reaching for a frying pan from the cabinet. "Every young'un's got to climb Fool's Mountain—"

"—just don't climb so far you can't come back down," I finished for her.

She gave me a slight smile. I finished my coffee and took my cup to the sink. I hugged Mama while she put bacon into the frying pan on the stove. She didn't turn around to hug me back, but she did sort of nuzzle her head back into my shoulder.

"Thank you, Mama," I said.

Gently, she pulled herself away and reached for the eggs. "You better go on. If you don't get started you won't never get there," she said over her shoulder.

I wondered if she meant the beach, Fool's Mountain, or back to where she wanted me to be.

Shane waited for me patiently as I waded back in from those deep waters. I knew he needed some kind of explanation. "I didn't want to worry them, I guess. That's one reason," I told him. He nodded in reply, but didn't really seem satisfied.

"Well, I'd want Dad to know if I got hurt. My mom too," he said. "If people love you, they don't mind being worried. My dad worried about you."

I thought for a full minute, looking for some way to explain. "Shane, when you get older, sometimes it's like people love you too much, it's smothering." I offered.

Shane considered this for a minute. "You mean like being overprotective or something?" he asked in all earnestness.

"Yeah, like that, only a little different. It's more like, you don't need to be loved so much like a little kid. You need to be loved like a grown man. Somebody who's strong and can take care of himself," I said.

Shane gave me a long look that said I hadn't done too good of a job looking out for myself the other day, but he didn't say it.

"Shane, even if you fall down, or wipe out and end up in the hospital, sometimes you got to know you can get back up on your feet all by yourself."

Shane nodded. The car grew quiet for a long time except for the radio. "Matt?" he asked.

"Yeah," I responded.

Shane hesitated and said finally, "You know you're my friend and like a brother to me and everything, so I can be totally up front with you, right?"

"Yeah, I know that."

Shane looked out his window to speak. "You got to learn to trust people better."

I didn't say anything in reply. We drove on down into Atlantic Beach in silence until we got to the surf shop. I parked and shut off the truck.

Shane looked at me uneasily. "You're not mad at me, are you?"

I had driven along with the truth of needing to trust more since he said it. It kind of hurt me to recognize I'd forgotten how to trust anybody a long way down the road. I was always too busy looking to see how they could hurt me.

I looked at Shane and smiled. "No way, buddy. I can't be mad at you for telling the truth."

Shane nodded his head seriously and said, "So work on it then."

I lightly popped him upside the head. He grinned back at me.

We found the ding repair kit in the surf shop and took it up to the register. While I was paying for it, I heard the door chime go off and a familiar voice behind me said, "What's up, rod dog?" It was Tillett and his buddy Eddie, the guy who spit all the time. The girl behind the counter handed me my change and I turned to face them.

Eddie whistled and said, "I heard you got popped upside the head. Damn. Nice one too." Tillett looked at my face and I watched him fight away the concern that flickered across his eyes. "How many stitches?" Eddie asked.

"Just six. No big deal," I said.

"He had a concussion too," Shane volunteered. "He had to spend the night in the hospital."

Eddie looked down at Shane. "Were you out with him?"

Shane shook his head no. "Matt was out by himself." Eddie glanced at Tillett. "My dad and his friend Tiger found him passed out. He'd bled a lot."

Tillett raised his eyebrows at me.

"Lone wolf," Eddie said admiringly. I shrugged. "Hey, ain't you the little dude that was ripping up the pier that day?"

"Maybe," Shane said. "There were a lot of guys out."

Eddie laughed. "Naw, man. I seen you." Shane looked embarrassed while Eddie half teased and half praised him for his surfing.

I looked at Tillett again to find him studying my face, a haunted look in his eyes. "Scar's gonna make a man out of you," he said.

I looked him in the eye. "Didn't take no scar for that," I said quietly.

He nodded abruptly and walked away. I turned away from his retreating back. "We gotta go, Eddie. Take it easy," I said.

Eddie nodded. "See you around, rod-dog. You too, little dude."

In the truck, Shane asked me, "Matt, who are those guys?"

I shrugged and put the truck on the road toward home. "Just some guys I know from working job sites. They're roofers." Shane busied himself taking the ding kit out of the bag and examining it. Tillett read my mind. He was good at it.

"Who's the wolf-looking guy?" Shane asked.

"His name is Tillett; why come?" I asked him carefully.

Shane stuffed the ding kit back into the bag and laid it on the seat between us. "I think he likes you, you know, like that." Shane looked at me with an infantile lecherous grin.

"Ah, man," I said, exasperated, "What makes you say that?"

Shane gave me a sharp look. "Just the way he looked at you," he said.

Shane was no dummy. Growing up surfing the emotional currents between his mother and father, not to mention Tiger and his stepfather. His perceptions were dead on, but I wondered about his judgment. "Do you think I could trust him?"

Shane shook his head. "Never. Not in a million years."

I laughed. Shane looked at me like he didn't get what was so funny, but he joined in.

The rest of the week, Shane kept me company and I kept him distracted. We worked on fixing my big board, and spent as much time on the beach as we could without violating Mark's grounding. I even helped Shane with a term paper he had to do for school on Aztec culture. I cheated by using the research for my own essay that was due for my English Comp class.

The day finally came for me to get my stitches out. That was the day that signaled the end of Shane's and my own restriction. Tiger drove me by the doctor's office on the way home from work. I submitted to another set of head X rays, which the doctor declared okay. He removed the stitches and examined my eyebrow and the skin above it.

"I'll refer you to a plastic surgeon," he said as he moved away from the examining table where I was sitting.

"Naw, you don't have to do that," I said defiantly.

The doctor left off writing in my chart to look over at me curiously. "Why not, for God's sake? If it's a matter of money . . . "

I slid off the table and walked over to the small mirror over the sink where he scrubbed up. I had grown attached to the stitches over my eye. Now, the wound was still a little red, but in time it would just be a thin line rising across my eyebrow and up a bit over my eye. I liked it. It made me look rougher, more intense somehow, as if the grave accent mark over my eye was emphasizing some menacing scrutiny of what I was seeing.

"It's not that," I told him firmly. Tiger was fronting me the money to pay my hospital bill and deducting it, fifty dollars a week, from my pay. I could have the scar removed if I wanted to, and pay Tiger indefinitely. The truth was, the scar was my own red badge of courage. I wasn't the kind of guy to get a tattoo. This scar, however, was the same thing, if a lot more hard won. It was a part of my dues as a man and as a surfer. "A man doesn't hardly seem like a man without a scar or two," I told the doctor.

I turned away from the mirror and looked him in the eye. He searched my face for a moment, started to say something, then bent his head back over my chart and continued scribbling. Finally, he said, "No problem. If you tire of the novelty of it, you can always have it done later."

He finished writing and stood abruptly. I extended my hand and said, "Thanks for everything, Doc. I appreciate you looking after me."

The doctor took my hand in his and shook it warmly. "Did you have any questions about the brochures I gave you in the hospital?"

I reached in my back pocket, took out my wallet and pulled out a three-pack of rubbers that were packed in some antiseptic shit called Nonoxynal-9 to show him. "And spit, don't swallow," I said quietly.

The doctor shook his head around a grin. "You're one of a kind, Matt. Just don't get so hung up playing this macho surfer bullshit that you do yourself some real harm."

I nodded and headed for the door. Just before I walked out, I turned and gave him a grin saying, "Don't worry, and don't take this personally, but I hope I never have to see you again." The doctor smiled back and waved me away.

The sunset on the way home was totally awesome. The air had been getting heavier all week as the moisture was pushed ahead of a cold front moving down from Canada. Daylight saving time ended this coming weekend. Tiger and I had stopped at a 7-Eleven to buy a six-pack to celebrate my stitches coming out.

We rode in companionable silence over the bridge from Morehead City to the beach, enjoying the beer and the last gasp of summer. It never ceased to fill my heart up, coming over the rise of the bridge. Atlantic Beach and the ocean beyond was like the entire world laid at my feet. I was home now, where I belonged.

I looked over at Tiger. He finished his beer and crumpled the can. Without taking his eyes from the road, he put the empty back in the bag and popped the seal on another one. I grinned to myself. Tiger was pretty much it as far as I was concerned. All the questions I'd had about him all my life had been answered, either by him telling me or by living and working with him day after day.

If anything, my admiration for him had grown. I imagined I knew him as good as I did my own brother, except for one detail.

Gliding down the hump of the bridge, Tiger looked around to catch me studying him. "What the hell are you doing, peeking at me?" he asked good-naturedly.

Taking his tone as an invitation to talk, I said, "All this time I've been spending with you, I ain't never asked you to tell me about Nathan Willis."

Tiger glanced at me sideways, then turned his attention back to the road and his beer. He took a long swallow as he braked at the light by the Circle. He put on the turn signal and gave me a brief look. "What brought that up again?"

I finished my own beer, crumpled the can, and got another from the bag. "Hell, I don't know. It's just always there, like some big mystery in the back of my mind."

Tiger sighed. "You really care about all that old mess? Don't you have enough with learning everything about your own self?"

I didn't say anything. I knew what he was talking about. The truth of it was, learning about Tiger had always been a part of learning about me. He was the other queer relation in my family. He had blazed the trail where I wanted to go. He had taught me how good and how difficult it was sometimes to have a lover and a life together. He taught me a profession. He taught me to surf.

"I don't sometimes see the difference between you and me," I told him bluntly.

The light turned green and Tiger turned to go home. He said, "So if you know all about me, it'll give you all the clues to figure out yourself."

I nodded in response. I was on shaky ground. Tiger was always generous on his terms, but grew distant if you got too greedy. He was one of the most intensely private people I'd ever met. I knew surfaces of him, but never what was underneath.

Tiger caught my nodded response and chuckled. "This is where you and me really are different, son." I looked over at him. Tiger was slender and fair. I looked for the word I came across in class the week before. Tiger was fey. I was dark, and promising to have a mass Tiger would never have, as soon as I grew into my raw bones. I felt stolid next to him.

The differences were more than physical, though. Tiger had always had an otherness about him that I always thought had to do with him being gay. It wasn't that, either.

"Who the fuck is Nathan Willis?" I asked impatiently.

Tiger looked at me sharply, but continued on the road toward home. "Nathan Willis was my father. He had an affair with your grandmother when he was stationed at the base. They didn't see each other again for years. He showed up one day in 1957 with what she took to be a bundle of dirty laundry. It was me. My mother died of complications a few weeks after I was born." Tiger paused and took a long swallow of beer.

Never looking over at me, he continued. "Your grandmama thought I was cute. She also figured if she kept me, he'd come back. He gave me to her, and it didn't take a lot of talking for him to give me up." Tiger drove on then in silence.

After a while, I said, "Did he ever come back?" Tiger poured the rest of his beer down his throat. I never even saw his Adam's apple bob once. He crumpled the can and nodded as he reached for another one.

"He came back once in awhile for a couple of years. Then he got killed, driving drunk outside of Layfayette, Louisiana. He played guitar and sang in juke joints and bars. I never knew him except for a picture Mama kept in that alligator pocketbook." Tiger fell silent then.

I finally had all the pieces to the Tiger puzzle. Nathan Willis had been much less of a mystery for me than Tiger had. I forgot when I started being satisfied with thinking all the family fuss was because he was gay, anticipating the same response to me when I came out.

I looked across the truck at Tiger. Even in the last of the daylight, he still seemed to gather it all up and hold it. He looked golden. I felt dusky in comparison. I had heard my mama say that God made love children prettier than other babies to hide their parents' sin. Sneaking looks across at him, I understood what she meant.

"What the hell do you keep peeking at me for?" Tiger asked again, and with more irritation this time. He sounded tired.

"I think I'm just seeing you a little better right now," I answered as gently as I could. Tiger didn't say anything and I looked over at him. The anger in his eyes startled me.

"You don't see shit," he spat. He looked cornered and mean. It scared me just seeing him; then he went off.

"Nobody gave you away like a damn puppy. You didn't grow up named like somebody would name a pet. You didn't see Heloise and Dordeen grudging every single scrap Mama handed me. You didn't see her watching you, wanting for you to turn into somebody she wanted and couldn't have. You never lived feeling like being loved was just a favor you got till you turned eighteen and then owing for that."

I could feel his eyes burning me and I wouldn't look around at him.

"What the fuck do you know about me?"

All of this coming out of him shocked the hell out of me. Tiger always walked around like he was so sure of himself, like he didn't give a fuck what anybody thought. How could I know where that came from? How was I to know what kind of pain it took to look out from behind those yellow eyes like nobody was ever going to hurt him again?

I heard him crack open another beer and gulp it down. It wasn't until we were almost home that he turned off at the pier. He parked the car away from the few others in the lot, then shut off the truck. I sat quietly across from him. I'd gone too far. Tiger rolled down his window and lit a cigarette.

"Matt, I'm sorry. I never meant to let all that loose on you. You were just the closest piece of family handy. I'm sorry. I really am." His normally scratchy voice was as rough as if he'd been swallowing gravel. The cool breeze pouring in the window from the ocean blew out the pain of his earlier outburst, but it still had left its mark on Tiger. The sun gone now, he looked tired and pale in the dull light of the parking lot.

He was right. I didn't know that much about him. But I loved him a lot.

"Tiger, I didn't mean to piss you off. I'm really sorry for—"

Tiger waved me off and thumbed his cigarette out the window. He gave me a brief smile to let me know it was okay. I just knew he'd taken a lot from whatever store of love he had for his family built up from his past and tried to pay it all back to me. I felt humble and grateful, even a little guilty.

"I owe you a lot, Tiger. I would have been crazy or as good as dead now if it hadn't of been for you. Daddy knows it too. Why else do you think he made it so easy for me to leave home? He knew you'd pick up where he had to leave off, raising me."

Tiger nodded as he kept on staring out the window, listening to me.

"I love, you, Tiger. You gave me a whole new kind of life," I said sincerely.

Tiger sighed and opened his last beer. "Well, hoss, I love you too. But it ain't got nothing to do with owing your daddy or your grandmama nothing." He burped and threw what was left of the beer and the can out the window. "Well, maybe it did at first. But not no more. You're part of my real family now." I smiled at him and he grinned back. "Understood?"

I nodded.

"Okay. Let's go home," he said and started up the Bronco.

When we got home, Tiger excused himself and went

to bed. Mark seemed a little concerned and shortly followed him. I sat with Shane and Billy watching TV until they fell asleep on the living room floor. Jeep appeared on the news again, getting interviewed by some sportscaster guy about the next day's game against State. I felt a rush of affection for him. He was so earnest and cool. I smiled to myself too because I knew I could make him sweat. Jeep was the only guy I'd been with that made me feel really good about myself.

I was too keyed up to go to bed. The news went off and I switched off the television. The dogs and the boys were all sprawled on the floor, sleeping lightly. I stood and the dogs raised their heads eagerly. I made a slight motion with my hand and they stood and shook. Their rabies tags tinkled softly against the small collection of other things that had become attached to their collars. Tiger had placed a small seashell on the ring with their name tags. Mark and Shane had put Saint Francis of Assisi medals along with that after having them blessed on his feast day at the parish church.

They looked at me expectantly. I decided to walk on the beach. I moved to the door and they followed, picking their way carefully over Shane and Billy's sleeping forms to join me at the door.

The night was peaceful. Fall was appraching, but the cicadas were still singing, the wind was still warm and the sound of it kept me company as the dogs and I made our way across the street and over the dune to the beach. The ocean looked as if someone had tossed handfuls of diamonds across the surface of the water where it caught and refracted the meager moonlight.

Walking on the beach late at night with only the dogs for company was one of the singular joys I had discovered since coming to live here. Now, there was a bite underneath the warm wind. I found myself shivering slightly as the approaching cold front stole in on the edges of the wind.

I hadn't been back to The Circle since I had met Tillett there the first time, and by mid-August, I had quit Tillett. On the nights when I felt most restless and horny, I'd just let myself quietly out of the house and walk down the beach a couple of miles or so to the pier. I found myself doing just that one night before Labor Day.

The pier was open twenty-four hours a day and so even in the middle of the night people were there to populate my solitary sleeplessness. Most were elderly fishermen and their wives. Sometimes I'd see a guy I'd look at twice, but I would no more strike up a conversation with him out on the pier than I would dive off the end buck naked.

Along the dark and deserted beach, I felt myself expand out into the night with some relief. There was enough moonlight to illuminate the low scut of clouds that were moving in from the ocean. I never watched the weather even though I worked outdoors. The whole summer had been practically rainless except for the huge thunderstorms that blew up late in the afternoons. Whole days of rain were rare.

I made my way to the pier, enjoying the breeze on my bare chest and the warm pull of the low run of beach break against my calves. I needed some touch so bad that I felt the night was licking me. As the lights from the pier got closer and I realized I was sporting a hard-on that a cat couldn't scratch. I laughed, imagining me, with my dick swinging out in front of me, wandering among all those old people out fishing on the pier. They probably wouldn't even notice. Nobody else did. Sometimes I felt like the whole world was fishing and I was just cutting bait. Hell, I was supposed to be queer bait.

The inside of the pier was quiet except for an old lady watching the news on a TV behind the lunch counter. I bought myself a Coke, and moved out onto the pier. It was a view to nowhere that I loved. A few people clung to the sides, endlessly casting and waiting just outside the cones of yellow light from the lamps in the center.

I walked slowly into the increasing wind as the pier moved offshore. Under my feet, the ocean roiled around the pilings and the deck shifted softly with the impact of each succeeding wave. It was like walking down the length of some huge benevolent creature's back. The smell of old bait, fish guts, and salt air rushed past me as I followed the pier out into the open ocean.

"Matt? What are you doing out here?" a man called from the dimness near the railing.

I was pretty surprised to hear my name called. In my whole summer here, I had never run into anyone from back home. As the man propped his fishing pole against the rail, he strode toward me, followed reluctantly by a larger figure. It was Mr. Loftin and Jeep.

"You look like a regular beach boy, son," Mr. Loftin said as he enthusiastically pumped my hand. Jeep gave me a shy look and took my hand to shake when his dad stopped. He looked really good.

"I live here now. I'm working for a surveyor and I'm planning to go to Carteret Community this fall," I explained. Jeep nodded and tried not to look embarrassed as his father went on and on about his achievements at the ECU football training camp over the summer.

" . . . so I told him, son, let's me and you head down to the trailer and go fishing for a few days before school starts." Mr. Loftin chatted along heedlessly.

"You guys have a place down here?" I asked.

Mr. Loftin grinned. "Sure do. It's just a trailer over in the park across the road, but it's plenty nice to come stay at for a week or so fishing."

I felt Jeep staring at me. I wondered if he was still uncomfortable around me. We had not spoken a single word to each other since that day in the dentist's office back in January.

"What's biting?" I asked Mr. Loftin.

He took my arm and pulled me over to look in his cooler. "I want you to just look at all them spot," he said proudly. A dozen sad fish lay on the ice, in various stages of dying. One convulsed, flipping itself wildly in a futile attempt to escape the cooler and get back into the warmer ocean.

"Damn," I said respectfully.

"Jeep was just about ready to call it a day, but hell, I don't reckon I'm going to miss my last night fishing," Mr. Loftin said as he looked offshore.

I knew a born fisherman when I saw one. A born pier fisherman was a totally different kind of breed from a surfcaster or a boat fisherman. Like the rest, Mr. Loftin was as in love with the night and the pier as I was, but for totally different reasons.

"Daddy'll be out here to watch the sun come up, but I have to get back to Greenville tomorrow morning," Jeep said and yawned.

"I got to work tomorrow or I'd stay right here and visit awhile," I said. "It was nice seeing y'all." I turned to go.

"Hold up a minute and I'll walk with you," Jeep said suddenly. I waited while he collected his things and told his daddy good night. Mr. Loftin waved us off, telling Jeep not to leave until he came back the next morning.

Jeep and I walked silently down the length of the pier back toward shore. I had forgotten what a big guy he was, even bigger than Mark. The summer in training camp had made him hard as a rock; however, there was none of the slight pudginess of mass he'd had in high school.

Neither of us spoke; we just walked, and I thought about the day on his bed. I knew he was thinking about it too, but it seemed like such a long time ago. It just made me want to say good-bye and head away from a memory that didn't belong here with my new life.

Where the pier joined the pier house a set of steps led to the beach. That was the way I'd come and the way I intended to leave. I stopped by the steps and held out my hand for Jeep to shake. "This is where I get off," I said. "It's been good to see ya. Good luck at school and everything."

Jeep hesitated, but then shook my hand briefly. His hand was warm over mine. He looked at me and seemed to resolve something before he said, "You want to walk over to our place and have a beer?"

Jeep held onto my hand. I thought about how late it was getting. Jeep seemed to realize he was still holding my hand and dropped it suddenly. "I mean, I know it's late and all. I guess you probably don't want to." From the lights over the door I could see he really looked like he wanted me to go. "I could run you back down to your place. It can't be that far if you walked up here." He looked a little humble when he said it. I figured it wouldn't do any harm.

"I guess one beer wouldn't hurt," I said.

Jeep smiled. He looked genuinely pleased. "C'mon then. Our trailer's just across the road."

Jeep began to talk then, like he always did back when we had skipped out of Youth Now and hung out in the storeroom on the fourth floor of the Christian Life Activities Center. He talked all the way to his trailer and continued as we settled on the screened porch outside. It seemed as though he had stored up eight months of things he wanted to tell me. It took him exactly four beers to get to what was the hardest to discuss.

"I'm really sorry about how I acted toward you after . . . " Jeep began, then nervously finished his beer. After all that had happened to me with Chris and everything, it seemed like no big deal to be nice about it.

"Don't worry about it, Jeep. It's okay," I said.

Jeep stood up and looked out over the sleeping trailer park. The cicadas' whine rose and sustained itself; seemed to go on forever. Jeep turned to me and whispered fiercely, "No it's not. I blew you off like you were nothing. You didn't deserve that. I'm sorry."

Although it was nice to hear him say it, I was sort of taken aback by the force he put behind what he was saying. I got up and walked over to stand beside him in the dark. He didn't look at me. "Look, man, apology accepted. I just figured you were freaked and that's okay. I'm gay; you're not. It's no big deal."

Jeep looked at me, incredulously. "You still don't get it, do you?" he said.

"Get what?" I asked shortly. I was starting to get pissed. I had done everything to make him feel better but cry for him. I didn't know what the hell else he wanted.

Jeep looked around us nervously. "I can't talk about this out here and I got to take a leak, bad," he said, and grabbed my arm. He steered me inside the tidy trailer and pointed to a door across the living room. "If you have to piss, there's another bathroom in there."

I nodded and went. I did have to pee awful bad. In the trailer's tiny bathroom, I let out the Coke and all the beers I'd had and then washed my hands. I was feeling a little buzzed and it was getting late. I wondered what the hell Jeep had on his mind. I had to be getting on home.

When I went back into the living room, Jeep handed me another beer and pushed me gently toward the sofa. I sat down, and he pulled up a kitchen chair opposite me. Jeep took a long swig of his beer and then set the can carefully on the floor by his feet. He leaned forward, resting his forearms on his elbows and said earnestly, "There's something I got to tell you. It's been eating at me since my mom died."

"Jeep, you ain't got to—"

"Shut up!" Jeep said pleadingly. "Just shut up and let me finish."

I took another hit off my beer and fished in my pocket for my cigarettes. Jeep let me light one and slid an ashtray toward me before he began to speak.

"I didn't stop talking to you because I was upset about what happened the day of my mama's funeral, you asshole. I was weirded out because I thought you were upset. Before I could get it sorted out, you were always around Chris."

This hit me like a ton of bricks. It had never occurred to me that Jeep was anything other than a straight arrow. I mean there was Gwen and all the other girls he dated. "You ain't queer. Why should you care?" I said, stunned.

Jeep stood up and began to pace around like something caged. Finally he said, "Would it blow your mind to find out I was curious, maybe?"

I didn't have anything to say about that. I was really shocked.

Jeep stopped pacing and slumped into a chair across the room. "That time with you, after Mom died, I didn't want to stop. It did have me weirded out for awhile, but then I decided that maybe . . . I don't know."

I sat in silence, smoking. This was too weird. After awhile, I ground out my cigarette and asked him why he never said anything about it.

"Chris," Jeep said quietly. "I knew you were real tight."

I nodded. Chris and I were real tight all right. It sort of made me glad that somebody noticed.

"Did you and Chris ever do it?" Jeep asked. There was a hot look in his eyes.

"Yeah. We did it a lot," I said proudly.

Jeep nodded and looked away. He stood up and retrieved his beer. "Yankee asshole," he said and belched deeply. Then he half laughed. "I bet you'd be pretty fucking amazed to find out I was jealous as hell."

I was amazed, but I was also pleased. I decided this honesty shit cut both ways. For once, this was fun. "Why? I mean . . ."

Jeep looked down at me and his shoulders sagged. "Goddamn Matt, you're good-looking as hell. I mean, I think you're very attractive." Jeep blurted this out, crushed his beer can and went to the refrigerator for another.

I watched him, my mind going ninety miles an hour. Jeep stood at the refrigerator drinking his beer, looking at me. I was getting horny. I felt a sense of meanness and power swimming up through my beer buzz. I'd had some pretty good teachers at this. Some of my lessons still hadn't quit hurting. I looked at Jeep like a cat looks at a mouse shivering in a corner.

"So, are you still curious?" I said.

Jeep watched me seriously. I knew he was trying to figure out if I was making fun of him. Finally, he nodded. I was driving and I knew where we were going; I'd been there before. "Have you ever done it . . . you know, with another guy?" I asked him gently.

Across the room, Jeep drained his beer and shook his head no. In a voice too small to be coming out of his giant frame, he said, "Never; not with nobody."

I couldn't resist being mean. "I thought—you know—since you went out with Gwen . . . "

Jeep looked at me, but all he said was, "Nobody."

I looked at the door, but I didn't get up. "Is your dad really not coming back for awhile?" I asked. My heart was pounding like I'd run a mile in under a minute flat. I knew I was about to get to a place I'd been wanting to go for a long time. It was almost too much.

Jeep sort of arched his feet and bobbed up and down a couple of times nervously. "He won't be back until dawn, maybe six-thirty, seven o'clock."

I stood up and walked the six steps to the kitchen. Jeep looked at me and licked his lips. "Do you really want to?" he asked hoarsely.

I nodded at him. He looked at me and clumsily put his hand on my bare shoulder. He gripped it and then began stroking it with his thumb. I focused my eyes on the hollow of his throat above the collar of his T-shirt. Suddenly, he turned and walked down the darkened hall beyond the kitchen. I followed him.

Jeep paused by a doorway in the tiny hall. I stopped in front of him and followed his glance into the tiny room. There was a small lamp burning softly by the bedside. The bed nearly filled the entire room. A breeze pushed at the white polyester curtains through the high, narrow jalousie window. To step into that room was literally to go to bed.

I looked up at Jeep, finding so much desire and anxiousness in his face that it broke my heart. This had to be his decision. As bad as I wanted to fuck with him, I wasn't Tillett. It wasn't in me to make his decisions for him.

"I want to, Jeep, but it's up to you. We don't have to do this if you're not sure," I said quietly.

Jeep looked toward the bed and back to my face. He reached toward me and placed his hands under my lats and pulled me to him. I felt his heart beating through his T-shirt as he simply held me against him and stroked my sides down toward my waist and back up again. I looked up at him and realized he simply didn't know how to proceed. I could feel his dick pushing against my groin through his cut-offs. He had his foot on the gas, but just didn't know where to go from here.

I ran my hands up under his T-shirt and stroked his sweaty back before bringing them down again to lift the T-shirt up by the hem. Jeep grasped the hem of the T-shirt himself and pulled it over his head. Sweat ran down his sides in the hot, close hallway. Gently, I bent my head and licked along a trail of perspiration running down the deep cut between the broad planes of his chest.

I watched his nipples contract and harden as I found the source of that slightly salty stream in the hollow of his throat. Stepping away, I saw Jeep looking at me with the sweetest disbelief. I grabbed him by his thick wrists and pulled him into the bedroom. I sat on the edge of the bed, Jeep still standing before me in the narrow space left between the bed and the wall.

I unsnapped his cut-offs and pulled down the zipper. I half expected him to be wearing a jock strap, but found instead a pair of boxer shorts, compressed into wrinkles which expanded like a cumulus cloud as I ran my hands behind Jeep and down over his full ass to let the cut-offs fall away.

Jeep leaned back into the wall until his shoulders rested solidly against it as I grasped his waist and pulled his belly toward my lips. I licked the hard rim of his navel and then the sparse dark fish bone of hair leading down from it to the gathered elastic of the waistband of the boxer shorts. Neatly as a cat, I smoothed the dark hairs to each side with my tongue.

Below my chin, I could feel the heat of Jeep's arching dick as it strained against the flimsy white cotton. I bent to find the head of it and only caressed it with my breath. I looked up at Jeep's face. His eyes were closed in intense concentration. I wanted him to look at me as I went on. I stared up at him until he looked down worriedly to see why I had stopped.

"Are you okay?" I asked him.

He responded with a quick nod and an embarrassed grin. "It's great. Are you okay?"

In answer, I let go of his waist with one hand and ran it up to find his right nipple under my palm. Jeep shifted his weight nervously. His knees shook.

I took the waistband of his boxers and stretched them away from his dick before I pulled them down to his ankles. His dick arched up and away from his body in the same thick symmetry as the rest of him. I ignored it and reached for the fat pad of his scrotum. Jeep whimpered softly as I forced it into my mouth, sucking hard enough to make his dick bob against my cheek.

I released his balls and licked my way up the shaft of his dick. I pulled it down forcibly to take only the plum-shaped head in my mouth. Briefly, I thought of Tillett. I stayed perfectly still, but for caressing the bottom of the glans with my tongue.

Jeep cried out and tried to pull away. I moved forward suddenly, his dick sliding to the back of my throat as I forced him up on the balls of his feet and back against the wall. He moaned and pulled at my hair as I contracted my throat. He managed to pull out before I felt the head of his dick swell and he came hard against my lips.

Jeep sagged against the wall. When his breathing slowed some, he said, "I'm so sorry. I'm so sorry."

I looked up at him, bewildered. He gently wiped my face with his hand and then sat down heavily on the bed next to me. His shoulders slumped as he looked at the smeared jism on his fingers guiltily. "I'm so sorry," he repeated.

I reached down and coaxed his feet from his boxer shorts, then handed them to him. "What are you sorry for?" I asked him gently.

Jeep wiped his hand thoroughly with the underwear. "I wanted it to be special," he said simply. He balled up and threw the soiled underwear across the narrow room. The wadded cotton expanded immediately upon hitting the wall and fell harmlessly onto the bed. Jeep stared at it with disgust.

I put my hand on his shoulder and asked him, "Didn't you like that?"

He turned to me quickly and said, "Yeah, I liked it. It was incredible. I just didn't want it to be over so quick." The earnestness in his eyes surprised me. "I wanted to please you too. Then it was just . . . over," he said and looked away.

In a way, I was amused, but I didn't want him to know it. Even with all my newfound experience, I could remember the lack of it. I wanted him to please me too. I stood up and pulled off my shorts. My own dick was still hard and thumped impressively against my belly as I turned and took Jeep by the shoulders and pushed him down on the bed, straddling his waist.

He looked up at me, confused and wary. I leaned down and kissed him. He kissed me back, harder, fitting his mouth to mine.

"You don't think I'm some kind of spaz?" he asked me when we broke off. I looked down into his eyes.

"No way," I said gently. I traced from the bridge of his nose down across his lips to the hollow of his throat with my tongue.

Jeep wrapped his arms around me and pulled me down onto his chest. The slight hair that gathered there tickled my nose. I felt his dick stir under me and I reached between us to fit it in the space between my legs, under my nuts.

"We've been here before," Jeep said quietly.

"I remember," I said.

"Want to try again?" he asked. With my ear against his chest, it sounded as if he was asking from somewhere deep inside himself.

"I've been waiting to for a long time," I told him.

After that first short scrimmage, we started playing for real. It turned out to be a long night of trying again and succeeding more than once.

Jeep and I managed to make it out of the house before the rain and his father both came down to the trailer. We hardly spoke in the car driving back to my place. It was an easy silence though. It was shared tiredness and shy smiles between friends who understood each other perfectly at last.

Tonight was a forever since then. I walked after the

dogs as they chased themselves in and out of the darkness. The ocean didn't lap at the shore as it had in August. Now, in mid-autumn, it roared in the distance, but was strangely quiet near the shore. The salt in the air was less cloying and more astringent. The wind held a promise of cold as it stroked my face. I was looking forward to winter, the quiet beach, the uncrowded waves, the days of ice burning in the cold light.

I sat down on the cool sand and looked out over the water. The dogs noticed my desertion of the path and trotted back to where I sat. After they had nosed me to see if I was okay, they lay down by my side, panting their satisfaction.

In front of me, the ocean moved gently, its own voice in constant conversation with the wind. A few restless terns and a large placid gull scavenged for any tiny morsel the sea left in the retreat of the wash. Over me, the sky shifted its own shades of darkness like an indecisive girl trying on different clothes. Below me, the sand held the heat of the day under a cooler crust.

In the midst of all of this, I felt completely myself, as elemental to the scene as any part of it. I imagined that if I stayed perfectly still, the wash of the shore break would reach me and dissolve me as surely as it would a sand sculpture. I felt so much a part of where I was, right then, that there were no separations between me and every other part of the night.

I found a crumpled pack of cigarettes in my pocket and lit one. I stroked the dogs, luminous gray smudges on the dark night sand, and let the breeze argue with me against needing to have Jeep around. I made it through the rough time, when I was banged up and sick, all by myself. I was just fine, I told myself. Let Jeep come or let Jeep go, I wasn't going to let it worry me. I wanted to be cool on my own.

Shane had told me I needed to trust people more. Trusting was a whole lot harder than giving yourself away, for quick and for cheap. I was just getting used to trusting myself. Jeep was different from what I had ever expected, or thought to need. The surprise of it began to grow from the first.

"There's a cat who's been in the cream," Mark said when I got home after the night I spent with Jeep.

Tiger snorted from the coffee pot, "I hope he wasn't drinking out of somebody else's bowl again." I heard Jeep's car driving away in the rain down below.

I stuffed my hands in the back pocket of my cut-offs and checked for the piece of envelope Jeep had scratched on in the car. Jeep had asked me for my address and phone number and gave me his own. With Chris gone and Tillett finished, I had every reason to be happy at finding Jeep back where I'd left him so long ago. If he hadn't asked for the bridge between us, I would have.

"Why come Matt's drinking cream in a bowl?" Billy asked, his mouth full of Sugar Smacks. "He ain't no cat. Why come he don't just drink milk in a glass like everybody else?"

Shane gave him an exaggerated shrug and went back to his comics.

"Sit down, son; you look rough," Mark said as he kicked out my chair and leaned back in his own with a smirk on his face.

Tiger brought me a cup of coffee. "Think you're going to be worth a shit outside today, boy?" he said as he went around the table to sit by Mark. I looked outside at the rain hopefully.

"Tiger? What's that on Matt's neck?" Mark asked seriously.

Billy pushed his cereal away and climbed down from his chair to examine me closer. A worried look crept over Tiger's lips before he closed them around a cigarette and lit it. "There's another one back here on his shoulder," Billy cried. "Did a dog bite you?"

I met Tiger's stare over my coffee cup. "It wasn't who you think, Tiger. I promised, remember?" I said. I knew Tiger thought I'd hooked up with Tillett. He nodded at me and looked away, relieved.

Mark started snickering.

"Was it a big dog, Matt?" Billy insisted.

"More like a wolf," Mark said, laughing.

Billy reached out a finger tentatively to touch a hickey on my shoulder. Shane sighed deeply and looked at me accusingly. "I told you you couldn't trust that guy," he said and left the table with the paper.

"It wasn't that guy, Shane," I said to his back.

"Good," he replied from the living room.

"What guy? Not Tillett again?" Mark asked.

Tiger warned Mark with his eyes and glanced toward Billy. Mark nodded in reply. Billy left my side and went to stand by Tiger. He always gravitated to him when he was hurt, scared, or confused. "Tiger, you reckon a wolf could get me?"

Tiger put his arm over the little boy's shoulder and said, "Naw. You don't run across wolves that'll do you like that unless you're out hunting them. Ain't that right, Matt?"

I nodded and reached across the table for one of Tiger's cigarettes. My own were still on the table by the sofa in Jeep's trailer. Mark and Tiger looked at each other, amused. I felt a little guilty, but it was funny.

"Oh, how the mighty have fallen," Mark intoned deeply.

"Did you fall down too?" Billy asked worriedly. Across his open face passed a million horrors I must have endured during the night.

"Matt's okay, half-pint. You go wash your face and get ready to go with Mark to the airport. You and Shane are going to help him out today since it's raining," Tiger said.

When Billy had left, Tiger looked at me and smiled. "Normally, I'd be pissed at you staying out all night so bad you couldn't work the next day, but it looks like God's let you off the hook." The rain rattled the windows with a wet bit of laughter from God himself.

Mark stood and stretched. "Anybody we know?" I explained it was an old friend from high school. Mark nodded and rubbed my head as he passed by. "Looks like that football player to me," he said.

I blushed and asked how he could tell. Mark laughed, "I remember when I couldn't tell the difference between a good time in bed and going after a blocking dummy." Mark snickered again as he walked away. "I hope you didn't just get to play center."

Tiger looked at me anxiously for a moment. I'd given him the brochures the doctor gave me to read.

"It's okay, Tiger. It was hot, but not dangerous," I said.

Tiger nodded. Then smiled at me gently. "There's no way we're going to make it out today. This mess is a tropical disturbance."

I stretched, I felt as relaxed and coddled as a cat. "Will it make waves?" I asked.

Tiger glanced out the door toward the ocean. "It'll be slop until the winds go offshore. Then it ought to be pretty nice."

I looked at Tiger and grinned.

"You okay with this?" he asked.

I just nodded. I wasn't interested in any self-analysis right then. I just felt exultant.

"I'm going to catch up on billing after Mark and the boys leave. You ought to get some sleep. You look like hell," Tiger said.

I stood up, sore and tired, but happy without an edge to it. I gave Tiger a long, just-got-fucked grin.

"Matt, go get a shower, man; you're disgusting," Tiger said.

After my shower, I lay naked on my bed, listening to the wind and rain, thinking about what happened the night before with Jeep. Even though I'd had my share of beers, every minute of it was crystal clear. For me now, it was as real as the memories of my first time with Chris. Knowing it was Jeep's first time, I did everything I knew how to do to make it great for him. I'd had a good teacher and I wanted to be a good one too.

As good as I'd been, I also had my own agenda. Jeep was willing and eager and I enjoyed having someone to compare with Chris and Tillett. I'd surveyed Jeep's body with the same precision as Tiger had taught me in the field, only with softer instruments. I remembered finding his nipples in the hair on his chest and tracing their circumference with my tongue. I remembered holding his dick in my hand, calculating its weight, heft, and length against Chris's, then Tillett's. I noted how the head of it swelled. I judged the weight of his balls in my hand and the long length of him as he strained over me.

Jeep was different, but much the same. His thrusts were deeper and more searching, but he was a much bigger man than the others. It came down to longer stroke and more torque. Yet Jeep seemed to have the same awareness of his size that a big dog must have. Even in his own hunger, he was careful not to hurt me or make me uncomfortable. When he finally rolled over and yielded himself to my own dick, an event that was rare with Chris, unthinkable with Tillett, it was not with a patient resignation, but with a hunger as big as the rest of him.

The hickeys on my neck and shoulders were my own fault. I wanted to keep Jeep out on the edges of the actual act as long as possible. Considering how quickly he came the first time, I kept Jeep going for an hour the next time before I even found his dick in my hand.

Jeep shuddered when he came. It was a deep shudder that he seemed to have held back all of his life. When he finally shot off, I measured it, as well, against Chris's and Tillett's own loads. I compared the taste of it. I compared how Jeep surrounded me and kept at his own exploration long after we were both spent and sweaty. Jeep's mouth continued to find and pull at the exposed spaces of my own body long after our dicks had retreated and coiled.

I had a basis of comparison. Jeep had given me some way to understand the whys of both Chris and Tillett. Honestly, I had enjoyed fucking Jeep as much as I ever enjoyed fucking either one of the other two. Jeep was hot and he was as into it as I was. But it was more than that.

First off, I had been wanting Jeep for years. That day in his room after his mama's funeral was real, just like all those Wednesday nights up in the Christian Life Activities Center when I wanted just to lean up next to him. The memory of that never left me.

The night before I finally had the chance to act on the stillborn fantasies of all those years. It was as real for me as any of the times I thought I cherished with Chris or was left hurting but still hungry by Tillett. I didn't want to admit it, but Jeep was first. Chris might have been easier, because he knew what to do, but I had been loving Jeep for years and I just couldn't admit it.

One thing kept coming back to me that morning in the dim light of my room at Tiger's house. In the night, I had watched as Jeep stood in the doorway of his room on the way back from a visit to the bathroom. He stood there naked, just looking at me on his bed. His tall form filled up the narrow door jamb. The patterns of light and dark stood in high relief on his chest and belly where his hair deepened the shadows and contrasted the lightness of his slick skin. Jeep looked warm, not made of moonlight and mother of pearl. He looked real and warm and secure, not like something made of empty promises or dirty dreams.

I wanted the comfort of his realness. I sat up on the edge of the bed and reached out for Jeep with my hand. He had stepped forward certainly, no longer afraid that I would reject him or afraid of his own self-doubts. He was the sweet awkward boy who had shared my scared years, before I could understand the power of my own body and spirit against all the things we both were taught not to trust.

We fitted ourselves into each other. Right then, I wanted him like I'd never let myself want him all the years before now. I wanted Jeep. I also wanted me, innocent and learning all over again. Jeep was my way back to myself from the new world shores of Chris and the darker interior of Tillett.

In the weeks that followed that night, Jeep came and went. At this point, I hadn't seen him in weeks. In times when I was a little down, I wondered if he had just satisfied his curiosity and drifted away. Worse, I wondered if he'd found some other surfer boy lounging around the campus, all sleepy eyes and knowing grin. Some hungers it didn't take anything or anybody special to fill.

I wanted to think that our history bore witness to the fact that we simply moved in and out of each other's gravitational pull, but our orbits were as set as the planets'. That was a wonderful little metaphor I kept close as a secret picture tucked in my wallet.

Jeep never came to the beach on weekends. Most of his life was regimented by school and football practice and games. When he did come, it was mainly late in the evening and late in the week. Early in October, he called me just as Tiger and I were getting in from work. He asked if I'd like to come down to his dad's place for dinner. I told him sure. "Can you spend the night?" he said shyly. "I don't have to leave until the morning." Before I could answer, he added, "That is, if you want to."

I felt a hot run of lust under a quieter thrill at his solicitousness. Jeep was always respectful to the point of timidity. It wasn't something I was used to. With Chris, our infatuation with each other was so complete that it was seamless. His demands dovetailed so completely with my own desires that everything was assumed. Tillett's courtship technique was as uncomplicated as whistling for a dog. I just jumped in the truck with my tail wagging. Jeep's shyness, which took nothing for granted, excited me unreasonably.

"I'd like that a lot," I told him.

"Great," he said. The relief and happiness sounding in that one word almost broke my heart. When I asked him what time he wanted me to be there, he asked if he could pick me up. I was a little flustered by the question. I never considered anything like introducing him to my family. I'd never had a reason, or an opportunity, really, to bring my partners home to Mark, Tiger, and the boys.

Jeep took my silent consideration for reluctance. "I don't have to. I just have to go out and pick up some stuff for supper, anyway," he offered.

"That's cool. I just need a little while to get cleaned up," I said, as Shane rushed in the door, hugging a football against his chest. Mark ran in behind him reaching for his shoulders. Shane tried to twist away from his father's grasp, throwing the football at me simultaneously.

"Shane passes to Matt," he yelled.

I tried to tuck the phone between my neck and shoulder to grab the football. The dogs went for it as well, jumping against me hard enough to dislodge the phone. I caught the ball. The phone fell on the floor.

Tiger yelled, "Hey, testosterone level unacceptable," from somewhere down the hall.

Shane retrieved the ball and looked sheepishly at his dad, who only shrugged and nodded at me. "Good save," he said.

I picked up the phone and apologized to Jeep. "I kinda got caught in the line of scrimmage there for a minute." Jeep laughed. "Give me a half hour," I said.

"Should I wear my helmet and pads?" he asked.

I thought about the reception he might be getting. "It might not be a bad idea," I said, and hung up.

"Who was that?" Shane asked.

"Don't be so nosy," Mark said and then added, "Who was that?"

I looked at the two of them, playing a shallow game of keep-away with the dogs, pitching the football between the living room and dining room. "My friend, Jeep. He's coming over to pick me up," I said.

"Matt's got a boyfriend; Matt's got a boyfriend," Shane started in a singsong voice. Mark chimed in along with him. The dogs scrambled back and forth, their claws providing a counterpoint scratch track on the hardwood floor.

Tiger came in and shouted, "Dogs! Children! Enough!" The dogs sat instantly, their stubbed tails wagging in confusion and submission. Mark caught Shane's last short pass and hung his head like an overgrown disobedient child. Shane slumped panting into a chair.

"What the hell?" Tiger demanded.

Mark began tossing the football between his hands and admitted, "Matt's got a boyfriend." Shane snickered.

"So all y'all gone crazy?" Tiger demanded.

"He's coming to pick him up in a half hour," Shane said.

Tiger grinned and pulled out a chair from the table. The dogs went to him for assurance, their heads down, but smiles on their faces.

"In that case, Matt had better go get a shower," Tiger said.

"And put on aftershave and deodorant," Shane said.

Mark tossed him the football and went to sit across the table from Tiger. "We'll need to discuss whether this young man is appropriate," Mark said seriously to Tiger.

"Hell, anybody'd be an improvement over the last one," Tiger said.

"Fuck all y'all," I said.

"No, just you," Shane yelled to my back as I headed down the hall toward the bathroom, dreading how far they might take this little rite of passage I'd never had to endure at the hands of my parents or my brother.

Jeep was as early as he was earnest. I came out of my room to find him sitting at the kitchen table, drinking a beer, flanked by Shane and Mark, all long legs sprawled, born-again jocks, discussing football. Tiger sat at the end of the table, watching Jeep as intently, a half-smile on his face.

No one noticed me for a full minute. Finally, I said, "Well, Jeep, I see you've met everybody."

Jeep gave me a small grin, suddenly shy when faced with the real reason he was here.

"We like him," Shane said to me. "He's a lot nicer than that roofer."

Mark rolled his eyes and smacked Shane lightly upside the head. "When did you get to be such a mouthy brat?"

Jeep looked at me, with some surprise, but no other hints as to what he was thinking.

"What's for supper?" I asked him directly.

Jeep reared back on the hind legs of the kitchen chair and stretched. He had obviously been made to feel at home. "Dad was down yesterday and left some bluefish he caught. I thought I'd fry them up and we'd have some slaw and french fries. There's enough for everybody if y'all all want to come down," he offered to Tiger.

Tiger smiled and shook his head. "As good as that sounds, I think we'll let you off the hook."

Mark gave me a teasing grin and said, "I don't know. I love bluefish."

Shane chimed in, "Yeah, bluefish is great."

Tiger stood and said, "Shane, we have food for supper." To Jeep, he said, smiling, "You guys better take off."

Mark stood as well and offered Jeep his hand. "It was good to meet you. Don't be a stranger."

Jeep grasped his hand and shook it. I watched something pass between their eyes that I envied. It wasn't anything erotic, it was just an easy masculine familiarity that passed between jocks of all ages. I had never been a jock, nor was I ever that easy around other males. The waves I rode broke over sexual shoals.

Jeep turned to Shane and grabbed him in a headlock. "Roofer, huh?" Shane struggled good-naturedly against Jeep's rough embrace. "You and me'll have to talk. Okay, buddy?"

Shane got loose and shook himself, like the dogs would have. "Sure, no problem."

Jeep turned to Tiger and extended his hand. "Nice to meet you. When I come down again, maybe we will have dinner," Jeep said. Tiger favored him with a crooked smile as he shook his hand.

As we made our way to the door, the dogs milled around Jeep's knees; even they wanted his self-assured touch. Usually they were aloof. They hadn't warmed to me so quickly. I was a bit overwhelmed by how easily Jeep had insinuated himself into the weave of the household. Only Billy was missing. I wondered if he, too, would be so easily won over by Jeep's effortless goodwill. I was almost jealous.

Back at his trailer, Jeep had me sit at the table with a beer while he busied himself cooking dinner. I half listened to him talk as he moved certainly in the small space. For a big guy, his movements were precise as he went about the small tasks of preparing the meal. I found a great deal of pleasure just watching him chop an onion or stir cornmeal batter.

After dinner, we sat at the table over another round of beers. I found myself comforted by the little rituals of domesticity. There was something satisfying about just sitting and smoking a cigarette after the good food. It was so easy and uncomplicated. The smells of dinner chased themselves around the room, pushed by a cool breeze coming in the open windows. The local radio station played beach music. The songs by The Drifters and the Tams were thirty years old, but they seemed as constant as the beach itself.

"Your beach family is pretty different from your mom and dad," Jeep said. I nodded. "What's their story?" he asked.

I briefed him on the essentials and he nodded sympathetically. "Mark and Shane are pretty cool," he said, "but Tiger is scary, kind of." Jeep admitted.

I laughed. "How is he scary?"

Jeep thought a minute, I could tell he was choosing his words carefully to avoid saying anything that would sound offensive.

"He's like some kind of big cat. He just watches you," Jeep said finally. He peered across the table at me, hoping I understood. I smiled at him.

"I think it's just his eyes. He's really warm once you get to know him."

Jeep nodded, but added, "He's still a little scary. He's like a shape shifter or something. You look at him one time and he's too beautiful to be a guy. The next time, he looks like he could break your neck with a swipe of his paw, just for the fun of it."

Jeep had Tiger down cold. I wished I could explain the cause of that blend of menace and beauty to him, but Jeep wasn't that complex. He was too much like a straight person to understand. I told him I could see his point and then added, "But Mark loves him to death."

Jeep grinned and said, "I noticed."

Jeep went to the refrigerator for more beer. He snapped the tab on one and gave it to me before opening his own and resuming his seat. "My mom and dad loved each other a lot. I hope that's what I have one day." He looked in my eyes searchingly for an instant, and then away quickly as though he'd been caught saying way too much.

"I hope you don't mind the music," he said suddenly. "I could change it if it's getting on your nerves."

I heard the Tams singing in the background. It would have been nostalgic for my parents, but it was even nostalgic to me. Beach music, old even when I was little, still seemed to be a link for me to the innocence of the days when my parents courted. I actually liked it. I told Jeep I did.

"I'm sorry I never learned to shag," I said.

That dance went with beach music like rum went with Coke and seemed as precise and mannered as a minuet these days.

"I remember peeking in clubs down at The Circle when I was a kid, thinking how grown up it looked. I thought it would be so cool to dance with somebody while you were falling in love," I said.

Jeep was staring at me, his hand still on his beer. "I know it sounds lame," I said, suddenly embarrassed by my own dated sense of romance.

The Tams died in a quick fade. There was a second or two of complete silence before an audible pop and hiss as the DJ placed a needle on an actual old record. The Drifters began singing *"Sweets for my sweet, sugar for my honey, your tasty kiss it thrills me so . . ."*

Jeep's intense stare eased into a grin. "You want to learn?"

I looked at him incredulously. Dusk was coming down and the trailer had dimmed to almost darkness. The beat of the song was infectious.

"Are you serious?" I asked him.

Jeep scrubbed the legs of the chair against the floor as he stood up suddenly. Walking past me, he grasped my hand and pulled me into the living room. From the middle of the floor, he reached over to the old radio and turned up the volume. Then he swung back to me and put his arm around my waist, pulling me close. "Now, check it out. All you have to do is like this, when I do like this," he said and demonstrated.

He swung out and away from me with an agility that belied his size. Awkwardly, I tried to follow the pattern of step, shuffle, step that he demonstrated. Never letting go of my hand, he corrected me gently, and encouraged me when I got it basically right. It really wasn't that complicated, but I felt stiff dancing in front of the open curtains.

Jeep noticed my discomfort and swung me out and away from him. He pulled me back to the solidity of his chest over my own dissonant feet and said, "Relax, get into it."

I had to laugh. It was so odd and fun and weird all at the same time.

"Fuck it," I said and swung out once more. The rhythm felt good, Jeep's hard hands felt even better.

We danced through an entire side of some old Drifters album, before a slow song came on. I went to break away, but Jeep pulled me up to him with a conviction that seemed undeniable. I laid my face against his chest, his sweat-dampened T-shirt soft and sweet.

"My mom and dad used to do this. They'd dance and laugh. I used to go to sleep hearing them moving to this music," Jeep said. His arms tightened around me. "I always wanted to dance with somebody I loved too," he said simply.

I put my hand up under his T-shirt into the wet small of his back and pulled him closer. I let my other hand find its way into the back pocket of his jeans. I didn't want to give in to what I was feeling. It seemed too simple, too old-fashioned. Too much like what my parents had. But I couldn't deny the comfort in it, the easy knowing of somebody so warm and wonderful near enough to smell and touch and count heartbeats.

I'd walked out on the edges with Tillett. I'd done all of the things that was supposed to make gay sex so hot and uninhibited. I'd sucked his fat dick in a men's room, been fucked half to death on the open deck of a boat by him on more than one occasion. But I'd done that already. I felt as jaded as old whore, but I had to admit, this is what I wanted. Not that.

I let myself merge against the hard denim and cotton of Jeep's long body and sighed. There wasn't any fighting this. I was raised by a mama and daddy who loved each other, who worked hard all day and came home drained to the simple comfort of a good meal and a welcoming smile. "You can't get above your raising," my grandmama used to say. I knew how low you could get under it. That wasn't what I wanted. This was.

The song ended and a commercial for marine outfitters came on. Jeep didn't let me go. He held on to me as surely as I was holding on to him. Both of us continued to sway to a remembered beat of an old familiar song. It was in every memory, what we looked for in every face we saw. Before I could push the thought away, I hoped he'd found it in mine.

I felt Jeep's erection through our clothes and ran my hands up along his sides. He let me go and pulled his T-shirt over his head as another golden oldie spoon song came on the radio. I put my mouth against his throat as he put his arms around me once more.

In my limited experience sleeping with guys, there always seemed to be one perfect moment that you reminded yourself to catch and hold on to. It impressed itself with a piercing realization that this was the doorway you were walking through, for good or bad. You were in the process off breaking off a piece of your own soul and offering it to the man in your grasp. All the willingness and wonder, the fear and exhilaration of trying to connect was suspended and defined by that exact moment. Jeep stroked the back of my hair and placed his mouth, open, on the top of my head.

The sex that followed the dance was as slow and filled with arch meaning as the old songs that carried us onto the bed in Jeep's daddy's trailer. Afterward, we lay wrapped up in each other and Jeep talked.

"I bet you can't guess what I'm gonna major in," he said as he stroked my back.

"Nah. Tell me," I said. He could have said anything. I just liked to hear his voice rumbling from under my ear against his chest.

"Early childhood education. I want to teach kids with learning disabilities."

I raised up on an elbow to look at him. He found my eyes in the dark and I saw a kind of shyness there. He looked away and said, "When I was a little kid, all the teachers told my folks I was slow. Everybody else did too. They called me a big dumb ox. Then, you remember Mrs. Ragland, in eighth grade?"

"Sure," I said softly.

"She didn't think I was dumb. She called up my folks and had them make an appointment with this specialist lady in Greenville. I have dyslexia. Nobody before cared enough to try and see I wasn't stupid."

Jeep turned his head back and looked up at the ceiling, "I want to be like Mrs. Ragland, you know. I want to make kids like me feel like they're something good and smart."

"I always thought you were smart. You remember hanging out on Wednesday nights? I thought you were so smart, and hell, you knew all this interesting stuff. I loved just listening to you," I admitted.

Jeep didn't say anything. He just took one of his huge paws and gently brought my face down to kiss.

Under the gentling stroke of his hands, I felt myself calmed and reassured. I had no doubts that he would be terrific with kids. What grew in my head after we slept and he departed again was the improbabilities of our being together.

Jeep was only able to go to college because of his athletic scholarship. It was convenient to have me as a lover, living an hour and a half away. I couldn't imagine him risking losing his ride if anybody were to get wind of his extra-curricular queer affair. Then too, I wondered about the complications of us being together if he did become a teacher.

Everybody in the world assumes that if you're queer, you automatically want to fuck little kids. It's total bullshit, but Southerners cling to their prejudices as they do to the old rugged cross. I couldn't imagine myself following Jeep like a dirty secret through the long years I wanted to walk with somebody. Then too, I damn sure didn't want to spend my life in some suck-ass small town back inland, even if it was with Jeep.

The dogs sensed something heavy-handed and hard-stepped in the night. They stood rapidly and bayed, a deep, hollowed sound. Their backs bristling and tense, they peered out into the blackness, distracted briefly by the sudden flight of the startled shore birds.

I sat still and impassive. Dogs find scents on the air and wager instinct against embarrassment. I waited and watched an elderly couple make their way hesitantly toward us in the dark. The old man responded to the dog's warning by stepping lightly between the dogs and his wife. She in turn, grasped his arm, not so much in fear, but in an attempt to pull him away from any sudden lunge.

I stood and grabbed the dogs' collars. Shushing them, I nodded a friendly apology to the older couple. Reassured, they stepped past us with wary smiles. I watched them walk away. The old guy put his arm around the old girl's shoulder; she placed hers around his waist.

The dogs sat on their haunches, looking up at me as if waiting for a decision of some sort. I wanted to call Jeep right then. I missed him so bad that my earlier assertions to myself seemed as hollow as a little boy's bravado. I wagered instinct against embarrassment and found I didn't even trust myself. I began walking toward home.

I followed behind the dogs, not like I was going home, but projecting myself years ahead into the future. My bare feet weren't squeaking on sand, but on the slippery slope of denial and lies that it took to be queer and married in a place like where I grew up. I felt myself choking, remembering the hot, close familiarity of a place lived in too long.

As much as I wanted to fall in love with Jeep, as safe and sure as I felt in his hands and his way of life, I was scared of it. The freedom I'd found at the beach was too new. I was too new. I knew the bounds I could live within. I knew the kind of relationship I had with Tillett, as hot as it was, was out of bounds for me. Being Chris's butt buddy was too narrow in its dimensions to build anything on. I just couldn't measure the distance I could go with Jeep.

I followed the dogs up the stairs to the deck and let them in the house. Never in my life had I forgotten the hard lessons of learning to see a month down the road. If this, then that, was something I'd only recently learned to ignore. It was scary. Every time I gave myself up to the moment, I got whomped upside the head. I had the scars to prove it. I sat down on one of the rockers and fought with the future for a really long time.

Me

and Tiger had a difference of opinion. I didn't think the waves were worth going out. Tiger pointed down toward a hollow wave breaking about fifty yards out to our left. The sets were smallish, but consistent. The little break had survived the storm, if it wasn't as big or as clean as it had been.

It had threatened rain all day under gray and uncharacteristically muggy skies for early November. The winds had built all day from the southeast, bushing up some surf. At four o'clock, the winds shifted offshore. Tiger and I finished getting grade shots for the topographic survey we were working on and packed it in. On the way home, we stopped at the new road leading to the break where I ate it so bad a couple of weeks before.

Tiger whooped as a nice set rolled in, head high and hollow. He looked at me with a sparkle in his eyes and turned, peeling off his T-shirt as he headed down the dune and back toward the truck. I looked back at the waves and felt a clammy hand worm its way under my nuts.

I turned away from the building sets and followed Tiger to the Bronco. He pulled out the bag with our wetsuits in it from behind all the equipment and tossed it to me. I watched him strip down until he was completely naked except for his socks. He looked up at me. "What the hell are you waiting for, Matt? Get the bag open and hand me my wetsuit."

He sat down awkwardly on the edge of the driver's seat waiting, while I tore into the bag and tossed him his wetsuit. I stripped with less enthusiasm, all the while eyeing my new O'Neil full suit, half hanging out of the bag where I'd tossed it in the back of the Bronco.

By the time I was naked, Tiger was pulling the zipper of the suit up with the cord that hung down the back with one hand and reaching for the boards on top of the truck. I could hear the water over the wind. It ground along the bottom, dragging sand and shell bits with a force loud enough to come all the way back to where I stood. I could feel it pounding under my feet.

"Matt, this ain't a peep show. Quit standing there with your dick hanging out and your thumb up your ass. There ain't an hour and a half of daylight left," Tiger commanded.

I sat my cold ass on the tailgate of the truck and pulled my suit up over my thighs. That accomplished, I pulled off my socks and stood to get the wetsuit up around my waist and tucked in my unit.

I could feel the water's vibrations traveling up through my bare feet. As if in slow motion I pulled my arms through the stiff sleeves. Before I could reach for the zipper cord, Tiger was pulling it up for me. I shrugged my shoulders to get myself situated in the second skin of neophrene. It was a new and odd feeling to be so packed into something.

Tiger had my long board down off the racks and stood offering it to me as I turned. The look on his face was determined. I took the board from him and ran my hands down the side to the ugly patch Shane and I had put on the glassing where it had cracked in contact with my head. It was like feeling a scab. I looked up to find Tiger watching me.

"Are you okay?" Tiger asked directly.

I nodded at him and he hesitated before taking his board down from the roof of the Bronco. I looked up into the gray scut overhead. The damp air that promised rain, the barometric oppressiveness, the loudness of the waves, it was all eerily familiar. I felt the place over my right eye throb slightly.

"Time to get back on the horse, Matt," Tiger reminded.

"Saddle up then, boss," I told him.

Tiger took his board off the racks as I turned toward the beach. The roadbed aggregate of crushed shells didn't even phase the leathery soles of my feet anymore. They had toughened in the months I'd pushed them on the hot sands and asphalt, oyster shells and gravel. I walked toward the dune line with Tiger following behind me.

The last time I'd crossed the slope I'd been carried. Today, I dug the balls of my feet into the sandy face and clenched my toes into it purposefully. On the crest, the wind pushed at my back and tried to force my board away from my side. The ocean laughed, as if a party was going on. I felt like a crasher for an instant.

Ahead of me to my left, the break made clean faces of the disorganized milling all around it. I could feel Tiger behind me, making his way up the dune. I didn't want to hear any more from him. I didn't need any more encouragement. The party was going on and if I hadn't been invited, I knew the way in.

I took off down the dune, digging my heels in hard with the same determination as I had coming up the other side. At the base, I knelt and strapped on my leash. Standing again, I was already moving into a stride, by the time I was on hard pack, I was running. The shock of the cold water was brief as the shore break slowed me. I laid my board down first and then myself on top of it using the backwash to pull me out.

Inside the stiffer skin of my wetsuit, I felt the chill, but not the wet as I paddled over the first wave and down its back. The mechanics of making it outside took over. The greatest comfort of surfing comes in the sureness of instinct. There is no thinking, no analysis or brooding. There is only waiting, moving, and then the rush of action, balance, and movement.

It's a goddamn lie that you become one with the wave. The wave tolerates you, entices you, challenges you, but it never loves you. It never recognizes you for being its master or its friend. No. You are a brightly colored blur on its back and across its face. You and the wave exist together for as long as the physics of time and space allow you to touch and create a seam together. Then, it's only you and it has gone.

The gift comes in the repetition and the knowledge that every time is different and the same. I turned my board back toward shore in a lull between sets. Tiger was just paddling out. I looked back over my shoulder and watched for my first wave.

A good whomp upside the head doesn't make you a better surfer; it makes you a more careful one. But the waves laugh at timidity. They have no respect for caution. You either take risks or the inside of your thighs get sore from gripping the rails of your board as you sit and wait for the ocean to be just right. The ocean is never just right.

I slipped around the corner of my fear first, and then crossed over the caution. It felt good. It would have been foolish after everything I'd learned to trust the buoyancy of the board or the surge of water under it. What I did was trust myself. I got some good rides in before the sun went below the cloud line and spilled thin gold across the water.

Tiger yelled at me and motioned it was time to go in. I held up one finger. One more ride. Tiger signaled okay and waited for his last ride as well. He caught one fairly quickly. It wasn't very big, but he worked it over pretty good before pitching out in waist-high water. I watched him stand and make his way onto the beach.

My last wave was okay. I was too far to the left to make the best of it. I took off late and it spanked me pretty hard. I remembered to check the tug of my leash when I found the bottom in chest-high water and pushed off. It was good to be reminded who was who and what was what. It made me laugh out loud.

Tiger waited for me on the beach. I felt his arm come over my shoulder and briefly pull me close. I turned and looked into his yellow eyes. Water caught in his hair had dripped down to collect in his fine white eyebrows. He looked back at me steadily with no hint of judgment or comfort, measuring the distance covered in my face with the practice of a professional.

I shivered slightly; the wind held the promise of winter and cold. Tiger moved to squeeze the back of my neck briefly, then let his hand fall away. We listened to the roar of the ocean for a long time.

"Let's pack it up and hit it again big tomorrow," Tiger said finally.

Silently, we made our way back to the Bronco.

By the time we turned off the beach road for the house, some blue was still trying to peek through the deepening rose of the sky. Out in the street, Mark, Shane, and Billy were tossing a football back and forth with Jeep.

"Looks like you've got company," Tiger said.

Mark threw a long pass to Jeep. Billy and Shane took off chasing him as he ran down the street toward the beach. Jeep picked the football cleanly out of the air, lowered his head, and began rushing back toward Mark. He neatly swerved to avoid Shane's attempt at a block by running up on the sand across the street, but collapsed as Billy hit his knees. As he rolled, Billy gleefully threw himself on him and Shane ran back to add his own body to the mess. Mark laughed into the wind.

Hearing the truck, Mark turned around and waved us into the driveway as if guiding an airplane to a jet bridge. Before he shut off the truck, Tiger turned to look at me.

"Time to get back on the horse, Matt."

I gave him a smile and opened the door.

As I got out, I heard Shane yell, "Matt's open." He threw the football and I ran to catch it as it flew at me. I remembered to watch the ball, but I caught a glimpse of Shane, Billy, and Jeep rushing toward me.

"He's mine; he's mine," Jeep yelled. I jumped to catch the ball and found it neatly. I saw Jeep reaching for me, strong, grinning, and happy.

I faked right, but Jeep was quicker. I wanted to believe he was getting good at reading my fake moves by now. He hunched and caught me in my midsection. The unexpected force of him knocked out my breath, but I hung onto the ball as he lifted me on his shoulder and began to spin us around. The cottage moved around us and I caught a glimpse of the ocean between the houses down the block as Jeep's arms held me tight.

"I've got him now," he shouted to nobody and everybody.

I couldn't believe much in what I'd always felt about life or love anymore. I had serious doubts if I was even a Matt I liked very much. But I knew Jeep from way back. Still spinning on his shoulder, I spiked the ball toward Shane and Billy. I put my arm around Jeep's neck and pulled his head into my side. His laughter vibrated on my ribs and spread into the waiting hollow near my heart.

I knew magnetic north could tear you apart. I really wanted true north to be as constant as Tiger taught me.

ABOUT THE AUTHOR

Jay Quinn is a native of coastal North Carolina. He is the author of *The Mentor: A Memoir of Friendship and Gay Identity,* and editor of *Rebel Yell: Stories by Contemporary Southern Gay Authors.* A frequent contributor to *The Lambda Book Report,* he lives and works in South Florida with his partner of nine years and their two huge Doberman/Lab-mix dogs.

Order Your Own Copy of
This Important Book for Your Personal Library!

METES AND BOUNDS

_____in hardbound at $39.95 (ISBN: 1-56023-184-X)

_____in softbound at $19.95 (ISBN: 1-56023-185-8)

COST OF BOOKS_____

OUTSIDE USA/CANADA/
MEXICO: ADD 20%____

POSTAGE & HANDLING_____
*(US: $4.00 for first book & $1.50
for each additional book)
Outside US: $5.00 for first book
& $2.00 for each additional book)*

SUBTOTAL_____

in Canada: add 7% GST____

STATE TAX____
*(NY, OH & MIN residents, please
add appropriate local sales tax)*

FINAL TOTAL____
*(If paying in Canadian funds,
convert using the current
exchange rate, UNESCO
coupons welcome.)*

❏　**BILL ME LATER:** ($5 service charge will be added)
(Bill-me option is good on US/Canada/Mexico orders only;
not good to jobbers, wholesalers, or subscription agencies.)

❏ Check here if billing address is different from
shipping address and attach purchase order and
billing address information.

Signature_____

❏　**PAYMENT ENCLOSED: $**_____

❏　**PLEASE CHARGE TO MY CREDIT CARD.**

❏ Visa　❏ MasterCard　❏ AmEx　❏ Discover
❏ Diner's Club　❏ Eurocard　❏ JCB

Account #_____

Exp. Date_____

Signature_____

Prices in US dollars and subject to change without notice.

NAME_____

INSTITUTION_____

ADDRESS_____

CITY_____

STATE/ZIP_____

COUNTRY_____ COUNTY (NY residents only)_____

TEL_____ FAX_____

E-MAIL_____

May we use your e-mail address for confirmations and other types of information? ❏ Yes　❏ No
We appreciate receiving your e-mail address and fax number. Haworth would like to e-mail or fax special
discount offers to you, as a preferred customer. **We will never share, rent, or exchange your e-mail address
or fax number.** We regard such actions as an invasion of your privacy.　.

Order From Your Local Bookstore or Directly From
The Haworth Press, Inc.
10 Alice Street, Binghamton, New York 13904-1580 • USA
TELEPHONE: 1-800-HAWORTH (1-800-429-6784) / Outside US/Canada: (607) 722-5857
FAX: 1-800-895-0582 / Outside US/Canada: (607) 722-6362
E-mail: getinfo@haworthpressinc.com
PLEASE PHOTOCOPY THIS FORM FOR YOUR PERSONAL USE.
www.HaworthPress.com

BOF00